From the orbiting observatory nearly 6 million miles out from the giant world, the meteorologist sent down the latest weather information to the stranded Mesklinite landship.

"Dondragmer, you should have about nineteen hours of reduced visibility. The temperature is going down, and the fog will change to ammonia crystals. In about five hours the temperature will be a lot lower, so you don't have to worry about melting—"

The next instant, he wished he could somehow outrace and stop the radio waves that would carry his confident prediction to the Mesklinite captain in 32 seconds.

For Dondragmer was on the screen, talking urgently: "Please get a special report to Barlennan. The temperature has gone up six degrees, to one hundred three . . . the ice has melted from the windows . . . and we're afloat!"

Also by Hal Clement
Published by Ballantine Books:

STAR LIGHT

by Hal Clement

A Del Rey Book

BALLANTINE BOOKS • NEW YORK

A Del Rey Book
Published by Ballantine Books

Copyright © 1971 by Hal Clement

All rights reserved under International and Pan-American Copyright Conventions. Published in the United States by Ballantine Books, a division of Random House, Inc., New York, and simultaneously in Canada by Ballantine Books of Canada, Ltd., Toronto, Canada.

ISBN 0-345-27358-3

Manufactured in the United States of America

First Ballantine Books Edition: September 1971
Second printing: February 1978

Cover art by H. R. Van Dongen

CONTENTS

I
PIT STOP

Beetchermarlf felt the vibrations die out as his vehicle came to a halt, but instinctively looked outside before releasing the *Kwembly's* helm. It was wasted effort, of course. The sun, or rather, the body he was trying to think of as *the* sun, had set nearly twenty hours before. The sky was still too bright for stars to be seen, but not bright enough to show details on the almost featureless dusty snow field around him. Behind, which was the only direction he could not see from the center of the bridge, the *Kwembly's* trail might have provided some visual reference; but from his post at the helm there was no clue to his speed.

The captain, stretched out on his platform above and behind the helmsman, interpreted correctly the latter's raised head. If he was amused, he concealed the fact. With nearly two human lifetimes spent on Mesklin's unpredictable oceans he had never learned to like uncertainty, merely to live with it. Commanding a "vessel" he did not fully understand, travelling on land instead of sea and knowing that his home world was over three parsecs away did nothing to bolster his own self-confidence, and he sympathized fully with the youngster's lack of it.

"We're stopped, helmsman. Secure, and start your

1

hundred hour maintenance check. We'll stay here for
ten hours."

"Yes, sir." Beetchermarlf slipped the helm into its
locking notch. A glance at the clock told him that
over an hour of his watch remained, so he began
checking the cables which connected the steering bar
with the *Kwembly's* forward trucks.

The lines were visible enough, since no effort had
been made to conceal essential machinery behind
walls. The builders of the huge vehicle and her eleven
sister "ships" had not been concerned with appearance.
It took only a few seconds to make sure that the few
inches of cable above the bridge deck were still free
of wear. The helmsman gestured an "all's well" to the
captain, rapped on the deck for clearance, waited for
acknowledgement from below, opened the starboard
trap and vanished down the ramp to continue his inspection.

Dondragmer watched him go with no great concern. His worries were elsewhere, and the helmsman
was a dependable sailor. He put the steering problem
from his mind for the moment, and reared the front
portion of his eighteen-inch body upward until his
head was level with the speaking tubes. A sirenlike
wail which could have been heard over one of Mesklin's typhoons and was almost ridiculous in the silence
of Dhrawn's snow field secured the attention of the
rest of the crew.

"This is the captain. Ten hours halt for maintenance
check; watch on duty get started. Research personnel
follow your usual routine, being sure to check with the
bridge before going outside. No flying until the scouts
have been overhauled. Power distribution, acknowledge!"

"Power checking." The voice from the speaking tube
was a little deeper than Dondragmer's.

"Life support, acknowledge!"

"Life support checking."

"Communication, acknowledge!"

"Checking."

"Kerverser to the bridge for standby! I'm going outside. Research, give me outside conditions!"

"One moment, Captain." The pause was brief before the voice resumed, "Temperature 77; pressure 26.1; wind from 21, steady at 200 cables per hour; oxygen fraction standard at 0.0122."

"Thanks. That doesn't seem too bad."

"No. With your permission, I'll come out with you to get surface samples. May we set up the drill? We can get cores to a fair depth in less than ten hours."

"That will be all right. I may be outside before you get to the lock, if you take time to collect the drill gear, but you are cleared outside when ready. Tell Kerverser the number of your party, for the log."

"Thank you, Captain. We'll be there right away."

Dondragmer relaxed at his station; he would not, of course, leave the bridge until his relief appeared, even with the engines stopped. Kerverser would be some minutes in arriving, since he would have to turn his current duties over to a relief of his own. The wait was not bothersome, however, since there was plenty to think about. Dondragmer was not the worrying type (the Mesklinite nervous system does not react to uncertainty in that way) but he did like to think situations out before he lived them.

The fact that he was some ten or twelve thousand miles from help if the *Kwembly* were ever crippled was merely background, not a special problem. It did not differ essentially from the situation he had faced for most of his life on Mesklin's vast seas. The principal ripple on his normally placid self-confidence was stirred up by the machine he commanded. It resembled in no way the flexible assemblage of rafts which was his idea of a ship. He had been assured that it would float if occasion arose; it actually had floated during tests on distant Mesklin where it had been built. Since then, however, it had been disassembled, loaded into shuttle craft and lifted into orbit around its world of origin, transferred in space to an interstellar flier, shifted back to another and very different shuttle after the three-parsec jump, and brought to Dhrawn's surface before being reassembled. Dondragmer had personally supervised the disassembly and reconstruction of the *Kwembly* and her sister machines, but the intervening steps had not been carried out under his own eye. This formed the principal reason for his wanting to go outside now; high as was his opinion of Beetchermarlf and the rest of his picked crew, he liked first-hand knowledge.

He did not, of course, mention this to Kervenser when the latter reached the bridge. It was something which went without saying. Anyway, the first officer presumably felt the same himself.

"Maintenance checks are under way. The researchers are going out to sink a well, and I'm going out to look things over," was all Dondragmer said as he resigned his station. "You can signal me with outside lights if necessary. It's all yours."

Kervenser snapped two of his nippers light-heartedly. "I'll ride it, Don. Enjoy yourself." The captain left by way of the still open hatch which had admitted his relief, telling himself as he went that Kervenser wasn't as casual as he sounded.

Four decks down and sixty feet aft of the bridge was the main air lock. Dondragmer paused several times on the way to talk to members of his crew as they worked among the cords, beams, and piping of the *Kwembly's* interior. By the time he reached the lock four scientists were already there with their drilling gear, and had started to don their air suits. The captain watched critically as they wriggled their long bodies and numerous legs into the transparent envelopes, made the tests for tightness, and checked their hydrogen and argon supplies. Satisfied, he gestured them into the lock and began suiting up himself. By the time he was outside the others were well on with setting up their apparatus.

He glanced at them only briefly as he paused at the top of the ramp leading from lock to ground. He knew what they were doing and could take it for granted, but he could never be that casual about the weather. Even as he latched the outer lock portal behind him, he was looking at as much of the sky as the towering hull of his command permitted.

The darkness was deepening very, very slowly as Dhrawn's two-month rotation carried the feeble sun farther below the horizon. As at home, the horizon itself seemed to be somewhat above his level of sight all around. The gravity-squeezed atmosphere responsible for this effect would also set the stars twinkling violently when they became visible. Dondragmer glanced toward the bow, but the twin stars which guarded the south celestial pole, Fomalhaut and Sol, were still invisible.

A few cirrus clouds showed above, drifting rapidly toward the west. Evidently the winds a thousand or two feet above were opposed to the surface ones, as was usual during the daytime. This might change shortly, Dondragmer knew; only a few thousand miles to the west was country in which the setting of the sun would make a greater temperature change than it did here, and there might be weather changes in the next dozen hours. Exactly what sort of changes, was more than his Mesklinite sailors background, even fortified with alien meteorology and physics, enabled him to guess.

For the moment, though, all seemed well. He made his way down the ramp to the snow and a hundred yards to the east, the lock was on the starboard side, partly to make sure of the rest of the sky and partly to get an overall view of his command before commencing a detailed inspection.

The western sky was no more threatening than the rest, and he favored it with only a brief glance.

The *Kwembly* looked just as usual. To a human being it would probably have suggested a cigar made of dough and allowed to settle on a flat table for a time. It was slightly over a hundred feet in length, between twenty and twenty-five in breadth, and its highest point was nearly twenty feet above the snow. Actually there were two such points; the upper curve of the hull, about a third of the way back, and the bridge itself. The latter was a twenty-foot crosspiece whose nearly square outlines somewhat spoiled the smooth curves of the main body. It was almost at the bow, permitting helmsman, commander, and conning personnel to watch the ground as they travelled almost to the point where the forward trucks covered it.

The flat bottom of the vehicle was nearly a yard off the snow, supported on an almost continuous set of tread-bearing trucks. These were individually castered and connected by a bewildering rigging of fine cables, allowing the *Kwembly* to turn in a fairly short radius with reasonably complete control of her traction. The trucks were separated from the hull proper by what amounted to a pneumatic mattress, which distributed traction and adapted to minor ground irregularities.

A caterpillarlike figure was making its way slowly along the near side of the land-cruiser, presumably Beetchermarlf continuing his inspection of the rigging. Twenty yards closer to the captain the short tower of the core drill had been erected. Above, clinging to the holdfasts which studded the hull but could hardly be seen at the captain's distance, other crew members were climbing about as they inspected the seams for tightness. This, to a Mesklinite, was a nerve-stretching job. Acrophobia was a normal and healthy state of mind to a being reared on a world where polar gravity was more than six hundred times that of Earth, and even "home" gravity a third of that. Dhrawn's comparatively feeble pull, scarcely thirteen hundred feet per second squared, took some of the curse off climbing, but hull inspection was still the least popular of duties. Dondragmer crawled back across the hard-packed mixture of white crystals and brown dust, interrupted by occasional sprawling bushes, and made his way up the side to help out with the job.

The great, curved plates were of boron fiber bonded with oxygen- and fluorine-loaded polymers. They had been fabricated on a world none of the Mesklinites had ever seen, though most of the crew had had dealings with its natives. The human chemical engineers had designed those hull members to withstand every corrosive agent they could foresee. They fully realized that Dhrawn was one of the few places in the universe likely to be even worse in this respect than their own oxygen-and-water world. They were quite aware of its gravity. They had all these factors in mind when they synthesized the hull members and the adhesives which held them together: both the temporary cements used during the testing on Mesklin and the supposedly permanent ones employed in reassembling the vehicles on Dhrawn. Dondragmer had every confidence in the skill of those men, but he could not forget that they had not faced and never expected to face the conditions their products were fighting. These particular parachute packers would never be asked to jump, though that paradox would have been lost on a Mesklinite.

Much as the captain respected theory, he very well knew the gap between it and practice, hence he devoted full attention to examining the joints between the great hull sections.

By the time he had satisfied himself that they were still sound and tight, the sky had become noticeably darker. Kervenser, in response to a rap on the outside of the bridge and a few gestures, had turned on some of the outside lights. By their aid the climbers finished their work and made their way back onto the snow.

Beetchermarlf appeared from under the great hull and reported his tiller lines in perfect shape. The workers at the drill had recovered several feet of core, and were taking this into the laboratory as soon as each segment was obtained, in view of the ambient temperature. Actually the local "snow" seemed to be nearly all water at the surface, and therefore safely below its melting point, but no one could be sure how true this would be deeper down.

The artificial light made the sky less noticeable. The first warning of changing weather was a sudden gust of wind. The *Kwembly* rocked slightly on her treads, the tiller lines singing as the dense air swept past them. The Mesklinites were not inconvenienced. In Dhrawn's gravity blowing them away would have been a job for a respectable tornado. They weighed about as much as a life-sized gold statue would have on Earth. Dondragmer, digging his claws reflexively into the dusty snow, was not bothered by the wind; but he was much annoyed at his own failure to notice earlier the clouds which accompanied it. These had changed from the fleecy cirrus perhaps a thousand feet above to broken stratus-type scud at half that height. There was no precipitation yet, but none of the sailors doubted that it would come soon. They could not guess, however, what form it would take or how violent it might be. They had been a year and a half on Dhrawn, by human measure, but this was not nearly long enough to learn all the moods of a world far larger than their own. Even had that world completed one of its own revolutions, instead of less than a quarter of one, it would not have been time enough and Dondragmer's crew knew it.

The captain's voice rose above the song of the wind. "Inside, everyone. Berjendee, Reffel, and Stakendee to me to help with the drilling gear. First man inside tell Kervenser to stand by on engines and be ready to swing bow to wind when the last of us is aboard." Dondragmer knew as he gave the command that it might be impossible to obey it. It was quite likely that the maintenance check might be at a stage which would prevent engine start. Having issued the order, however, he thought about it no further. It would be carried out if possible, and his attention was needed elsewhere. The drilling equipment was top priority; it was research apparatus, which was the entire reason for the Mesklinites' presence on Dhrawn. Even Dondragmer, comparatively free of that suspicion of human intentions and motives which affected many Mesklinites, suspected that the average human scientist would value the drilling equipment more highly than the lives of one or two of the crew.

The researchers had already withdrawn the bit and started inside with it when he reached them. The crank and gear box of the muscle-powered device followed, leaving only the supporting frame and guide towers. These were less critical, since they could be replaced without human assistance, but since the wind was growing no worse, the captain and his helpers stayed to salvage them also. By the time this had been done, the others had vanished inside and Kervenser was clearly impatient on the bridge above.

Thankfully Dondragmer shepherded his group up the ramp and through the lock door, which he latched behind them. They were now standing on a yard-wide shelf running the length of the lock, facing an equally

wide pool of liquid ammonia which formed the in-
board half of the compartment. The most heavily bur-
dened of the group climbed into the liquid grasping
holds similar to those on the outer hull; others, like
the captain, simply dived in. The inner wall of the lock
extended four feet below the surface, and had a three-
foot clearance between its lower edge and the bottom
of the tank. Passing under this and climbing the far
side, they emerged on a ledge similar to that at the
entrance. Another door gave them ingress to the mid-
section of the *Kwembly*.

There was a slight stink of oxygen about them—a
few bubbles of outside air usually accompanied anything which went through the lock—but the ubiquitous
ammonia vapor and the catalyst surfaces exposed at
many sites within the hull had long ago proven capable
of keeping this nuisance under control. Most of the
Mesklinites had learned not to mind the odor too much
especially since, as far as anyone knew, really small
traces of the gas were harmless.

The researchers doffed their suits and made off with
their apparatus and the cases which had protected their
cores from the liquid ammonia. Dondragmer dismissed
the others to their regular duties, and headed for the
bridge. Kervenser started to leave the command station
as the captain came through the hatch, but the latter
waved him back and went to the starboard end of the
superstructure. Portions of its floor were transparent.
The human designers had originally intended it all to
be so, but they had failed to allow for Mesklinite psychology. Crawling about on the hull was bad enough,
but standing on a transparent floor over fifteen feet
or so of empty air was beyond all reason. The captain
stopped at the edge of one of the floor panes and
looked down gingerly.

The grayish surface about the huge vehicle was
unchanged; the wind which shook the hull was making

no apparent impression on the snow which had been packed by two-score Earth gravities for no one knew how much time. Even the eddies around the *Kwembly* showed no signs of their presence, though Dondragmer had rather expected them to be digging holes at the edges of his treads. Farther out, to the limit reached by the lights, nothing could be seen on the expanse except holes where the cores had been dug and the whipping branches of an occasional bush. He watched these closely for several minutes, expecting the wind to make some impression there if anywhere, but finally shifted his attention to the sky.

A few bright stars were beginning to show between the patches of scud, but the Guardians of the Pole could not be seen. They were only a few degrees above the southern horizon—much of that due to refraction —and the clouds further blocked the slanting view. There was still no sign of rain or snow, and no way of telling which, if either, to expect. The temperature outside was still just below the melting point of pure ammonia and far below that of water, but mixed precipitation was more than likely. What these would do to the nearly pure water-ice under him was more than Dondragmer cared to guess; he knew about the mutual solubility of water and ammonia, but had never attempted to memorize phase diagrams or freezing-point tables of the various possible mixtures. If the snow did dissolve, the *Kwembly* might get a chance to show her floating ability. He was not eager to make the test.

Kervenser interrupted his thoughts.

"Captain, we will be ready to move in four or five minutes. Do you want driving power?"

"Not yet. I was afraid that the wind would cut the snow out from under us and tip us over, like backwash on a beached ship, and I wanted to be bow-on if that happened; but there seems to be no danger of it so far. Have the maintenance checks continue except for items which would interfere with a five-minute warning for drive power."

"That's what we're doing, Captain. I set it up when your order came in a few minutes ago."

"Good. Then we'll keep outside lights on and watch the ground around us until we're ready to go again, or until the blow ends."

"It's a nuisance not being able to guess when that will be."

"It is. At home a storm seldom lasts more than a day, and never more than an hour or so. This world turns so slowly that storm cells can be as big as a continent, and could take hundreds of hours to pass. We'll just have to wait this one out."

"You mean we can't travel until the wind goes down?"

"I'm not sure. Air scouting would be risky, and we couldn't go fast enough without it for scouting to be worth the trouble, as far as the human crowd is concerned."

"I don't like going so fast anyway. You can't really look over a place unless you stop for a while. We must be missing a lot that even the human funnies would find interesting."

"They seem to know what they want—something about being able to decide whether Dhrawn is a planet or a star—and they pay the bills. I admit it gets boring for people with nothing to occupy them but routine."

Kervenser let that remark pass without comment, if not without notice. He knew his commander would not have been deliberately insulting, even after the mate's slighting remark about human beings. This was a point on which Dondragmer differed rather sharply from many of his fellows, who took for granted that the aliens were out for what they could get, like any good traders. The commander had spent more time in close communication with human, Paneshk, and Drommian scientists than had almost any other Mesklinite and, having a rather tolerant and accommodating personality to start with, had become what many of the other Mesklinites regarded as soft with respect to the aliens.

Discussion of the matter was rare, and Beetchermarlf's arrival foretsalled it this time. He reported completion of checkout. Dondragmer relieved him, ordered him to send the new helmsman to the bridge, and fell silent until the latter arrived. Takoorch, however, was not the sort to live with silence; and when he reached the bridge lost little time in starting what he doubtless considered a conversation. Kervenser, amused as usual by the fellow's imagination and gall, kept him going; however, Dondragmer ignored all but occasional snatches of the conversation. He was more interested in what was going on outside, little as that seemed to be at the moment.

He cut off the bridge lights and all the outside ones but the lowest floods, giving himself a better view of the sky without completely losing touch with the surface. The clouds were fewer and smaller, but they seemed to be moving past quite as rapidly as before. The sound of the wind remained about the same. More stars were slowly appearing. Once he glimpsed one of the Guardians, as the Mesklinite sailors had so quickly named them, low to the south. He could not tell which it was; Sol and Fomalhaut were about equally bright from Dhrawn, and their violent twinkling through the huge world's atmosphere made color judgment unreliable. The glimpse was brief anyway, since the clouds were not completely gone.

"—the whole starboard group of rafts peeled off, with everyone but me on the main body—"

Still no rain or snow, and the clearing skies made them seem less likely now, to the captain's relief. A check with the laboratory through one of the speaking tubes informed him that the temperature was dropping; it was now 75, three degrees below ammonia melting point. Still close enough for trouble with mixtures, but heading in the right direction.

"—of the islands south and west of Dingbar. We'd been ridden ashore by a storm bulge, and were high and dry with half the drift boards broken. I—"

The stars overhead were almost uninterrupted now; the scud had nearly vanished. The constellations were familiar, of course. Most of the brighter stars in the neighborhood were little affected by a three-parsec change in viewpoint. Dondragmer had had plenty of time to get used to the minor changes, anyway, and no longer noticed them. He tried to find the Guardians once more, but still had no luck. Maybe there were still clouds to the south. It was too dark now to be sure. Even cutting the rest of the floods for a moment didn't help. It did, however, attract the attention of the other two, and the flow of anecdote ceased for a moment.

"Anything changing, Captain?" Kervenser's jocular attitude vanished at the possibility of action.

"Possibly. Stars are showing above, but not to the south. Not anywhere near the horizon, in fact. Try a spot."

The first office obeyed, and a spear of light flicked upward from a point behind the bridge as he touched one of the few electrical controls. Dondragmer manipulated a pair of pull cables, and the beam swung toward the western horizon. A wail, the rough equivalent of a human grunt of surprise, came from Kervenser as the descending beam became more visible parallel to the ground.

"Fog!" exclaimed the helmsman. "Thin, but that's what's blocking the horizon." Dondragmer gave a gesture of agreement as he reared to a speaking tube.

"Research!" he hooted. "Possible precipitation.

Check what it is, and what it could do to this water-ice under us."

"It will take a while to get a sample, sir," came the answer. "We'll be as quick as we can. Are we cleared outside, or will we have to work through the hull?"

The captain paused for a moment, listening to the wind and remembering how it had felt.

"You're cleared out. Be as quick as you can."

"On the way, Captain."

At Dondragmer's gesture, the first officer cut off the spot, and the three went to the starboard end of the bridge to watch the outside party.

They moved quickly but the haze was becoming more noticeable by the time the lock opened. Two caterpillarlike forms emerged carrying a cylindrical package between them. They made their way forward to a point almost under the watchers, and set up their equipment—essentially a funnel facing into the wind and feeding into a filter. It took several minutes to convince them that they had a big enough sample, but eventually they dismantled the equipment, sealed the filter into a container to preserve it from the lock fluid and made their way back to the entrance.

"I suppose it will take them a day to decide what it is, now," grumbled Kervenser.

"I doubt it," replied the captain. "They've been playing with quick tests for water-ammonia solutions. I think Borndender said something about density being enough, given a decent sized sample."

"In that case, why are they taking so long?"

"They could hardly be out of their air-suits yet," the captain pointed out patiently.

"Why should they get out of them before making delivery to the lab? Why couldn't—"

A hoot from a speaking tube interrupted him. Dondragmer acknowledged.

"Just about pure ammonia, sir. I think it was super-cooled liquid droplets; it froze into a froth in the filter, and let quite a bit of outside air loose when it melted in here. If you should smell oxygen for the next few minutes, that's it. It may start icing up the hull, and if it coats the bridge, as it did the filter, it will interfere with your seeing, but that's all I can guess at right now in the way of trouble."

It was not all Dondragmer could imagine, but he acknowledged the information without further comment.

"This sort of thing hasn't happened since we've been here," he remarked. "I wonder whether it's some sort of seasonal change coming on. We are getting closer to this body's sun. I wish the human crowd had watched this world for a longer time before they sold us on the idea of exploring it for them. It would be so nice to know what comes next. Kervenser, start engines. When ready, turn bow into wind and proceed ahead dead slow, if you can still see out. If not, circle as sharply as possible to port, to stay on surface we know. Keep an eye on the treads—figuratively, of course; we can't see them without going out—and let me know if there's evidence that anything is sticking to them. Post a man at the stern port; our trail might show something. Understand?"

"The orders, yes, sir. What you're expecting, no."

"I may be wrong, and if I'm right there's probably nothing to do anyway. I don't like the idea of going outside to clear the treads manually. Just hope."

"Yes, sir." Kervenser turned to his task, and as the fusion engines in the *Kwembly's* trucks came to life, the captain turned to a block of plastic about four inches high and wide and a foot long, which lay beside his station. He inserted one of his nippers in a small hole in the side of the block, manipulated a control, and began to talk.

II
GRANDSTAND

His voice travelled fast, but it was a long time on the way. The radio waves carrying it sped through Dhrawn's heavy but quickly thinning atmosphere and through the space beyond for second after second. They weakened as they travelled, but half a minute after they had been radiated their energy was still concentrated enough to affect a ten-foot dish antenna. The one they encountered was projecting from a cylinder some three hundred feet in diameter and half as long: it formed one end of a structure resembling a barbell, spinning slowly about an axis perpendicular to its bar and midway between its weights.

The current induced by the waves in the antenna flicked, in a much shorter time, into a pinhead-size crystal which rectified it, enveloped it, used the envelope to modulate an electron stream provided by a finger-sized generator beside it and thus manipulated an amazingly old-fashioned dynamic cone in a thirty-foot-square room near the center of the cylinder. Just thirty-two seconds after Dondragmer uttered his words they were reproduced for the ears of three of the fifteen human beings seated in the room. He did not know who would be there at the time, and therefore spoke the human tongue he had learned rather than his own language; so all three understood him.

"This is an interim report from the *Kwembly*. We stopped two and a half hours ago for routine maintenance and investigation. Wind was about 200 cables at the time, from the west, sky partly cloudy. Shortly after we got to work the wind picked up to over 3,000 cables—"

One of the human listeners was wearing a puzzled expression, and after a moment managed to catch the eye of another.

"A Mesklinite cable is about 206 feet, Boyd," the latter said softly. "The wind jumped from about five miles an hour to over sixty."

"Thanks, Easy." Their attention returned to the speaker.

"Fog has now closed us in completely, and is getting ever thicker. I don't dare move as I had planned; just in circles to keep the treads from icing. The fog is supercooled ammonia according to my scientists, and the local surface is water snow. It doesn't seem to have occurred to my research people, but with the temperature in the seventies it seems to me there's a chance of the fog's dissolving some of the water ice to make a liquid. I realize this machine is supposed to float, and I don't suppose the surface would melt very deeply anyway, but I'm wondering whether anyone has thought much about what will happen if a liquid freezes around our treads. I have to admit I never have, but the thought of chipping the ship loose by muscle power isn't inviting. I know there's no special equipment on board to handle such a situation, because I assembled and loaded this machine myself. I'm simply calling to report that we might possibly be here a good deal longer than planned. I'll keep you informed, and if we do get immobilized we'll be glad of projects to keep our scientists busy. They've already done most of the things you set up for an ordinary stop."

"Thanks, Don," replied Easy. "We'll stand by. I'll

ask our observers and aerologists whether they can make a guess about the size of your fog bank, and how long it's likely to stay around you. They may have some useful material already, since you've been on the night side for a day or so. For that matter, they may even have current pictures; I don't know all the limits of their instruments. Anyway, I'll check and let you know."

The woman opened her microphone switch and turned to the others as her words sped toward Dhrawn.

"I wish I could tell from Don's voice whether he's really worried or not," she remarked. "Every time those people run into something new on that horrible world, I wonder how we ever had the gall to send them there or how they had the courage to go."

"They certainly weren't forced or tricked into it, Easy," pointed out one of her companions. "A Mesklinite who has spent most of his life as a sailor, and covered his home planet from equator to south pole, certainly isn't naive about any of the aspects of exploring or pioneering. We couldn't have kidded them if we'd wanted to."

"I know that in my head, Boyd, but my stomach doesn't always believe it. When the *Kwembly* was bogged in sand only five hundred miles from the settlement, I was grinding enamel off my teeth until they worked her loose. When Densigeref's *Smof* was trapped in a cleft by a mud flow that formed under it and let it down, I was almost the only one who backed up Barlennan's decision to send another of the big landrovers to the rescue. When the *Esket's* crew disappeared with a couple of very good friends of mine, I fought both Alan and Barlennan on the decision *not* to send a rescue crew. And I still think they were wrong. I know there's a job to be done and that the Mesklinites agreed to do it with a clear understanding of its risks, but when one of those crews gets into trouble I just can't help imagining myself down there with them and I tend to take their side when there's an argument about rescue action. I suppose I'll be fired from this place eventually because of that, but it's the way I'm made."

Boyd Mersereau chuckled.

"Don't worry, Easy. You have that job just because you do react that way. Please remember that if we do disagree strongly with Barlennan or any of his people, we're six million miles and forty g's of potential away and he's probably going to do what he wants anyway. Whenever it gets to that point, it's very much to our advantage to have someone up here whom he can regard as being on his side. Don't change a bit, please."

"Humph." If Elise Hoffman was either pleased or relieved, she failed to show it. "That's what Ib is always saying, but I've been writing him off as prejudiced."

"I'm sure he is, but that doesn't necessarily disqualify him from forming a sound opinion. You must believe some things he says."

"Thanks, Easy," Dondragmer's answer interrupted the discussion. He was using his own language this time, which neither of the men understood very well. "I'll be glad of any word your observers can supply. You needn't report to Barlennan unless you particularly want to. We aren't actually in trouble yet and he has enough on his mind without being bothered by maybe's. The research suggestions you can send down straight to the lab on set two; I'd probably mix them up if I relayed. I'll sign off now, but we'll keep all four sets manned."

The speaker fell silent, and Aucoin, the third human listener, got to his feet, looking at Easy for a translation. She obliged.

"That means work," he said. "We had a number of longer programs planned for later in the *Kwembly's* trip, but if Dondragmer may be delayed long where he is, I'd better see which of them would fit now. I got enough of that other speech to suggest that he doesn't really expect to move soon. I'll go to Computation first and have them reproduce a really precise set of position bearing for him from the shadow satellites, then I'll go to Atmospherics for their opinion and then I'll be in the planning lab."

"I may see you in Atmospherics," replied Easy. "I'm going now to get the information Dondragmer wanted, if you'll stand watch here, Boyd."

"All right, for a while. I have some other work to do myself, but I'll make sure the *Kwembly's* screens are covered. You'd better tell Don who's here, though, so he won't send up an emergency message in Stennish or whatever he calls his native language. Come to think of it, though, I suppose sixty seconds extra delay wouldn't matter much, considering what little we could do for him from here."

The woman shrugged, spoke a few words of the little sailor's language into the transmitter, waved to Mersereau, and was gone before Dondragmer received her last phrase. Alan Aucoin had already left.

The meteorology lab was on the "highest" level of the cylinder, enough closer to the spin axis of the station to make a person about ten percent lighter than in the communication room. Facilities for exercise being as limited as they were, powered elevators had been omitted from the station's design, and intercoms were regarded as strictly emergency equipment. Easy Hoffman had the choice of a spiral stairway at the axis of symmetry of the cylinder or any of several ladders. Since she wasn't carrying anything, she didn't bother with the stairs. Her destination was almost directly "above" Communications, and she reached it in less than a minute.

The most prominent features in this room were two twenty-foot-diameter hemispherical maps of Dhrawn.

Each was a live-vision screen carrying displays of temperature, reference-altitude pressure, wind velocity, where it was obtainable, and such other data as could be obtained either from the low-orbiting shadow satellites or the Mesklinite exploring crews. A spot of green light marked the Settlement just north of the equator, and nine fainter yellow sparks scattered closely around it indicated the exploring land-cruisers. Against the background of the gigantic planet their spread made an embarrasingly small display, scattered over a range of some eight thousand miles east and west and twenty or twenty-five thousand north and south, on the western side of what the meteorologists called Low Alpha. The yellow lights, except for two well out in the colder regions to the west, formed a rough arc framing the Low. Eventually it was to be ringed with sensing stations, but little more than a quarter of its eighty thousand mile perimeter had so far been covered.

The cost had been high—not merely in money, which Easy tended to regard as merely a measure of effort expended, but in life. Her eyes sought the red-ringed yellow light just inside the Low which marked the position of the *Esket*. Seven months—three and a half of Dhrawn's days—had passed since any human being had seen a sign of her crew, though her transmitters still sent pictures of her interior. Easy thought grimly, now and again, of her friends Kabremm and Destigmet; and occasionally she bothered Dondragmer's conscience, though she had no way of knowing this, by talking about them to the *Kwembly's* commander.

"H'lo, Easy," and "Hi, Mom," cut into her gloomy thoughts.

"Hello, weather men," she responded. "I have a friend who'd like a forecast. Can you help?"

"If it's for here in the station, sure," answered Benj.

"Don't be cynical, son. You're old enough to understand the difference between knowing nothing and not knowing everything. It's for Dondragmer of the *Kwembly*." She indicated the yellow light on the map, and outlined the situation. "Alan is bringing an exact position, if that will help."

"Probably not much," Seumas McDevitt admitted. "If you don't like cynicism I'll have to pick my words carefully; but the light on the screen there should be right within a few hundred miles, and I doubt that we can compute a precise enough forecast for that to make a significant difference."

"I wasn't sure you'd have enough material for any predictions at all," Easy countered. "I understand that weather comes from the west even on this world, and the area to the west has been out of sunlight for days now. Can you see such places well enough to get useful data?"

"Oh, sure." Benj's sarcasm had vanished and the enthusiasm which had caused him to put down atmospheric physics as his post-primary tentative was taking over. "We don't get much of our measurement from reflected sunlight anyway; nearly all is direct radiation from the planet. There's a lot more emitted than it receives from the sun anyway; you've heard the old argument as to whether Dhrawn ought to be called a star or a planet. We can tell ground temperature, a good deal about ground cover, lapse rates, and clouds. Winds are harder—" he hesitated, seeing McDevitt's eye on him and unable to read the meteorologist's poker face. The man read the trouble in time and nodded him on before the rush of self-confidence had lost momentum. McDevitt had never been a teacher, but he had the touch.

"Winds are harder because of the slight uncertainty in cloud heights and the fact that adiabatic temperature changes often have more to say about the location of clouds than air mass identities do. In that gravity, the air density drops by half about every hundred yards of climb, and that makes for terrific PV changes in temperature—" he paused again, this time eying his mother. "Do you know about that sort of thing, or should I slow down?"

"I'd hate to have to solve quantitative problems on what you've just been saying," Easy replied, "but I think I have a fair qualitative picture. I get the impression that you're a little doubtful about telling Don to the nearest minute when his fog is going to clear. Would a report from him on surface pressures and winds be any help? The Kwembly has instruments, you know."

"It might," McDevitt admitted as Benj nodded silently. "Can I talk to the Kwembly directly? And will any of them understand me? My Stennish doesn't exist yet."

"I'll translate if I can keep your technical terms straight," replied Easy. "If you plan to do more than a one-month tour here, though, it would be a good idea to try to pick up the language of our little friends. Many of them know some of ours, but they appreciate it."

"I know. I plan to. I'd be glad if you'd help me."

"When I can, certainly; but you'll see a lot more of Benj."

"Benj? He came here three weeks ago with me, and hasn't had any better chance to learn languages than I have. We've both been checking out on the local observation and computer nets, and filling in on the project background." Easy grinned at her son.

"That's as may be. He's a language bug like his mother, and I think you'll find him useful, though I admit he got his Stennish from me rather than the Mesklinites. He insisted on my teaching him something that his sisters wouldn't be able to listen in on. Write as much of that off to parental pride as you like, but give him a try. Later, that is; I'd like that information for Dondragmer as soon as we can get it. He said the wind was from the west at about sixty miles an hour, if that helps at all."

The meteorologist pondered a moment.

"I'll run what we have through integration, with that bit added," he said finally. "Then we can give him something when we call, and if the numerical details he gives us then are too different we can make another run easily enough. Wait a moment."

He and the boy turned to their equipment, and for several minutes their activities meant little to the woman. She knew, of course, that they were feeding numerical data and weighting values into computing devices which were presumably already programmed to handle the data appropriately. She was pleased to see Benj apparently handling his share of the work without supervision. She and her husband had been given to understand that the boy's mathematical powers might not prove up to the need of his field of interest. Of course, what he was doing now was routine which could be handled by anyone with a little training whether he really understood it or not, but Easy chose to interpret the display as encouraging.

"Of course," McDevitt remarked as the machine was digesting its input, "There'll be room for doubt anyway. This sun doesn't do very much to the surface temperature of Dhrawn, but its effect is not completely negligible. The planet has been getting closer to the sun almost ever since we really got going here three years ago. We didn't have any surface reports except from half a dozen robots until the Mesklinite settlement was set up a year and a half later, and even their measurements still cover only a tiny fraction of the planet. Our prediction work is almost entirely empirical, no matter how much we want to believe in the laws of physics, and we really don't have enough data for empirical rules yet."

Easy nodded. "I realize that, and so does Dondrag-mer," she said. "Still, you have more information than he does, and I guess anything is welcome to him at this point. I know if I were down there thousands of miles from any sort of help, in a machine which is really in the test stage, and not even able to see what was around me—well, I can tell you from experience that it helps to be in touch with the outside. Not just in the way of conversation, though that helps, but so they could more or less see me and know what I was going through."

"We'd have an awful time seeing him," put in Benj. "Even when the air at the other end is clear, six million miles is a long way for telescope work."

"You're right, of course, but I think you know what I mean," his mother said quietly. Benj shrugged and said no more; in fact, a rather tense silence ensued for perhaps half a minute.

It was interrupted by the computer, which ejected a sheet of cryptic symbols in front of McDevitt. The other two leaned over his shoulders to see it, though this did Easy little good. The boy spent about five sec-onds glancing over the lines of information, and emitted a sound halfway between a snort of contempt and a laugh. The meteorologist glanced up at him.

"Go ahead, Benj. You can be as sarcastic as you like on this one. I'd advise against letting Dondragmer have these results uncensored."

"Why? What's wrong with them?" asked the woman.

"Well, most of the data, of course, was from shadow satellite readings. I did plug in your wind report, with a bit of uncertainty. I don't know what sort of instru-ments the caterpillars have down there, or how pre-cisely the figures were transmitted to you; and you did say *about* sixty for the wind speed. I didn't mention the fog, since you didn't tell me any more than the fact that it was there, and I had no numbers. The first line of this computer run says that visibility in normal light—normal to human eyes, that is, and about the same to Mesklinite ones, I gather—is twenty-two miles for a one-degree blur."

Easy raised her eyebrows. "Just how do you account for something like that? I thought all the old jokes about weather men had gone pretty well out of date?"

"Actually, they just got stale. I account for it by the simple fact that we don't and can't have complete information for the machine. The most obvious lack is a detailed topographic chart of the planet, especially the couple of million square miles west of the *Kwembly*. A wind coming up or down a slope of six inches per mile at any respectable speed would change its air mass temperature rapidly just from PV change, as Benj pointed out a few minutes ago. Actually, the best maps we have of the topography were worked out from just that effect, but they're pretty sketchy. I'll have to get more detailed measurements from Dondragmer's people and give them another run. Did you say Aucoin was getting a more exact position for the *Kwembly?*"

Easy had no time to answer; Aucoin himself appeared in the room. He did not bother with greetings, and took for granted that the meteorologists would have the background information from Easy.

"Eight point four five five degrees south of the equator, seven point nine two three east of the Settlement meridian. That's as close as they'll swear to. Is a thousand yards or so too much uncertainty for what you need?"

"Everybody's being sarcastic today," muttered McDevitt. "Thanks, that'll be fine. Easy, can we go down to Comm and have that talk with Dondragmer?"

"All right. Do you mind if Benj comes along, or is there work he should be doing here? I'd like him to meet Dondragmer, too."

"And incidentally display his linguistic powers. All right, he may come. You, too, Alan?"

"No. There's other work to do. I'd like to know the details on any forecast you consider trustworthy, though, and anything Dondragmer reports which might conceivably affect Planning. I'll be in PL."

The weather man nodded. Aucoin took himself off in one direction, and the other three made their way down ladders to the communication room. Mersereau had disappeared, as he had intimated he might, but one of the other watchers had shifted his position to keep an eye on the *Kwembly's* screens. He waved and returned to his place as Easy entered. The others paid the party little attention. They had been aware of Easy's and Mersereau's departures simply because of the standing rule that there were never to be fewer than ten observers in the room at once. The stations were not assigned on a rigid schedule; this had been found to lead to the equivalent of road hypnosis.

The four communication sets tied to the *Kwembly* had their speakers centered in front of a group of six seats. The corresponding vision screens were set higher, so that they could also be seen from the general seats further back. Each of the six "station" seats was equipped with a microphone and a selector switch permitting contact with any one or all four of the *Kwembly's* radios.

Easy settled herself in a comfortably central chair and switched its microphone to the set on Dondragmer's bridge. There was little to be seen on the corresponding screen, since the transmitter's eye was pointed forward toward the bridge windows and the Mesklinites' report of fog was perfectly correct. The helmsman's station and its occupant could be partly seen in the lower left-hand corner of the screen; the rest was gray blankness marked off into rectangles by the window braces. The bridge lights were subdued, but the fog beyond the windows was illuminated by the *Kwembly's* outside floods, Easy judged.

"Don!" she called. "Easy here. Are you on the bridge?" She snapped on a timer and shifted her selector switch to the set in the laboratory. "Borndender, or whoever is there," she called, still in Stennish, "we can't get a reliable weather prediction with the information we have. We're talking to the bridge, but we'd be glad if you could give us as exactly as possible your present temperature, wind velocity, outside pressure, anything quantitative you have on the fog, and—" she hesitated.

"And the same information for the past few hours, with times given as closely as possible," Benj cut in in the same language.

"We'll be ready to receive as soon as the bridge finishes talking," continued the woman.

"We could also use whatever you have on air, fog, and snow composition," added her son.

"If there is any other material you think might be of help, it will also be welcome," finished Easy. "You're there and we aren't, and there must be some ideas about Dhrawn's weather you've formed on your own." The timer sounded a bell note. "The bridge is coming in now. We'll be waiting for your words when the captain finished."

The speaker's first words overlapped her closing phrase. The timer had been set for the light-speed lag of a round-trip message between Dhrawn and the station, and the bridge had answered promptly.

"Kervenser here, Mrs. Hoffman. The captain is below in the life-support room. I'll call him here if you like, or you can switch to the set down there, but if you have any advice for us we'd like it as quickly as possible. We can't see a body-length from the bridge and don't dare move, except in circles. The fliers gave us an idea of the neighborhood before we stopped and it seems solid enough, but we certainly can't take a chance on going forward. We're going dead slow, in a circle about twenty-five cables in diameter. Except when we're bow or stern to the wind, the ship feels as though it were going to capsize every few seconds. The fog has been freezing as it hits the windows, which is why we can't see out. The tracks still seem to be clear, I suppose because they're moving and ice gets cracked off before it can hurt, but I expect the tiller lines to freeze up any time, and getting the ice off them will be a glorious job. I suppose it will be possible to work outside, but I'd hate to do it myself until the wind stops. Having an air-suit ice up sounds unpleasant. Any thoughts?"

Easy waited patiently for Kervenser to finish. The sixty-four second message delay had had a general effect on everyone who did much talking between station and planet; they developed a strong tendency to say as much as possible at one time, guessing at what the other party wanted to hear. When she knew that Kervenser had finished and was waiting for an answer, she quickly summarized the message which had been given the scientists. As with them, she omitted all mention of the computer result which had insisted that the weather must be clear. The Mesklinites knew that human science was not infallible—most of them had, in fact, a much more realistic and healthy idea of its limitations than many human beings—but there was no point in making one's self look too silly if it could be helped. She was not, of course, a meteorologist, but she was human and Kervenser would probably lump her in with the others.

The group waited almost silently for the first officer's answer when she finished. Benj's muttered translation for the benefit of McDevitt took only a few seconds longer than the message itself. When the response finally came it was merely an acknowledgement and a polite hope that the human beings could furnish useful information soon; the *Kwembly* scientists were sending up the requested material at once.

Easy and her son readied themselves for the data. She started a recorder to check any technical terms before attempting translation, but the message came through in the human language. Evidently Borndender was sending. McDevitt recovered promptly from his surprise and began taking notes, while the boy kept his eyes on the pencil point and his ears on the speaker.

It was just as well that Easy was not needed for translation. Well as she knew Stennish, there were many words strange to her in both languages; she couldn't have interpreted either way. She knew that she should not be embarrassed by the fact, but she couldn't help it. She could not help thinking of the Mesklinites as representing a culture like that of Robin Hood or Haroun al Raschid, though she knew perfectly well that several hundred of them had received very comprehensive scientific and technical educations in the last half century. The fact had not been widely published, since there was a widespread notion that it was bad to release much advanced knowledge to "backward" peoples. It was likely to give them an inferiority complex and prevent further progress.

The weather men didn't care. When the final "over" came through, McDevitt and his assistant uttered a hasty "Thank You" into the nearest microphone and hurried off toward the laboratory. Easy, noting that the selector switch had been set for the bridge radio, corrected it and returned a more careful acknowledgement before signing off. Then, deciding that she would be useless in the meteorology lab, she settled back on the chair which gave her the best view of the *Kwembly's* four screens, and waited for something to happen.

Mersereau returned a few minutes after the others had left, and had to be brought up to date. Otherwise, nothing of note occurred. There was an occasional glimpse of a long, many-legged form on one of the screens, but the Mesklinites were going about their own affairs with no particular regard for the watchers.

Easy thought of starting another conversation with Kervenser; she knew and liked this officer almost as well as she did his captain. However, the thought of the lag between remark and answer discouraged her, as it often did when there was nothing of importance to be said.

Even with no lag, conversation languished. There was little for Easy and Mersereau to say to each other which had not already been said; a year away from Earth could be counted on to exhaust most subjects of conversation except professional shop talk and matters of private, personal interest. She had little of the latter in common with Mersereau, though she liked him well enough, and their professions overlapped only in connection with talking to Mesklinites.

In consequence there was little sound in the communication room. Every few minutes one or another of the exploring land-cruisers would send in a report, which would be duly relayed to the Settlement; but most of the human beings on watch had no more occasion for small talk than Easy and Boyd Mersereau. Easy found herself trying to guess when the weather men would be back with their forecast and how reliable the new one would be. Say, two minutes to the lab, or one, if they hurried; one more to feed the new material into the computer; two for the run; five minutes of arguing, since she knew her son, over whether this prediction was really any better than the last; a repeat run with modified weights on the variables; two minutes back down to the comm room, since they certainly wouldn't hurry this time. They'd still be arguing. They should be here soon.

But before they made it, things changed. Quite suddenly, the bridge screen demanded attention. It had been quiet, with gray windows masked by frozen ammonia dominating the foreshortened image of part of the helmsman. The latter had been almost motionless, his tiller bar well over to one side as the *Kwembly* pursued the circular path described by Kervenser.

Then the windows were suddenly clear, though little could be seen beyond them; the communicator's angle of view was not depressed enough to reach ground within range of the lights. Two more Mesklinites appeared and flowed over to the windows, looking out and gesturing with obvious excitement. Mersereau pointed to another screen; there was excitement in the lab, too. So far, none of the little explorers had seen fit to report what was going on. Easy judged they were too occupied with immediate problems, furthermore it was customary for them to keep their sound volume down, or off completely, unless they specifically wanted to speak to the human beings.

At this point the weather men returned. Easy saw her son out of the corner of her eye, and asked without looking around, "Do you have anything useful this time?"

McDevitt answered briefly, "Yes. Shall I have Benj translate it to them?"

"No. They're in some sort of trouble, it seems. Give them the word yourself. Dondragmer would certainly be on the bridge, or will be by the time your words get there, when anything like this is going on. Here, use this seat and mike."

The meteorologist obeyed without question. It would be the last time for many months that he would pay Easy that compliment. He began talking as he settled into the seat.

"Dondragmer, you should have about nineteen hours of reduced visibility. The freezing fog should last for less than another hour; the temperature is going down, and the fog will change to ammonia crystals which shouldn't stick to your windows. If you can get rid of the ice already there, you should at least see through them into the snow. The wind will decrease gradually for about five more hours. By that time, the temperature should be low enough so you needn't worry about eutectic melting. There will be higher clouds for another forty-five hours—" He went on, but Easy had stopped listening.

Near the end of McDevitt's second sentence, long before the beginning of his message could have reached Dhrawn, a Mesklinite had approached the bridge pickup so closely that his grotesque face nearly filled the screen. One of his nipper-equipped arms reached out of sight to one side, and Easy knew he was activating the voice transmitter. She was not surprised to hear the captain speaking in a much calmer tone than she could have managed under the circumstances.

"Easy, or whoever is on watch, please get a special report to Barlennan. The temperature has gone up six degrees, to one hundred three, in the last few minutes, the ice has melted from the windows, and we are afloat."

III
NERVE CENTER

Perhaps it was unkind for Dondragmer to have given his report in the human language. The time taken for translation might have eased the shock a trifle for Mc-Devitt. The worst part, as the meteorologist said later, was realizing that his own prediction was on its way to Dhrawn and nothing could stop it. For a moment he had a wild notion of getting a ship and racing the radio waves to the planet so as to shadow them from the *Kwembly's* receivers. The thought was only a flicker; only so much can be done in thirty-two seconds. Besides, none of the tenders then at the station was capable of faster-than-light flight. Most of them were used in servicing the shadow satellites.

Easy, in the next seat, didn't seem to have noticed the discrepancy between the prediction and Dondragmer's report; at least, she hadn't glanced at him with the expression which nine out of ten of his friends would have used. Well, she wouldn't, he thought. That's why she's on this job.

The woman was manipulating her selector switch again, with her attention focussed on a smaller screen above the *Kwembly's* four. At first an indicator beside it glowed red; as she worked her switches it turned green and the image of an office-like room with fully a dozen Mesklinites in view appeared on the screen. Easy began her report instantly.

She was brief. All she could give was a repetition of Dondragmer's few sentences. She had finished long before there was any evidence on the screen that her words were being received.

When the response came, however, it was satisfying. Every caterpillarlike body in sight looped toward the pickup. While Easy had never learned to read expression on the Mesklinite "face", there was no misunderstanding the wildly waving arms and snapping pincers. One of the creatures raced toward a semicircular doorway at the far side of the room and disappeared through it. In spite of the creature's red and black coloration, Easy found herself reminded of the sight, a few years before, of one of her daughters inhaling a strand of spaghetti. A Mesklinite in a hurry under forty Earth gravities appears legless to human eyes.

The sound was not on yet from the Dhrawn end, but there was a rising buzz of conversation in the human communication room. It was not unusual for exploring land-cruisers to run into difficulties. In general the working Mesklinites took such difficulties more calmly than the human beings who were watching helplessly. In spite of the lack of intercom in the station, people began entering the room and filling the general seats. Screen after screen in the front monitoring areas was tuned to the "headquarters" unit in the Settlement. Meanwhile Easy and Mersereau were dividing their attention among the four sets reporting from the *Kwembly,* with only an occasional glance at the other picture.

It was not obvious on the screens that the vehicle was afloat because the transmitters shared any motion it might have, and there was little loose equipment whose motion might have betrayed a pitch or a roll.

The bulk of the crew were sailors by training. Lifelong habit prevented them from leaving things unsecured. Easy kept closest watch on the bridge screen hoping to spot something outside which could give a clue to what was occurring, but nothing recognizable could be seen through the windows.

Then the panes were blotted out once more as Dondragmer came back into the foreground and expanded his report.

"There seems to be no immediate danger. The wind is pulling us along fairly rapidly, judging by our wake. Our magnetic course is 66. We are floating level, submerged to about deck two. Our scientists are trying to compute the density of this liquid, but no one has ever bothered to work out displacement tables for this hull as far as I know. If you human beings happen to have that information, my people would be glad to get it. Unless we run into something solid and I can't guess at the chances of that, we'll be safe. All machinery is functioning properly, except that the treads have nothing to bite on. They race if we give them power. That's all for now. If your shadow satellites can keep track of our location, we'll be glad of that information as often as you can manage. Tell Barlennan everything is all right so far."

Easy shifted microphone connections and repeated the captain's report as nearly verbatim as she could. She saw, in due course, that it was being taken down in writing at the other end. She rather hoped that the writer would have some question to ask: not that she was likely to be able to answer it, but she was beginning to get a helpless, useless feeling again. The Mesklinite, however, merely acknowledged the information and headed for the door with his notes. Easy was left wondering how far he had to go to get them to the commander. No human being had a very good idea of the layout of the Mesklinite base.

As a matter of fact, the trip was brief. Most of it appeared to be outdoors because of the settlers' attitude toward massive objects overhead: an attitude hard to overcome even on a world where gravity was only a fraction of its normal Mesklin value. The roofs of the Settlement were almost all of transparent film brought from their home world. The only departure from a common, city-wide floor level was dictated by terrain. The thought of either a basement or a second story would never have occurred to a Mesklinite. The many-decked *Kwembly* and her sister vehicles were of basically human and Paneshk design.

The messenger wove through a maze of corridors for some two hundred yards before reaching the commander's office. This was at the northern edge of the cluster of foot-high structures which formed the greater part of the Settlement. The Settlement itself was close to the edge of a six-foot cliff extending almost a mile east and west, broken by a dozen or so artificial ramps. On the ground below the cliff, but still with their bridges looming above the transparent coverings of the "city," were two of the huge land-cruisers. The wall of Barlennan's room was also transparent and looked directly out on the nearer of these vehicles; the other was parked some thousand feet to the east. A few air-suited Mesklinites were also visible outside, dwarfed by the monstrous vehicles they were tending.

Barlennan was watching this group of mechanics critically when the runner entered. The latter used no formality, but burst into Easy's relayed report as he entered the compartment. By the time the commander had swerved around to receive the written version, he had heard it all orally.

It was not satisfactory, of course. Barlennan had had time to think up a number of questions since the first messenger had arrived, and this message answered none of them. The commander controlled his impatience.

"I take it there hasn't been anything useful from the human weather experts yet."

"Nothing at all, sir, to us. They may have been talking to the *Kwembly* without our hearing, of course."

"True enough. Has word gone to our own weather people?"

"Not as far as I know, sir. There's been nothing very useful to tell them, but Guzmeen may have sent a message there, too."

"All right. I want to talk to them myself anyway. I'll be at their complex for the next half hour or more. Tell Guz."

The messenger made the affirmative nipper gesture and vanished through the door he had entered by. Barlennan took another, making his way slowly westward through building after building and over the enclosed connecting ramps which made the Settlement a single unit. Most of the ramps on his course sloped upward, so that by the time he turned south away from the cliff he was some five feet higher than his office, though not yet on a level with the bridges of the land-cruisers behind him. The roof fabric bulged a little more tautly above him, since the nearly pure hydrogen in the station did not drop as rapidly in pressure with increasing altitude as did Dhrawn's much denser gas mixture. The Settlement had been built at an elevation which was quite high for Dhrawn. The total outside pressure was about the same as that at Mesklin's sea level. It was only when the land-cruisers descended to lower elevations that they carried extra argon to keep their internal pressure balanced.

Since Dhrawn's air carried about two per cent oxygen, the Mesklinites were careful about leaks. Barlennan still remembered the awkward results of an oxygen-hydrogen explosion shortly after he had first encountered human beings.

The research complex was the westernmost and

highest side of the colony. It was fairly well separated from most of the other structures and differed from them in having a solid, though still transparent roof. It also came closer than any other part of the Settlement to having a second story, since a number of instruments were mounted on the roof where they could be reached by ramps and liquid-trap air locks. By no means all the instruments had been furnished by the alien sponsors of the Settlement; the Mesklinites had been using their own imaginations and ingenuity for fifty years, although they had not really felt free about doing so until reaching Dhrawn.

Like the exploring vehicles, the laboratory complex was a mixture of crudeness and sophistication. Energy was supplied by hydrogen-fusion units; chemical glassware was home-made. Communication with the orbiting station was by solid-state electromagnetic beam transmitter; but messages were carried physically about the complex by runners. Steps were being taken to change this, unknown to the human beings. The Mesklinites understood the telegraph and were on the verge of making telephones able to transmit their own voice range. However, neither telephone nor telegraph was being installed in the Settlement because most of Barlennan's administrative effort was being concentrated on the project which had provoked Easy's sympathy for the *Esket's* crew. It takes a lot of work to lay cross-country telegraph lines.

Barlennan was saying nothing about this to his sponsors. He liked human beings, though he did not go as far in that direction as Dondragmer: he was always aware of their amazingly short life span, which prevented him from getting to really know the people he worked with before they were replaced by others. He was rather concerned about the possibility of human, Drommian, and Paneshk finding out just how ephemeral they all were, for fear it might depress them. It had, in fact, become Mesklinite policy to evade discussion on the matter of age with aliens. It was also policy not to depend more heavily than could be avoided on them. You never knew whether the next ones to take over would have the same attitudes. They were intrinsically undependable, most Mesklinites felt; Dondragmer's confidence in them was a glaring exception.

All this was known to the Mesklinite scientists who saw the commander arrive. Their first concern was with the immediate situation. "Is someone in trouble, or are you just visiting?"

"Trouble, I'm afraid," replied Barlennan. He briefly outlined Dondragmer's situation. "Collect anyone you think may be useful and come to the map." He made way to the forty-foot-square chamber whose floor was the "map" of Low Alpha, and waited. Very little of the area had been "mapped," so far. He felt, as he had so often before, that there was a long, long job ahead. Still, the map was more encouraging to him than its human counterpart some millions of miles above was to its human viewers. Both showed the arc covered by the land cruisers and something of the landscape. The Mesklinites had indicated this in spidery black lines suggesting a sketch of human nerve cells, complete with cell bodies.

The specific Mesklinite data centered mostly around the spot where the *Esket* lay. This information, marked in red, had been obtained without direct human assistance. This was one place in the Settlement where there would be no vision transmitter as long as Barlennan was running things.

Now, however, he focused his attention several feet to the south of the *Esket*, where there was discouragingly little data in either red or black. The line representing the track of the *Kwembly* looked lonesome. Barlennan had raised his front end as high as was com-

fortable, bringing his eyes six or seven inches from the
floor, and was looking at the map gloomily when the
scientists began to arrive. Bendivence was either very
optimistic or very pessimistic. The commander couldn't
decide which was the more likely reason for his having
called nearly twenty people to the conference. They
gathered a few feet from him, reared up and waited
politely for his information and questions. He started
without preamble.

"The *Kwembly* was here at her last report," he indicated. "It had been crossing a field of snow, water
snow, nearly clear of dissolved material but quite dirty
according to Don's science people."

"Borndender?" queried someone. Barlennan gestured
affirmatively and went on.

"The snow field started here." He crawled to a spot
nearly four feet northwest of the position marker. "It
lies between a couple of mountain ridges, which we
have indicated only roughly. Destigmet's balloons
haven't gotten this far south yet, or at least word hasn't
reached us and Don's fliers haven't seen much. Just
now, while the *Kwembly* was stopped for a routine
maintenance check, a heavy wind came up, and then a
dense fog of pure or nearly pure ammonia. Then, quite
suddenly, the temperature rose several degrees and they
found themselves afloat, being blown roughly eastward
by the wind. We would like explanations and we badly
need constructive advice. Why did the temperature go
up, and why did the snow melt? Is there any connection
between the two? Remember that the highest temperature they mentioned was only about a hundred and
three, twenty-six or seven degrees below the melting
point of water. Why the wind? How long is it likely to
last? It's carrying the *Kwembly* toward the hot regions
inside Low Alpha south of the *Esket* site." He gestured
toward a heavily red-marked section of the floor. "Can
we tell how far they'll be carried? I didn't want Don-

dragmer to go out on this trip, and I certainly don't want to lose him even if we don't agree completely.

"We'll call for what help we can get from the men, but you'll have to use your brains, too. I know some of you have been trying to make sense out of Dhrawn's climatology; do you have any worthwhile ideas which might apply here?"

Several minutes of silence followed. Even those in the group most given to uttering rhetorical speeches had been working with Barlennan too long to risk them now. For some time no really constructive ideas came up. Then one of the scientists scuttled toward the door and vanished, with "Just a moment, I have to check a table" floating behind him. He was back within thirty seconds.

"I can account for the temperature and melting," he said firmly. "The ground surface was water ice, the fog ammonia. The heat of solution as they met and mixed would have caused the temperature rise. Ammonia-water solutions form eutectics which can melt as low as seventy-one."

Mild hoots of appreciation and approving gestures of nipper-equipped arms greeted this suggestion. Barlennan went with the crowd, though words had been used which were not entirely familiar to him. But he was not through with his questions.

"Does that give us any idea how far the *Kwembly* will be carried?"

"Not in itself. We need information about the extent of the original snow field," was the answer. "Since only the *Kwembly* has been in the area, about the only hope is the photo maps made by the humans. You know how little we can get from those. Half the time you can't differentiate between ice and clouds. Besides they were all made before we landed here."

"Give it a try, anyway," ordered Barlennan. "With luck, you can at least tell whether those mountain ranges to the east are blocking the *Kwembly's* present path. If they are, it's hard to see how the craft could be carried more than a few hundred thousand cables."

"Right," answered one of the investigators. "We'll check. Ben, Dees, come along; you're more used to the photos than I am." The three vanished through the door. The others broke up into small groups, muttering arguments to each other and waving excitedly, now at the map underfoot, now at items presumably in the nearby laboratories. Barlennan endured this for several minutes before deciding that a little more guidance was needed.

"If that plateau Don was crossing was such pure water, there couldn't have been any ammonia precipitation there for a long, long time. Why should things have changed so suddenly?"

"It almost has to be a seasonal effect," answered one of the men. "I can only guess, but I'd say it had something to do with some consistent change in the wind pattern. Air currents from different parts of the planet will be saturated with water or ammonia according to the nature of the surface they pass over, mostly its temperature, I suppose. The planet is nearly twice as far from its sun at one time as at another and its axis is much more inclined than Mesklin's. It's easy to believe that at one time of year only water is precipitated on that plateau and at another it gets supplied with ammonia. Actually, the vapor pressure of water is so low that it's hard to see what situation would get water into the atmosphere without supplying even more ammonia, but I'm sure it's possible. We'll work on it, but it's another of those times when we'd be a lot better off with world-wide, year-round information. These human beings seem to be in an awful hurry; they could have waited a few more years to land us here, I should think."

Barlennan made the gesture whose human equivalent

would have been a noncommittal grunt. "The field data *would* be convenient. Just think of yourself as being here to get it instead of having it given to you."

"Of course. Are you going to send the *Kalliff* or the *Hoorsh* out to help Dondragmer? This is certainly different from the *Esket* situation."

"From our point of view, yes. It might look funny to the humans, though, if I insisted on sending out a rescue cruiser this time after letting them talk me out of it before. I'll think it over. There's more than one way of sailing upwind. You do that theoretical work you've just been talking about, but be thinking about what you'd want to take on a field trip up toward the *Kwembly*."

"Right, Commander." The scientist started to turn away, but Barlennan added a few more words.

"And Jemblakee. No doubt you'll be strolling over to Communications to talk to your human colleagues. Please don't mention this, what was it, heat of solution and eutectic business. Let them mention it first, if they're going to, and be properly impressed when and if they do. You understand?"

"Perfectly." The scientist would have shared a grin of understanding with his commander if their faces had been capable of that sort of distortion. Jemblakee left, and after a moment's thought Barlennan did the same. The remaining researchers and technicians might possibly be the better for his presence to keep their centerboards down but he had other things to do. If they couldn't hold course without his pincers on their helms, they'd just have to drift for a while.

He should talk to the human station soon; but if there was going to be an argument, as seemed rather likely, he had better do a little course-plotting himself. Some of the two-legged giants, Aucoin, for example, who seemed to have a great deal to say about their policy, were reluctant to expend or even risk any sort of reserve equipment, no matter how important the action seemed from the Mesklinite viewpoint. Since the aliens had paid for it, this was perfectly understandable, even laudable. Still there was nothing immoral about talking them around to a more convenient attitude if it could be done. If he could arrange it, the best plan would be to work through that particularly sympathetic female named Hoffman. It was too bad the human beings kept such irregular hours; if they had set up decent, regular watches in their communication section Barlennan would long since have worked out their schedule and been able to pick his party. He wondered, not for the first time, whether the irregular schedule might not be deliberately set up to block that very action, but there seemed no way to find out. He could hardly ask.

The Settlement's comm center was far enough from the laboratories to give him thinking time en route. It was also close enough to his office to encourage a pause for making a few notes before actually opening the verbal fencing match.

The central theme would have to be the question of rescue, if Dondragmer's trouble wound up crippling his cruiser. If the previous situation involving the *Esket*, months before, were any indication, the tightwads up above would be basically against sending the *Kalliff*. Of course, there was nothing they could do if Barlennan chose to go his own way in that matter, or in any other, but the commander was hoping to keep that fact cushioned in the decencies of polite conversation. He would be happiest if that aspect of the situation never came up at all. This was one reason he hoped to work Easy Hoffman into the other end of the discussion. For some reason, she seemed prone to take the Mesklinite side when disagreements arose. She was certainly one reason that there had been no open argument during the *Esket* incident, though a more important reason was that Barlennan had never had the slightest intention of sending a rescue cruiser before and had therefore actually been siding with Aucoin.

Well, he could at least go as far as the comm room door and find out who was on duty above. With the rippling equivalent of a shrug, he lifted his sprawled eighteen inches from the office floor and made his way into the corridor. It was at that moment that the wind reached the Settlement.

There was no fog at first or for some minutes thereafter. Barlennan, promptly changing his plans as the roof began rippling, got all the way back to the laboratories; but before he had a chance to get any constructive information from his scientists the stars began to fade. Within a few minutes the lights showed a solid gray ceiling a body-length above the Mesklinites. The ceilings here were rigid and did not vibrate in the wind as those in the corridor had, but the sound outside was loud enough to make more than one of the scientists wonder how stable the buildings actually were. They didn't express the thought aloud in the commander's presence but he could interpret the occasional upward glances when the whine of the heavy outside air increased in pitch.

It occurred to him that his present location was about the most useless possible one for a commander who was not a scientist, since the people around him were about the only ones in the Settlement to whom he could not reasonably give orders. He asked just one question, was informed in reply that the wind speed was about half that Dondragmer had reported some ten thousand miles away, then headed for the communication room.

He thought briefly of going back to the office on the way, but knew that anyone wanting him would find him almost as quickly at Guzmeen's station. Meanwhile a question had crossed his mind which could probably be answered by relay from the human station faster than any other way, and that question seemed more and more important as the seconds passed. Forgetting that he wanted to make sure that Easy Hoffman was on duty above, he shot into the radio room and politely nudged aside the staff member in front of the transmitter. He began to speak almost before he was in position and the sight of Hoffman's features when the screen lit up was a pleasant surprise rather than a major relief.

"The wind and fog are here, too," he began abruptly. "Some people were outdoors. There's nothing I can do about them at the moment; but some were working in the cruisers parked outside. You could check through their communicators as to whether everything is all right there. I'm not too worried, since the wind speed is now much less than Don reported. Besides, the air is much less dense at this height; but we can't see at all through this fog, so I'd be relieved to know about the men in the cruisers."

Easy's image had started to speak part way through the commander's request, obviously not in answer, since there had not been time enough for the speed-of-light round-trip. Presumably the human beings had something of their own to say. Barlennan concentrated on his own message until it was done, knowing that Guzmeen or one of his crew would be writing down whatever came in. Message crossing under these circumstances was a frequent event and was handled by established routine.

With his own words on the way, the commander turned to ask what the humans had wanted but the question was interrupted. An officer shot into the room and began reporting as soon as he saw Barlennan.

"Sir, all groups but the two who checked out at the north gates are accounted for. One of these was working in the *Hoorsh*, the other was levelling ground for the new complex twenty cables north, on the other side of the parking valley. There were eight people in the first group, twenty in the second."

Barlennan made the gesture of understanding, all four nippers clicking shut simultaneously. "We may have radio reports from the space station shortly on the *Hoorsh* group," he replied. "How many who were actually outside after the wind and fog arrived have come in? What do they report on living and travelling conditions? Was anyone hurt?"

"No one hurt, Sir. The wind was only a minor inconvenience; they came in because they couldn't see to work. Some of them had trouble finding their way. My guess is that the ground-levelling crew is still groping its way back, unless they just decided to wait it out where they were. The ones on the *Hoorsh* may not even have noticed anything, inside. If the first bunch stays out of contact too long, I'll send out a messenger."

"How will you keep *him* from getting lost?"

"Compass, plus picking someone who works outside a lot and knows the ground well."

"I'm not—" Barlennan's objection was interrupted by the radio.

"Barlennan," came Easy's voice, "the communicators in the *Hoorsh* and the *Kalliff* are all working. As far as we can see, there is no one in the *Kalliff* and it's just sitting there; nothing is moving. There are at least three, and possibly five, men in the life-support section of the *Hoorsh*. The man covering those screens has seen as many as three at once in the last few minutes but isn't too confident of recognizing individual Mesklinites. The cruiser doesn't seem to be affected. The people aboard are going about their business and paying no attention to us. Certainly they weren't trying to send an emergency message up. Jack Bravermann is trying to get their attention on that set now but I don't think there's anything to worry about. As you say, slower wind and thinner air should mean that your settlement is in no danger if the *Kwembly* wasn't hurt."

"I'm not worried, at least not much. If you'll wait a moment, I'll find out what your last message but one was and try to answer it," returned Barlennan. He turned to the duty officer whose place at the set he had taken. "I assume you got what she said."

"Yes, Sir. It wasn't urgent, just interesting. Another interim report has come up from Dondragmer. The *Kwembly* is still afloat, still drifting, though he thinks it has dragged bottom once or twice and the wind is still blowing there. Because of their own motion, his scientists won't commit themselves to an opinion on whether the wind velocity has changed or not."

The commander gestured acceptance, turned back to the communicator, and said, "Thanks, Mrs. Hoffman. I appreciate your sending even 'no change' reports so quickly. I will stay here for a while, so if anything really does happen I will know as soon as possible. Have your atmospheric scientists come up with predictions they trust? Or explanations of what happened?"

To the other Mesklinites in the room it was obvious that Barlennan was doing his best to keep his expression unreadable as he asked this question. His arms and legs were carefully relaxed, chelae neither too tightly closed nor gaping open, his head neither too high nor too close to the floor, his eyes fixed steadily on the screen. The watchers did not know in detail what was in his mind, but could tell that he attached more than face value to the question. Some of them wondered why he bothered to control himself so, since it was most unlikely that any human being could interpret his body expression anyway; but those who knew him best realized that he would never take a chance on a matter like that. After all, there were some human beings, of whom Elise Rich Hoffman was emphatically one, who seemed to think very easily from the Mesklinite viewpoint, besides speaking Stennish as well as human vocal equipment would permit.

All watched the screen with interest, wondering whether the human being on it would show signs of having noticed the commander's attitude when her answer came back. All communication room personnel were reasonably familiar with human facial expressions; most of them could recognize at least a dozen different human beings by face or voice alone, the commander having long ago expressed a strong desire that such abilities be cultivated. Barlennan, his glance leaving the screen for a moment and roving around the circle of intent listeners, was amused at their expressions even while he was annoyed at his own obviousness. He wondered how they would react to whatever answer Easy returned, but he never found out.

The human female had evidently received the question and was starting to form a sentence in reply, when her attention was distracted. For several seconds she was obviously listening to something and her eyes shifted away from the pickup of the Settlement communicator. Then her attention came back to Barlennan.

"Commander. Dondragmer has reported again. The *Kwembly* has stopped, or almost stopped, aground. They are still being dragged a little, however; the flow of liquid has not slowed. They have been tipped so that the trucks are out of contact with whatever surface is below them. If they aren't dragged free by the river, they're there to stay; and Dondragmer thinks the level is going down."

IV
SMALL TALK

It was a curious, helpless sensation for Beetchermarlf. The *Kwembly's* helm was connected to the trucks by simple pulley-and-cord rigging; even Mesklinite muscles could not turn the trucks when the vehicle was at rest, and, while forward motion made steering possible, it certainly did not make it easy. Now, as the vehicle floated with the driving units clear of the bottom, the helm flopped limply in response to a casual nudge or even to a slight roll of the hull. In theory, the cruiser was maneuverable at sea, but this required installing driving paddles on the treads, something most easily done on land. Dondragmer had thought fleetingly, as he realized they were adrift, of sending out air-suited men to attempt the task, then decided it wasn't worth the risk even if everyone were attached solidly to the hull by life-lines. It was likely enough, as far as anyone could tell, that they might reach the end or the edge of the river or lake or whatever they were floating on before any such job could be completed, anyway. If men were outside when that happened, life-lines would be of little use.

The same thoughts had crossed the helmsman's mind as he lay at his station, but he did not voice them. Beetchermarlf was young, but not so young as still to assume that no one else could recognize the obvious.

He was quite prepared to grant his captain's professional competence.

As the minutes slipped by, however, he began to worry at Dondragmer's failure to issue any orders. Something should be possible; they couldn't just drift eastward. He glanced at the compass; yes, eastward, indefinitely. There had been hills that way according to the last flight reports, the same hills which had bordered the snow field on their left, sometimes showing slightly above the distant horizon, for the last three or four thousand miles. Judging by their color they were rock, not ice. If the surface the *Kwembly* was floating on was simply melted snow field, they almost had to hit something soon. Beetchermarlf had no more idea than anyone else how fast they were going but his confidence in the strength of the hull matched that of the captain. He had no more wish to strike a reef on Dhrawn than he had ever had on Mesklin.

Anyhow, the wind should not move them too fast, given the air density. The top of the hull was smoothly curved except for the bridge, and the trucks on the bottom should give plenty of drag. As far as the air scouts had been able to tell, the snow field had been level, so the liquid itself shouldn't be moving. Come to think of it, the outside pressure should give a check on that. The helmsman stirred at the thought, glanced up at the captain, hesitated, and then spoke.

"Sir, how about checking hull-squeeze watch? If there is any current where we're floating, we'd have to be going downhill, and that should show—" Dondragmer interrupted.

"But the surface was level—no, you're right. We should check." He reared up to the bank of speaking tubes and called the laboratory. "Born, how is the pressure? You're keeping track, of course."

"Of course, Captain. Both bow and stern safety bladders have been expanding ever since we began to float. We've descended about six body lengths in twice that many minutes. I'm about ready to tap more argon."

Dondragmer acknowledged, and looked back at his helmsman.

"Good for you. I should have thought of that. That means we are being carried by current as well as wind and all bets on speed, distance, and where we stop are off. There couldn't be a current unless the air scouts missed a slope, and if there's a slope this plateau must drain somewhere."

"We're secure for rough travel, Sir. I don't see what else we can do."

"There's one thing," Dondragmer said grimly. He reared to the tubes again, and emitted the sirenlike general quarters call. Reasonably sure that all were listening, he pulled his head back so as to be equally distant from all the tubes, and spoke loudly enough to get through them all.

"All hands into air suits as quickly as possible. You are relieved from stations for that purpose, but get back as soon as you can." He lowered himself to his command bench and addressed Beetchermarlf. "Get your suit and mine, and bring them back here. Quickly!"

The helmsman was back with the garments in ninety seconds. He started to assist the captain with his, but was dismissed by an emphatic gesture and went to work on his own. In two minutes both, protected except for head covering, were back at their stations.

The haste, as it turned out, was unnecessary. More minutes passed while Beetchermarlf toyed with the useless helm, and Dondragmer wondered whether the human scientists were ever going to come through with any information and what use it was likely to be if they did. He hoped that satellite fixes could give him some idea of the *Kwembly's* speed; it would, he thought rather cynically, be nice to know how hard they were likely to hit whatever finally stopped them. Such fixes were, he knew, hard to get on order; there were over thirty of the "shadow-satellites" in orbit but they were less than three thousand miles above the surface. No attempt had been made to arrange their orbits so that their limited fields of visual and microwave coverage would be either uniform or complete; communication was not their primary purpose. The main human base, in synchronous orbit over six million miles above the Settlement meridian, was supposed to need no help with that task. Also, the ninety-plus mile per second orbital speed of the lower satellites, helpful though the human observers claimed it to be for moving-base-line location checking, still seemed to Dondragmer an inevitable cause of difficulty. He was not at all hopeful about getting his speed from this source. That was just as well, because he never got it.

Once, about half an hour after they had gone adrift, a brief shudder ran through the *Kwembly* and the captain duly reported to the station that they had probably touched bottom. Everyone else on board made the same assumption and tension began to mount.

There was a little warning just before the end. A hoot from the laboratory speaking tube was followed by a report that pressure had started to rise more rapidly, and that an additional release of argon into the ship's atmosphere had been necessary to keep the safety bladders from rupturing. There was no sensation of increasing speed, but the implication of the report was plain enough. They were descending more rapidly. How fast were they going horizontally? The captain and helmsman looked at each other, not asking the question aloud but reading it in each other's expressions. More minutes passed; the tension mounted, chelas gripping stanchions and holdfasts ever more tightly.

Then there was a thunderous clang, and the hull swerved abruptly; another, and it tilted sharply to starboard. For several seconds it pitched violently, and those near bow and stern could feel it yawing as well, though the fog still blocked any outside view which might have explained the sensation. Then there was another, much louder clang and the *Kwembly* rolled some sixty degrees to starboard; but this time she did not recover. Scraping, grinding sounds suggested that she was moving slightly, but no real change of attitude accompanied them. For the first time, the sound of liquid rushing past the hull became noticeable.

Dondragmer and his companion were unhurt. To beings who regarded two hundred Earth gravities as normal and six hundred as a most minor inconvenience, that sort of acceleration meant nothing. They had not even lost their grips, and were still at their posts. The captain was not worried about direct injuries to his crew. His first words showed that he was considering matters much further ahead.

"By stations, report!" he bellowed into the speaking tubes. "Check hull soundness at all points, and report all cracks, open breaks, dents, and other evidence for leaks. Lab personnel to emergency stations, and check for oxygen. Life-support, cut tank circulation until the oxygen check is done. Now!"

Apparently the speaking tubes were intact, at least. Hoots of response began to return immediately. As the reports accumulated, Beetchermarlf began to relax. He had not really expected the shell which protected him from Dhrawn's poisonous air to withstand anything like such a shock and his respect for alien engineering went up several grades. He had regarded artificial structures of any sort as normally inferior in strength and durability to any living body. He had, of course, excellent reason for such an attitude. Nevertheless, it appeared when all the reports were finally in, that there were no major structural failures or even visible cracks. Whether the normal leaks, unavoidable in a structure which had to have entrances for personnel and equipment, not to mention hull openings for instruments and control lines, were any worse than they had been, would not be known for a while. Pressure monitoring and oxygen checking would of course continue as normal routine.

Power was still on, which surprised no one. The twenty-five independent hydrogen converters, identical modules which could be moved from any energy-using site in the *Kwembly* to any other, were solid-state devices with no moving parts larger than the molecules of gaseous fuel which were fed into them. They could have been placed under the hammer of a power forge without damage.

Most of the outside lights were gone, or at least inoperative, though these could be replaced. Some were still working, however, and from the submerged end of the bridge it was possible to see out. Fog still blocked the view from the upper end. Dondragmer made his way very gingerly to the low end and took a brief look at the conglomeration of rounded rocks with diameters from half his own length to twenty times that, into which his craft had managed to wedge itself. Then he climbed carefully back to his station, energized the sound system of his radio and transmitted the report which Barlennan was to hear a little over a minute later. Without waiting for an answer, he began issuing orders to the helmsman.

"Beetch, stand by here in case the men have anything to say. I'm going to make a complete check myself, especially of the air locks. With all there is to be said for our design, we didn't have this much of a roll in mind when we settled on it. We may only be able to use the small emergency locks, since the main one seems to be underneath us at the moment. It may be blocked on the outside even if we can open the inner door and find the septum still submerged. Chatter with the human beings if you want. The more of us who can use their language and the more of them who can use ours, the better. You have the bridge."

Dondragmer made the habitual, but now rather futile, gesture of rapping on the hatch for clearance; then he opened it and disappeared, leaving Beetchermarlf alone.

The helmsman had no urge at the moment for idle talk with the station above. His captain had left him with too much to think about.

He was not exactly delighted at being left in charge of the bridge, under the circumstances. He was not even too concerned about the main air lock's being blocked; the smaller ones were adequate, though not for life-support equipment, he suddenly remembered. Well, at the moment the desirability of going out seemed very small but if the *Kwembly* were permanently disabled that need would have to be faced.

The real question, in that event, was just what good going outside would do. The twelve thousand miles or so, which Beetchermarlf thought of as nearly fourteen million cables, was a long, long walk, especially with a load of life-support equipment. Without that apparatus it was not to be thought of. Mesklinites were amazingly tough organisms mechanically and had a temperature tolerance range which was still disbelieved by many human biologists, but oxygen was another matter. Its partial pressure outside at the moment was presumably about fifty pounds per square inch, quite enough to kill any member of the *Kwembly's* crew in seconds.

The most desirable thing at the moment was to get the big machine back on her treads. How, and whether, this could be done would depend largely on the stream of liquid flowing past the stranded hull. Working outside in that current might not be impossible, but it was going to be difficult and dangerous. The air-suited Mesklinites would have to be heavily ballasted to stay put at any task and life-lines would complicate the details.

The stream might not, of course, be permanent. It had apparently just come into existence with the change in weather and it might cease flowing as suddenly. However, as Beetchermarlf well knew, there is a difference between weather and climate. If the river were seasonal, its "temporary" nature might still turn out to be too long for the Mesklinites; Dhrawn's year was some eight times as long as that of Earth and over one and a half times that of Mesklin.

This was an area where human information might be useful. The aliens had been observing Dhrawn carefully for nearly half of one of its years and casually for much longer. They should have *some* idea of its seasons. The helmsman wondered whether it would be out of order for him to put such a question to someone in the orbiting station, since the captain had not. Of course, the captain *had* said he could use the radio for chatter and had made no mention of what might or might not be said.

The idea that there was anything except the *Esket* incident which should not be discussed with the human sponsors of the Dhrawn expedition had not gone down the chain of command as far as Beetchermarlf. The young helmsman had almost made up his mind to initiate a call to the station when the radio beside him spoke. It spoke, furthermore, in his own language, though the accent was not above reproach.

"Dondragmer. I know you must be busy but if you can't talk now I'd be glad if someone else could. I am Benjamin Hoffman, an assistant in the aerology lab here at the station, and I'd like two kinds of help if anyone can find time to give it.

"For myself, I'd like practice in language; it must be obvious that I need it. For the lab, we're in a very embarrassing position. Twice in a row we've worked out weather predictions for your part of the planet which have been way, way off. We just don't have enough detailed information to do the job properly. The observations we can make from here don't resolve enough and there aren't anywhere near enough reporting stations down there. You and the others have planted a lot of automatics on your trips, but they still don't cover much of the planet, as you know. Since good predictions will be as useful to you as they will be to us, I thought maybe I could talk things out in real detail with some of your scientists and maybe work out the weather patterns where you know enough to supplement the background calculations and really get good forecasts, at least right in your neighborhood."

The helmsman replied eagerly.

"The captain is not on the bridge, Benjaminhoffman. I am Beetchermarlf, one of the helmsmen, now on watch. Speaking for myself, I should be very glad to exchange language practice when duties permit, as now. I am afraid the scientists will be pretty busy for a while; I may be myself, most of the time. We are having some trouble, though you may not know all the details. The captain did not have time for the full story in the report I heard him send up a few minutes ago. I will give you as complete a picture as I can of the situation and some thoughts which have occurred to me since the captain left the bridge. You might record the information for your people and comment on my ideas if you wish. If you don't think they're worth mentioning to the captain, I won't. He'll be busy enough without them anyway. I'll wait until you tell me you're ready to record, or that you don't want to, before I start." Beetchermarlf paused, not entirely for the reason he had just given. He suddenly wondered whether he should bother one of these alien beings with his own ideas which began to seem crude and poorly worked out to him.

Still, the factual reports had to be useful. There was much detailed information about the *Kwembly's* present situation which the men could not possibly know yet. By the time Benj's approval came from the speaker, the helmsman had recovered some of his self-confidence.

"That will be fine, Beetchermarlf. I'm ready to tape your report. I was going to anyway, for language practice. I'll pass on whatever you want. Even if your weather men are busy, maybe the two of us could try to do what I suggested with the weather information. You can probably get their measurements, and you're on the spot and can see everything and if you're one of the sailors Barlennan recruited on Mesklin you certainly know something about weather. For all I know, you may have spent a couple of my lifetimes in that place on Mesklin learning engineering and research methods. Come ahead; I'm ready here."

This speech completed the restoration of Beetchermarlf's morale. It had been only ten of Mesklin's years since alien education had started for a selected few of its natives. This human being must be five years old or younger. Of course, there was no telling what that might mean in the way of maturity for his species, and one could not very well ask; but in spite of the aura of supernormality which tended to surround all the aliens, one just did not think of a five-year-old as a superior being.

As relaxed as anyone could well be on a floor with a sixty-degree tilt, the sailor began his description of the *Kwembly's* situation. He gave a detailed account of the trip down what now had to be recognized as a river, and of its conclusion. He described minutely what could now be seen from the bridge. He explained how they were now stranded off their tracks, and emphasized the situation which faced the crew if this could not be corrected. He even detailed the structure of the air

locks, and explained why the main one was probably
unusable and the others possibly so.

"It will help a great deal in the captain's planning,"
he concluded, "if we can have some trustworthy estimate of what will happen to this river, and especially
whether and when it will run dry. If the whole snow
field melts at this season and runs off the plateau
through this one drain, I suppose we're here for the
best part of a year and will have to plan accordingly.
If you can give any hope that we can work on dry
land without having to wait too long, though, it would
be very good to know."

Benj was rather longer than sixty-four seconds in
answering this; he, too, had been given material for
thought.

"I have your details on tape, and have sent it up to
Planning," his words came through at last. "They'll
distribute copies to the labs. Even I can see that figuring out the life story of your river is going to be a nasty
job; maybe an impossible one without a lot more knowledge. As you say, the whole snow field might be starting a seasonal melt. If the waters of North America had
to drain out through one river you'd be there for a
long time. I don't know how much of the place your
aerial scout reports cover, and I don't know how am-
biguous the photos from up here may be, but I'll bet
when it's all down on maps there'll still be room for
argument. Even if everyone agrees on a conclusion,
well, we still don't know much about that planet."

"But you've had so much experience with other
planets, many of them!" returned Beetchermarlf. "I
should think that would be of some help."

Again the answer was longer in coming back than
light-lag alone would explain.

"Men and their friends have had experience on a lot
of planets, that's true, and I've read a good deal of it.
The trouble is, practically none of it helps here. There

are three kinds of planet, basically. One we call Terrestrial, like my own home; it is small, dense, and practially without hydrogen. The second is the Jovian, or Type Two, which tends to be much larger and much less dense because they have kept most of their hydrogen from the time they originally formed, we think. Those two were the only kinds we knew about before we left our own star's neighborhood, because they are the only kinds in our system.

"Type Three is very large, very dense, and very hard to account for. Theories which had the Type One's losing their hydrogen because of their initially small mass, and the Twos keeping theirs because of their greater mass, were fine as long as we'd never heard of the Threes. Our ideas were perfectly satisfactory and convincing as long as we didn't know too much, if you'll forgive my sounding like my basic science teacher.

"Type Three is the sort you're on. There are none of them around any sun with a Type One planet. I suppose there must be a reason for that, but I don't know what it is. Well, nothing was known about them among the Community races until we learned to travel between stars and began to do it on a large scale, large enough so the principal interest of wandering ships wasn't just new habitable planets. Even then we couldn't study them first hand, any more than we could the Jovian worlds. We could send down a few special, very expensive and usually very unreliable robots, but that was all. Your species is the first we've ever encountered able to stand the gravity of a Type Three or the pressure of a Type Two, for that matter."

"But isn't Mesklin a Type Three, by your description? You must know a lot about it by now; you've been in touch with our people for something like ten years, and some of you have even landed at the Rim, I mean the equator."

"More like fifty of our years. The trouble is that Mesklin isn't a Type Three. It's a peculiar Two. It would have had all the hydrogen of any Jovian world if it hadn't been for its rotation, that terrific spin which gives your world an eighteen-minute day and a shape like a fried egg. There aren't any others like it which we've found yet, and no intermediate cases that anyone's recognized, or at least that I've heard of. That's why the Community races were willing to go to so much trouble and effort and spend so much time building up contact with your world and setting up this expedition to Dhrawn. We'll find out a good deal in thirty years or so about that world's makeup from the neutrino counters in the shadow-satellites but the seismic equipment you people have been planting will add a lot of detail and remove a lot of ambiguity. So will your chemical work. In five or six of your years we may know enough about that rock ball to make a sensible guess why it's there or at least, whether it ought to be called a star or a planet."

"You mean you only made contact with the people of Mesklin so you could learn more about Dhrawn?"

"No, I didn't mean that at all. People are people and worth getting to know for their own sake—at least, both my parents feel that way, though I've met folks who certainly don't. I don't think the idea for the Dhrawn project got started until long after your College was under way. My mother or Dr. Aucoin could tell you when. It was long before I was born. Of course, when it dawned on someone that you folks *could* make first-hand investigation of a place like Dhrawn, everyone jumped at the chance."

This, of course, forced Beetchermarlf to ask a question which he would ordinarily have regarded as a strictly human affair and none of his business, like the matter of how mature a five-year-old should be. It slipped out before he caught himself; for over an hour thereafter he and Benj were arguing over the reasons for such activities as the Dhrawn project and why such a vast amount of effort should be devoted to an activity with no obvious material return in prospect. Benj did not defend his side too well. He was able to give the usual answers about the force of curiosity, which Beetchermarlf could see up to a point; he knew enough history to have heard how close man and several other species had come to extinction from energy starvation before they had developed the hydrogen fusion converter; but he was too young to be really eloquent. He lacked the experience to be able to point out convincingly, even to himself, the complete dependence of any culture on its understanding of the laws of the universe. The conversation never became heated, which would have been difficult in any argument where there is a built-in cooling-down period between any remark and its answer. The only really satisfactory progress made was in Benj's mastery of Stennish.

The discussion was interrupted by Beetchermarlf's suddenly becoming aware of a change in his surroundings. For the last hour his entire attention had been on Benj's words and his own replies. The canted bridge and gurgling liquid had receded to the far background of his mind. He was quite surprised to realize abruptly that the pattern of lights twinkling above him was Orion. The fog had gone.

Alert once more to his surroundings, he noticed that the water line around the bridge seemed just a trifle lower. Ten minutes' careful watching convinced him that this was so. The river *was* falling.

Part way through the ten minutes he had, of course, been queried about his sudden silence by Benj, and had given the reason. The boy had immediately notified McDevitt, so that by the time Beetchermarlf was sure about the changing water level there were several

interested human beings on hand above to hear about
it. The helmsman reported briefly to them on the radio
and only then did he call through the speaking tubes
for Dondragmer.

The captain was far aft, behind the laboratory section and just forward of the compartment containing
the pressure bladder, when the call came. There was a
pause after the helmsman finished speaking, and
Beetchermarlf expected the captain to come bursting
through the bridge hatchway after a few seconds; but
Dondragmer did not yield to the temptation. The ports
in the rest of the hull, including the compartment
where he was, were much too small to permit a clear
estimate of the water level, so he had to accept his
helmsman's judgement. Dondragmer was willing to do
this, rather to the young sailor's surprise.

"Keep track as exactly as you can of the rate of fall,
until you are relieved," was his order. "Let me and the
human beings know the rate as soon as you can guess
it reliably; tell us thereafter whenever you change your
estimate."

Beetchermarlf acknowledged the order and clambered across the bridge to a point where he could
mark the water line with a scratch on one of the
window stanchions. Reporting the action to the captain and the human listeners, he returned to his station
keeping his eyes fixed on the mark. The ripples in the
liquid were several inches high, settling down only at
rare intervals, hence it was some time before he could
be at all sure of the change in depth. There were two
or three impatient queries from above, which he answered politely in the best he could muster of his
limited human language, before Benj reported that he
was once more alone except for nonentities watching
other cruisers. Most of the time thereafter until
Takoorch arrived as bridge relief was spent by the two
in describing their home worlds, correcting each others'

misconceptions about Earth and Mesklin by way of language practice and, though neither was fully aware of it, developing a warm personal friendship.

Beetchermarlf returned six hours later to let Takoorch go (actually the interval was twenty-four days by Mesklinite reckoning, a standard watch length) and found that the water was down nearly a foot from his reference mark. Takoorch informed him that the human Benj had just returned from a rest period. The younger helmsman wondered privately just how soon after Tak's arrival the other had found it was time to take a rest. Naturally he could not ask such a question, but as he settled back into his station he sent a call radiating upward.

"I'm back on, Benj. I don't know how recently Tak made a report to you, but the water is down over half a body length and the current seems much slower. The wind is nearly calm. Have your scientists anything to report?"

He had time during the answer delay to realize that the last question had been rather pointless, since the principal news wanted from the human scientists was the probable duration of the river, but there was nothing to be done about it now. Besides, maybe they *did* have something of value.

"Your friend Takoorch did tell us about the water and wind, among a good many other things," Benj's voice announced. "It's good to have you back, Beetch. I haven't heard anything from the labs, but it seems to me from what you've said about the way you're tipped and the rate the water's been dropping, and from what I can judge from the cruiser model I have here, that another sixty or seventy hours should leave you dry. That's if the water keeps dropping at the same rate, of course. It might do that if it's flowing away through a nice smooth channel but I wouldn't count on that. I hate to sound pessimistic but my guess is that it will slow down before all the liquid is gone."

"You may be right," agreed Beetchermarlf. "On the other hand, with the current easing off we can probably work outside safely enough before it's all gone." This was a prophetic remark. It was still on its way to the station when a speaking tube hooted for attention.

"Beetchermarlf! Inform the human beings that you will be relieved immediately by Kervenser, and report at once to the starboard after emergency lock in your air-suit. I want a check of the trucks and tiller lines. Two others will go with you for safety. I am more interested in accuracy than speed. If there is any damage which would be easier to fix while we are still tilted than it would be after we are level, I want to know about it. After you make that check, take a general look around. I want a rough idea of how solidly we are wedged into this position and how much work it will take to level us and get us loose. I will be outside myself making a similar check, but I want another opinion."

"Yes, Sir," the helmsman responded. He almost forgot to notify Benj, for this time the order was a distinct surprise, not the fact that he was to go outside, but that the captain had chosen him to check his own judgement.

The air-suits had been removed when Dondragmer was convinced that the hull was sound, but Beetchermarlf was back into his in half a minute and at the designated lock moments later. The captain and four sailors, all suited, were waiting. The crewmen held coils of rope.

"All right, Beetch," greeted the captain. "Stakendee will go out first and attach his line to the handiest climbing grip. You will follow, then Praffen. Each of you will attach his line to a different grip. Then go about your assignments. Wait—fasten these to your suit harness; you'll float without ballast." He handed four weights equipped with quick-release clips for harness attachment to the helmsman.

Egress was made in silence through the tiny lock. It was essentially a U-shaped liquid trap, fundamentally similar in operation to the main one and deep enough so that the *Kwembly's* tilt did not quite spoil its operation. The fact that the outer end was in liquid anyway may have made the difference. Beetchermarlf, emerging directly into the current, was glad of Stak's steadying grip as he sought anchorage for his own safety line.

A minute later the third member of their group had joined them, and together they clambered the short distance that separated them from the river bottom. This was composed of the rounded rocks which had been visible from the bridge, arranged in an oddly wavelike pattern whose crests extended across the direction of the current. At first glance, Beetchermarlf got the impression that the cruiser had stranded in the trough between two of these waves. Enough of the outside lights were still working to make seeing possible, if not quite ideal.

The trio made their way around the stern to get a look at their vehicle's underside. While this was much less well lighted, it was obvious at once that there would be a great deal to report to Dondragmer.

The *Kwembly* had been supported by a set of sixty trucks, each some three feet wide and twice as long, arranged in five longitudinal rows of twelve. All swivelled on casters and were interconnected by a maze of tiller ropes which were Beetchermarlf's main responsibility. Each of the trucks had a place to install a power unit, and had its own motor consisting of a six-inch-thick shaft whose micro-structure gave it a direct grip on the rotating magnetic field which was one of the forms in which the fusion units could deliver their energy. If no power box was installed, the truck rolled free. At the time of the accident, ten of the *Kwembly's* twenty-five converters had been on trucks, arranged in point-forward V patterns fore and aft.

Eighteen trucks from the rear of the cruiser, including all five of the powered ones at that end, were missing.

V

FRYER TO FREEZER

Strictly speaking, all of them weren't missing. Several could be seen lying on the boulders, evidently dislodged at the time of the final impact. Whether any had gone with the earlier bumps, presumably miles upstream, Beetchermarlf could not guess and was rather afraid to find out. That could be checked later. Inspecting what was left would have to come first. The helmsman set to it.

The front end seemed to have sustained no damage at all; the trucks were still present and their maze of tiller lines in proper condition. Amidships, many of the lines had snapped in spite of the enormous strength of the Mesklinite fiber used in them. Some of the trucks were twisted out of alignment; several, indeed, swung freely to the touch. The pattern of missing parts aft was regular and rather encouraging. Numbering from the port side, Row 1 had lost its last five trucks; Rows 2 and 3 their last four; Row 4 the last three; Row 5, on the starboard side, its last two. This suggested that they had all yielded to the same impact, which had wiped diagonally across the bottom of the hull; and since some of the detached units were in the neighborhood, there seemed a good chance that they all would be.

The inspectors were surprised at how little damage had been done by the trucks tearing away. Beetchermarlf and his companions had had nothing to do with the design of the *Kwembly* and her sister machines. None of them had more than the roughest idea of the sort of thinking which had been involved. They had never considered the problems inherent in building a machine powered by the most sophisticated energy sources ever developed, but operated by beings from a culture still in the muscle-and-wind stage; beings who would be cut off from *any* repair and replacement facilities once they were on Dhrawn. This was the reason the steering was done by tiller and rope rather than by powered selsyns or similar devices; why the air locks were so simple, and not completely foolproof; why the life-support system was not only manually operated (except for the lights which kept the plants alive) but had even been designed and built by Mesklinite scientists and technicians.

A few hundred of the beings had received an extensive body of "alien" education, though no attempt had been made to spread the new knowledge through the Mesklinite culture. Nearly all of the "college graduates" were now on Dhrawn, together with recruits like Beetchermarlf; mostly young, reasonably intelligent volunteers from among the sailors of Barlennan's maritime nation. These were the people who would have to perform any repairs and all regular maintenance on the land-cruisers, and this fact had to be kept constantly in the foreground of the designers' minds. Designing vehicles capable of covering thousands of miles of Dhrawn's environment in a reasonable length of time, and at the same time reasonably safely under Mesklinite handling, had inevitably resulted in equipment with startling qualities. Beetchermarlf should not have been surprised either that the pieces of his cruiser went back together so readily, or that the cruisers had suffered so little damage.

Of course, the intelligence of the Mesklinites had been

taken into account. It was the main reason for not depending on robots: these had proved unsatisfactory in the early days of space exploration. Mesklinite intelligence was obviously comparable to that of human beings, Drommians, or Paneshks: a fact surprising in itself, since all four planets appeared to have evolved their life forms over widely different lengths of geological time. It was also fairly certain that Mesklinites were much longer-lived, on the average, than human beings, though Mesklinites were oddly reluctant to discuss this; indeed, what this would mean in terms of their general competence was as problematic as Dhrawn itself. It had been a risky project from all angles, with most of the risk being taken by the Mesklinites. The giant barge drifting in orbit near the human station, which was supposed to be able to evacuate the entire Settlement in emergency, was little more than a gesture, especially for the beings afield in the land-cruisers.

None of this was in the minds of the three sailors inspecting the *Kwembly's* damage. They were simply surprised and delighted to find that the lost trucks had merely popped out of the sockets in which they normally swivelled and into which they could apparently be replaced with little trouble, provided they could be found. With this problem settled to his satisfaction, Beetchermarlf made a brief cast over the river bottom to the limits imposed by the safety lines and found twelve of the trucks within that radius. Some of these were damaged: tracks broken or with missing links; bearing wheels cracked; a few axles bent. The three gathered all the material they could reach and transport and brought it back to the *Kwembly's* stern. The helmsman considered doubling up on the safety lines and increasing their search radius but decided to report to Dondragmer and get his approval first. Indeed, the helmsman was a bit surprised that the captain had not appeared earlier, in view of his announced intention of checking outside.

He found the reason when he and his companions went back around the stern to the lock. Dondragmer, his two companions of the original sortie and six more crewmen, who had evidently been summoned in the meantime, were near the middle of the *Kwembly* laboring to remove boulders from the region of the main air lock.

The breathing suits had no special communication equipment, and the transmissive matching between their hydrogen-argon filling and the surrounding liquid was extremely poor; but the Mesklinite voice, built around a swimming siphon rather than a set of lungs (the hydrogen-using midgets lacked lungs) was another thing which had bothered human biologists. The helmsman caught his captain's attention with a deep hoot and gestured him to follow around the stern of the cruiser. Dondragmer assumed that the matter was important and came along after directing the others to continue their work. One look and a few sentences from Beetchermarlf brought him abreast of the situation.

After a few seconds' thought he rejected the idea of looking immediately for the missing trucks. The water was still going down; it would be safer and easier to conduct the search when it was gone, if this did not take too long. In the meantime repairs could be started on the ones which had already been found. Beetchermarlf acknowledged the order and began to sort the damaged equipment in order to plan the work.

Care was necessary; some parts were light enough to be borne away by the current when detached from the rest of the assemblies. Some such items were already missing, and had presumably gone in just that fashion. The helmsman had a portable light brought to the scene and stationed one of his helpers a few yards downstream to catch anything which got away from him. He thought how helpful a net would be but there was no such item aboard the *Kwembly*. It would be possible to make one from the miles of cordage she carried, but it hardly seemed worth the time.

Eight hours of labor, interrupted by occasional rests spent chatting with Benj, saw three of the damaged trucks again serviceable. Some of their parts were not of the original quality, Beetchermarlf and the others having improvised freely. They had used Mesklinite fabric and cord as well as alien polymers and alloys which were on hand. Their tools were their own; their culture had high standards of craftsmanship and such things as saws, hammers, and the usual spectrum of edged tools were familiar to the sailors. The fact that they were made of the Mesklinite equivalents of bone, horn, and shell was no disparagement to them, considering the general nature of Mesklinite tissue.

Replacing the repaired units in their swivels took muscle even by Mesklinite standards. It also took more tool work, as metal in the mountings had been bent out of shape when the trucks were torn free. The first three had to be placed in Row 4, since Row 5 was pressed against the boulders of the river bottom and the other three were too high to be reached conveniently. Beetchermarlf bowed to necessity, attached the trucks where he could, and went back to fixing more.

The river continued to fall and the current continued to decrease. Dondragmer ordered the helmsman and his helpers to move their work area from beneath the hull, anticipating what would happen as the bouyant force on the *Kwembly* decreased. His caution was justified when, with a grinding of boulders, the vehicle slipped from its sixty-degree tilt to about thirty, bringing two more rows of trucks within reach of the bottom and forcing two workmen to duck between stones to avoid being crushed.

At this point it became obvious that even if the water

fell further, the cruiser would not. A point on its port underside about a third of the way back from the bow and between Rows 1 and 2 was now resting on a single rock some eighteen feet in diameter and half buried in the river bottom: a hopeless object to dislodge even without the *Kwembly's* weight on it. Beetchermarlf kept on with his assigned job but couldn't help wondering how the captain proposed to lift his craft off that eminence. He was also curious about what would happen when and if he succeeded. The rocky surface which formed the river bed was the last sort of thing the cruiser's designers had had in mind as a substrate and the helmsman doubted seriously that she could run on such a base. High-gravity planets tend to be fairly level, judging by Mesklin (the only available example), and even if an area were encountered where traction seemed unpromising, the designers must have supposed that the crew need merely refrain from venturing onto it. This was another good example of the reason manned exploration was generally better than the automated kind.

Beetchermarlf, in a temporarily philosophical mood, concluded that foresight was likely to depend heavily on the amount of hindsight available.

Dondragmer, pondering the same problem, getting his vehicle free, was no nearer a solution than his helmsman some fifty hours after going aground. The first officer and the scientists were equally baffled. They were not worried, except for the captain, and even his feeling did not exactly parallel human "worry." He had kept to himself and Beetchermarlf (who had been on the bridge at the time) a conversation he had had with the human watchers a few hours before.

It had begun as a regular progress report, on an optimistic tone. Dondragmer was willing to admit that he hadn't thought of a workable plan yet but not that he was unlikely to think of one. Unfortunately, he had included in the remark the phrase "we have plenty of time to work it out."

Easy, at the other end, had been forced to disagree.

"You may not have as much as you think. Some of the people here have been considering those boulders. They are round, or nearly so, according to your report and what we can see on the bridge set. The most likely cause of that shape, according to our experience, is washing around in a stream bed or on a beach. Moving rocks that big would require a tremendous current. We're afraid that the stream which carried you there is just a preliminary trickle, the first thaw of the season, and if you don't get away soon you'll face a lot more water coming down."

Dondragmer had considered briefly.

"All right, but we're already doing all we can. Either we get away in time, or we don't; we can't do better than our best. If your scientists can give any sort of specific forecast of this super-flood we'll be glad of it, of course; otherwise we'll have to go on as we are. I'll leave a man on the radio here, of course, unless I have too much for them to do; in that case, try the lab. Thanks for the information, I guess."

The captain had gone back to work and to thought. He was not one to panic; in emergencies he seemed calmer than in a personal argument. Basically, his philosophy was the one he had just expressed: to do all one could in the time available, with the full knowledge that time would run out some day. At the moment, he only wished he knew what all he could do was.

The big rock was the main problem. It was keeping the drivers from traction, and until they not only touched bottom but bore heavily on it there was no moving the *Kwembly* with her own power. She might conceivably have been shifted by muscle power at Mesklin's Rim, or on Earth, but not under Dhrawn's gravity. Even a two-foot boulder was hard to move in that field.

There was rigging inside which could be set up as lifting tackle but none of it could begin to support the vehicle's weight as a static load even if its mechanical advantage were adequate.

Some trucks, four, to be exact, were in contact with the troublesome rock itself. Several more in Row 5 were touching bottom. None of these was powered at the moment but converters could be transferred to them. If the four on the rock, and the ones forward from them, and some of the Row 5 trucks, were all to be powered why couldn't the cruiser simply be backed off?

She could. No reason at all to doubt it. On level ground with reasonable traction any four well-spaced power units could drive her. With her weight concentrated on only a few trucks, traction should be better than normal and a backward move would be mainly downhill.

It was not lack of self-confidence which caused Dondragmer to outline this plan to the human being on communication watch; he was announcing his intentions, not asking for advice. The man who heard him was not an engineer and gave casual approval to the move. As a matter of routine he reported the situation to Planning so that the information could be distributed. Consequently it reached an engineer within an hour or so, long before Dondragmer was ready to execute his plan.

It caused a raising of eyebrows, a quick examination of a scale model of the *Kwembly,* and two minutes of rapid slide-rule work.

The engineer was a poor linguist, but this was not the only reason he went looking for Easy Hoffman. He did not know Dondragmer very well, had no idea how the Mesklinite would react to criticism; he had worked with Drommians, since there were some connected with the Dhrawn project and he felt it safest to have his point presented by the official oil-spreader. Easy, when found, promptly assured him that she had never known Dondragmer to resent reasonable advice, but agreed that her better knowledge of Stennish would probably help even though the captain was fluent in the human tongue. They went together to the communication room.

Benj was there, as was usual when he was not on duty. He had by now made friends with several more of the Mesklinites, though he still liked Beetchermarlf best. The latter's long work hours resulting from the accident had not entirely prevented them from conversing and Benj's Stennish had improved greatly; he was now almost as good as his mother believed.

When Easy and the engineer arrived, he was listening to Takoorch and was not too sorry to interrupt the exchange with the news that there was an important message for the captain.

It took several minutes to get Dondragmer to the bridge; like the rest of the crew he had been working almost constantly, though by luck he happened to be inside when the call came.

"I'm here, Easy," his voice finally came through. "Tak said you had a business call. Go ahead."

"It's about this way you plan to back off the rock, Don," she began. "We don't have the whole picture here, of course, but there are two things bothering our engineers. One is the fact that your forward truck will run off the stone while you still have ten feet or more of hull, including some of your bridge, over it. Have you measured to see whether there's any risk of bare hull slamming down on the stone as the truck rolls off? Also, toward the end of the maneuver, you'll have your hull supported almost entirely at the ends. The pneumatic undercarriage may distribute the load but my friend here isn't sure it will; further, if you get the bare hull instead of the mattress taking half the *Kwembly's* weight, Dhrawn's gravity is going to make a very respectable effort to break your land-ship in half. Have you checked those points?"

Dondragmer had to admit to himself that he had not and that he had better do so before the project went much farther. He conceded this on the radio, thanked Easy and her friend, and headed for the main lock, long since cleared for use.

Outside, the current had dropped to the point where life-lines were no longer necessary. Water depth was down to about seven feet, measured from the average level of the smallest boulders. The water line was, indeed, at about the most inconvenient possible level for seeing the whole picture. He had to climb part way up the rock, a difficult task in itself, though helped by the fact that he had some buoyancy; from there he had to follow the forward trucks to a point where he could compare the curvature of the big boulder and that of the *Kwembly's* lower bow. He could not be completely sure, since moving the hull backward would change its pitch, but he did not like what he saw. The human engineer was probably right. Not only was there risk of hull damage, but the steering bar came through the hull just ahead of the mattress by means of a nearly air-tight mechanical seal backed by a liquid trap and made its key connections with the maze of tiller-ropes. Serious damage to the bar would not actually cripple the vehicle, since there was a duplicate aft, but it was not a risk to be taken casually.

The answer to the whole situation was staring him in the face by that time but he was another hour or more in seeing it. A human psychologist, when he heard about this later, was very annoyed. He had been looking for significant differences between human and Mesklinite minds, and was finding what he considered an undue number of points of similarity.

The solution involved work, of course. Even the smallest boulders were heavy. Still, they were numerous, and it was not necessary to go far for a plentiful supply. With the entire crew of the *Kwembly* at the job except for Beetchermarlf and those still helping him with the trucks, a ramp of piled stones grew with fair speed from the stern of the trapped vehicle toward the key rock.

It was a help to Beetchermarlf. As fast as he readied a damaged bearing unit for service, he found himself able to get at new installation sites which had been out of reach before. He and the stone-carriers finished almost together, allowing for four trucks which he had been unable to repair because of missing parts. He had made thrifty use of these, cannibalizing them for the needs of some of the others, and had spotted the unavoidable gaps in traction widely enough to keep the cruiser's weight reasonably well distributed. To work on Row 5, practically buried in the river bottom, he had had to deflate that part of the mattress. Pumping it up again when the two trucks were replaced caused the hull to shift slightly, to the alarm of Dondragmer and several workers underneath; fortunately the motion was insignificant.

The captain had spent most of the time shuttling between the radio, where he kept hoping for a reliable prediction of the next flood, and the work site, where he divided his attention between the progress of the ramp and the view upstream. By the time the ramp was complete the water was less than a yard deep, and the current had ceased entirely; they were in a pool rather than a stream.

It was now full night; the sun had been gone for nearly a hundred hours. The weather had cleared completely, and workers outside could see the violently twinkling stars. Their own sun was not visible; it was barely so at the best of times this deep in Dhrawn's heavy atmosphere, and at the moment was too close to the horizon. Not even Dondragmer knew offhand whether it was slightly above or slightly below. Sol and Fomalhaut, which even the least informed of the crew knew to be indicators of south, glowed and wavered over a low eminence a few miles in that direction. The imaginary line connecting the two had tilted less than twenty degrees, human scale, since dark; the Mesklinite navigators would have said less than four.

Outside the range of the *Kwembly's* own lights it was almost totally black. Dhrawn is moonless; the stars provide no more illumination than they do on Earth or Mesklin.

Temperature was nearly the same. Dondragmer's scientists had been measuring the environment as completely as their knowledge and equipment allowed, then sending the results to the station above. The captain had been quietly hoping for some useful information in return, though he realized that the human beings didn't owe him any. The reports, after all, were simply part of the job the Mesklinites had engaged to do in the first place.

He had also suggested to his own men that they try some independent thinking. Borndender's answer to what he regarded as sarcasm had been to the effect that if the human beings would supply him with reports from other parts of Dhrawn and with computer time with which to correlate them, he would be glad to try. The captain had not intended sarcasm; he knew perfectly well the vast difference between explaining why a ship floats on water or ammonia and explaining why 2.3 millicables of 60-20 rain fell at the Settlement between Hour 40 and Hour 100 of Day 2. He suspected that his researcher's misinterpretation had been deliberate; Mesklinites were often quite human when in search of excuses and Borndender was currently feeling annoyed with his own lack of usefulness. Without bringing this aspect of the matter into the open, the captain merely repeated that useful ideas would be welcome, and left the lab.

Even the scientists were ordered outside when the time finally came to use the ramp. Borndender was irritated at this and muttered something as he went about the academic nature of the difference between being inside the *Kwembly* and outside her if anything drastic happened. Dondragmer, however, had not made a suggestion; he had issued an order, and not even the scientists denied either his right or his competence to do so. Only the captain himself, Beetchermarlf and a technician named Kensnee in the life-support compartment were to be aboard when the start was made. Dondragmer had considered acting as his own helmsman and taking a chance on the life equipment but reflected that Beetchermarlf knew the tiller cable layout better and was more likely to sense anything going wrong in that department. Inside power was not directly concerned with motion, but if any slip or collapse of the ramp caused trouble with the life-support system it was better to have someone on hand. This support system was even more important than the cruiser: in an emergency the crew could conceivably walk back to the Settlement carrying their air equipment even if the crusier were ruined.

The reasoning behind the evacuation order should have left Beetchermarlf and Kensnee as the only ones aboard, with even the captain watching from outside. Dondragmer was not prepared to be so reasonable. He had stayed aboard.

Tension in the crowd of caterpillarlike beings gathered outside the monster hull mounted as the drivers took up the slack in their treads. Because Dondragmer could not see the tense crowd from the bridge, he was calm; Beetchermarlf could feel their mood and was perturbed. The human watchers, observing by way of a set which had been taken from the life-support room and secured on a rock projecting from the water a hundred yards from the land-cruiser, could see nothing until the cruiser actually started to move. They were all calm except Easy and Benj.

The boy was paying little attention to the outside view, instead he was watching the bridge screen on which part of Beetchermarlf was visible. He had one set of chelae on the tiller, holding it fast; the other three sets were darting with almost invisible speed among the grips of the engine control lines, trying to equalize the pull of the different trucks. He had made no attempt to power more than the usual ten; the cords which normally cross-connected them, so that a single line would work them all, had been realigned for individual control. Beetchermarlf was very, very busy.

As the *Kwembly* began to inch backward, one of the human beings commented explosively.

"Why in blazes didn't they put remote controls or at least torque and thrust indicators, on that bridge? That poor bug is going crazy. I don't see how he can tell when a particular set of tracks is even gripping, let alone how it responds to his handling."

"If he had fancy indicators he probably couldn't," replied Mersereau. "Barlennan wanted no more sophisticated gear on those vehicles than his people could repair on the spot, except where there was really no choice. I agreed with him, and so did the rest of the planning board. Look—she's sliding off, smooth as ice."

A chorus of expressive hoots came from the speaker, muffled by the fact that most of the beings emitting them were under water. For a long moment, a score or so of the 'midship trucks were hanging free as the stern of the *Kwembly* came off the ramp and moved back over the river bed. The engineer who had been afraid of the bridge effect crossed his fingers and rolled his eyes upward. Then the bow dipped as the forward trucks came down onto the ramp in their turn, and weight was once more decently distributed. The twisting stress, which no one had considered seriously, lessened as the cruiser eased onto the relatively level cobbling of the river bed and came to a halt. The crew divided and poured around bow and stern to get to the main lock, no one thinking to pick up the communicator. Easy thought of reminding the captain, but decided that it would be more tactful to wait.

Dondragmer had not forgotten the instrument. As the first members of the crew emerged from the inner surface of the lock pool, his voice echoed through the speaking tubes.

"Kervenser! Reffel! Take the scout fliers out at once. Reffel, pick up the communicator outside; make sure the shutter is in the flier before you start; then make a ten-minute sweep north to east and back. Kervenser, sweep west and around to south for the same time. Borndender, report when all your measuring equipment is aboard. Beetchermarlf and Takoorch, outside and realign the engine control cords to normal."

His communicator at the bridge had the sound on, so Easy heard and translated these orders, though the reference to a shutter meant nothing to any of them. She and her colleagues watched the screen of the outside set with interest as the two tiny helicopters rose from the upper lock, one of them sweeping toward the pickup and presumably settling outside its field of view. The other was still climbing as it left the screen, heading west. The picture rocked as the set was picked up by Reffel and wrestled into its space aboard the flier. Easy flicked a switch absent-mindedly to record the scenes for future map work as the viewpoint lifted from the ground.

Dondragmer would have appreciated being able to watch the same screen but could only wait for a relayed verbal report from Reffel or a delayed but direct one from Kervenser. Actually, Reffel did not bother to relay. The ten-minute flights produced no information demanding speedy delivery. What it amounted to, as Dondragmer reported to the human audience, was that the *Kwembly* was in a valley some fifteen miles wide, with walls of bare rock quite steep by Dhrawn's standards. The pilots estimated the slope at twenty to thirty degrees. They were also remarkably high, fully forty feet. To the west there had been no sign of a new flood as far as Kervenser had flown. He noted that the boulders strewing the valley floor gave way to bare rock within a mile or two and there were numerous pools like the one in which the *Kwembly* was now standing. To the east, the stones and pools continued as far as Reffel had gone. Dondragmer pondered these data for a while after relaying this information to the satellite, then ordered one of the fliers back to work.

"Kerv, get back aloft. The helmsmen won't be done for hours yet. Go as far west along the valley as you can in an hour and check as closely as your lights will allow for any sign of more water starting down. Make that three hours, unless you have a positive finding, of course, or have to turn back because of bad visibility. I'm going off watch. Tell Stakendee to take the bridge before you leave."

Even Mesklinites get tired but Dondragmer's thought that this was the right time to get some rest was unfortunate, as Barlennan pointed out to him later. When the captain insisted that there would have been nothing for him to do even if he had been fully alert, his superior gave the Mesklinite equivalent of a snort of contempt.

"You'd have managed to find something. You did later."

Dondragmer refrained from pointing out that this proved that his omission was not a serious error; but he had to admit to himself that it had appeared so at the time.

It was almost eight hours after Kervenser's departure that a crewman hooted outside the door of the captain's quarters. When Dondragmer responded, the other squeezed the situation into a single sentence.

"Sir, Kervenser and the helmsmen are still outside, and the pool of water we're in has frozen."

VI
POLICY

Impatience and irritation were noticeable in the Planning Laboratory but so far no tempers had actually been lost. Ib Hoffman, back for less than two hours from a month-long errand to Earth and Dromm, had said practically nothing except to ask for information. Easy, sitting beside him, had said nothing at all so far but she could see that something would have to be done shortly to turn the conversation into constructive channels. Changing the Project's basic policy might be a good idea, it often was. But right now, it was futile for the people at this end of the table to spend time blaming each other for the present policy. Still less useful was the scientists' bickering at the other end. They were still wondering why a lake should freeze when the temperature had been rising. A useful answer might lead to some useful action but to Easy it seemed a question for the laboratory rather than for a conference room.

If her husband didn't take a hand in the other discussion soon, she would have to do something herself, she decided.

"I've heard all about that side of it before, and I still don't buy it!" snapped Mersereau. "Up to a point it's good common sense, but I think we're way past that point. I realize that the more complex the equipment, the fewer people you need to run it; but you also need more specialized apparatus and specially trained personnel to maintain and repair it. If the land-cruisers had been as fully automated as some people wanted, we could have gotten along with a hundred Mesklinites on Dhrawn instead of a couple of thousand *at first;* but the chances are that every one of these machines would be out by now because we couldn't possibly have landed all the backup equipment and personnel they'd need. There aren't enough technically trained Mesklinites in existence yet, for one thing. I agreed with that, Barlennan agreed with it; it was common sense, as I said.

"But you, and for some reason Barlennan, went even farther. He was against including helicopters. I know there were some characters in the Project who assumed you could never teach a Mesklinite to fly, and maybe it was racial acrophobia that was motivating Barlennan; but at least he was able to realize that without air scouting the land-crusiers wouldn't dare travel more than a few miles an hour over new ground, and it would take roughly forever to cover even Low Alpha at that rate. We did convince him on that basis.

"But there was a lot of stuff we'd have been glad to provide, which would have been useful and have paid its way, which *he* talked *us* out of using. No weapons; I agree they'd probably have been futile. But no short-range radio equipment? No intercoms in the Settlement? It's dithering nonsense for Dondragmer to have to call us, six million miles away and ask us to relay his reports to Barlennan at the Settlement. It's usually not critical, since Barl couldn't help him physically and the time delay doesn't mean much, but it's silly at the best of times. It *is* critical now, though, when Don's first mate has disappeared, presumably within a hundred miles of the *Kwembly* and possibly less than ten, and there's no way in the galaxy to get in touch with him either from here or from the cruiser. Why was Barl against radios, Alan? And why are you?"

"The same reason you've just given," Aucoin answered with just a trace of acerbity. "The maintenance problem."

"You're dithering. There isn't any maintenance problem on a simple voice, or even a vision, communicator. There were four of them, as I understand it, being carried around on Mesklin with Barlennan's first outside-sponsored trip fifty years or so ago, and not one of them gave the slightest trouble. There are sixty on Dhrawn right now, with not a blip of a problem from any of them in the year and a half they've been there. Barlennan must know that, and you certainly do. Furthermore, why do we relay what messages they do send by voice? We could do it automatically instead of having a batch of interpreters hashing things up (sorry, Easy) and you can't tell me there'd be a maintenance problem for a relay unit in this station. Who's trying to kid whom?"

Easy stirred; this was perilously close to feud material. Her husband, however, sensed the motion and touched her arm in a gesture she understood. He would take care of it. However, he let Aucoin make his own answer.

"Nobody's trying to kid anyone. I don't mean equipment maintenance, and I admit it was a poor choice of words. I should have said morale. The Mesklinites are a competent and highly self-reliant species, at least the representatives we've seen the most of. They sail over thousands of miles of ocean on these ridiculous groups of rafts, completely out of touch with home and help for months at a time, just as human beings did a few centuries ago. It was our opinion that making communication too easy would tend to undermine that self-confidence. I admit that this is not certain; Mesklinites are not human, though their minds resemble ours in many ways, and there's one major factor whose effect we can't evaluate and may never be able to. We don't know their normal life spans, though they are clearly a good deal longer than ours. Still, Barlennan agreed with us about the radio question—as you said, it was he who brought it up—and he has never complained about the communication difficulty."

"To us." Ib cut in at this point. Aucoin looked surprised, then puzzled.

"Yes, Alan, that's what I said. He hasn't complained to us. What he thinks about it privately none of us knows."

"But why shouldn't he complain, or even ask for radios, if he has come to feel that he should have them?" The planner was not completely sidetracked, but Easy noted with approval that the defensiveness was gone from his tone.

"I don't know why," Hoffman admitted. "I just remember what I've learned about our first dealings with Barlennan a few decades ago. He was a highly cooperative, practically worshipful agent for the mysterious aliens of Earth and Panesh and Dromm and these other mysterious places in the sky during most of the Gravity mission, doing our work for us just as we asked; then at the end he suddenly held us up for a blackmail jolt which five human beings, seven Panesh-ka, and nine Drommians out of every ten still think we should never have paid. You know as well as I do that teaching advanced technology, or even basic science, to a culture which isn't yet into its mechanical revolution makes the ecologists see red because they feel that every race should have the right to go through its own kind of growing pains; makes the xenophobes scream because we're arming the wicked aliens against us; gets the historians down on us because we're burying priceless data and annoys the administrative types because they're afraid we're setting up problems they haven't learned to cope with yet."

"It's the xenophobes who are the big problem," Mersereau snapped. "The nuts who take it for granted that every non-human species would be an enemy if it had the technical capacity. That's why we give the Mesklinites only equipment they can't possibly duplicate themselves, like the fusion units: things which couldn't be taken apart and studied in detail without about five stages of intermediate equipment like gamma-ray diffraction cameras, which the Mesklinites don't have either. Alan's argument sounds good, but it's just an excuse. You know as well as I do that you could train a Mesklinite to fly a reasonably part-automated shuttle in two months if the controls were modified for his nippers, and that there isn't a scientist in this station who wouldn't give three quarts of his blood to have loads of physical specimens and instruments of his own improvising bouncing between here and Dhrawn's surface."

"That's not entirely right, though there are elements of truth in it," Hoffman returned calmly. "I agree with your personal feeling about xenophobes, but it is a fact that with energy so cheap that a decently designed interstellar freighter can pay off its construction cost in four or five years, an interstellar war isn't the flat impossibility it was once assumed to be. Also, you know why this station has such big rooms, uncomfortable as some of us find them and inefficient as they certainly are for some purposes. The average Drommian, if there were a room here he couldn't get into, would assume that it contained something being deliberately kept secret from him. They have no concept of privacy, and by our standards most of them are seriously paranoid. If we had failed to share technology with them when contact was first made, we'd have created a planetful of highly competent xenophobes much more dangerous than anything even Earth has produced. I don't know that Mesklinites would react the same way, but I still think that starting the College on Mesklin was the smartest piece of policy since they admitted the first Drommian to M. I. T."

"And the Mesklinites had to blackmail us into doing *that*."

"Embarrassingly true," admitted Hoffman. "But that's all side issue. The current point is that we just don't know what Barlennan really thinks or plans. We can, though, be perfectly sure that he didn't agree to take two thousand of his people including himself onto an almost completely unknown world, certain to be highly dangerous even for a species like his, without having a very good reason indeed."

"We gave him a good reason," pointed out Aucoin.

"Yes. We tried to imitate him in the art of blackmail. We agreed to keep the College going on Mesklin, over the objections of many of our own people, if he would do the Dhrawn job for us. There was no suggestion on either side of material payment, though the Mesklinites are perfectly aware of the relation between knowledge and material wealth. I'm quite willing to admit that Barlennan is an idealist, but I'm not sure how much chauvinism there is in his idealism or how far either one will carry him.

"All this is beside the point, too. We shouldn't be worrying about the choice of equipment provided for the Mesklinites. They agreed with the choice, whatever their private reservations may have been. We are still in a position to help them with information on physical facts they don't know and which their scientists can hardly be expected to work out for themselves. We have high-speed computation. Right now we have one extremely expensive exploring machine frozen in on a lake on Dhrawn, together with about a hundred living beings who may be personnel to some of us but are personalities to the rest. If we want to change pol-

icy and insist on Barlennan's accepting a shuttleful of
new equipment, that's fine; but it's not the present
problem, Boyd. I don't know what we could send down
right now that would be the slightest help to Dondragmer."

"I suppose you're right, Ib, but I can't help thinking about Kervenser, and how much better it would
have been if—"

"He could have carried one of the communicators,
remember. Dondragmer had three besides the one on
his bridge, all of them portable. The decision to take
them or not was strictly on Kervenser himself and his
captain. Let's leave out the if's for now and try to
do some constructive planning."

Mersereau subsided, a little irritated at Ib for the
latter's choice of words but with his resentment of
Aucoin's attitude diverted for the moment. The planner
took over the conversational lead again, looking down
the table toward the end where the scientists had now
fallen silent.

"All right, Dr. McDevitt. Has any agreement been
reached as to what probably happened?"

"Not completely, but there is an idea worth checking further. As you know, the *Kwembly's* observers
had been reporting nearly constant temperature since
the fog cleared; no radiational cooling; if anything, a
very slight warming trend. Barometric readings have
been rising very slowly at that place ever since the machine was stranded; readings before that time are
meaningless because of the uncertain change in elevation. The temperatures have been well below the
freezing points of either pure water or pour ammonia
but rather above that of the ammonia monohydrate-
water eutectic. We're wondering whether the initial
thaw might not have been caused by the ammonia fog's
reacting with the water snow on which the *Kwembly*
was riding. Dondragmer was afraid of that possibility;

and if so, the present freeze might be due to evaporation of ammonia from the eutectic. We'd need ammidity readings—"

"What?" Hoffman and Aucoin cut in almost together.

"Sorry. Office slang. Partial pressure of ammonia relative to the saturation value—equivalent of relative humidity for water. We'd need readings on that to confirm or kill the notion, and of course the Mesklinites haven't been taking them."

"Could they?"

"I'm sure we could work out a technique with them. I don't know how long it would take. Water vapor wouldn't interfere; its equilibrium pressure is four or five powers of ten smaller than ammonia's in that temperature range. The job shouldn't be too hard."

"I realize this is an hypothesis rather than a full-blown theory, but is it good enough to base action on?"

"That would depend on the action." Aucoin made a gesture of impatience, and the atmospheric physicist continued hastily.

"That is, I wouldn't risk an all-or-nothing break-out effort on it alone, but I'd be willing to try anything which didn't commit the *Kwembly* to exhausting some critical supply she carries, or put her in obvious danger."

The planner nodded. "All right," he said. "Would you rather stay here and supply us with more ideas, or would it be more effective to talk this one over with the Mesklinites?"

McDevitt pursed his lips and thought for a moment.

"We've been talking with them pretty frequently, but I suppose there's more good likely to come from that direction than—" he stopped, and Easy and her husband concealed smiles. Aucoin nodded, appearing not to notice the *faux pas*.

"All right. Go on back to Communications, and good

luck. Let us know if either you or they come up with anything else that seems worth trying."

The four scientists assented and left together. The ten remaining conference members were silent for some minutes before Aucoin voiced what all but one were thinking.

"Let's face it," he said slowly. "The real argument is going to come when we relay this report to Barlennan."

Ib Hoffman jerked upright. "You haven't yet?" he snapped.

"Only the fact of the original stranding, which Easy told them and occasional progress reports on the repair work. Nothing yet about the freeze-up."

"Why not?" Easy could read danger signals in her husband's voice, and wondered whether she wanted to smooth this one over or not. Aucoin looked surprised at the question.

"You know why as well as I do. Whether he learned about it now or ten hours from now or from Dondragmer when he gets back to the Settlement a year from now would make little difference. There is nothing Barlennan could do immediately to help, and the only thing he could do at all is something we'd rather he didn't."

"And that is?" interjected Easy sweetly. She had about made up her mind which line to take.

"That is, as you well know, sending one of the two land-cruisers still at the Settlement off to rescue the *Kwembly,* as he wanted to do for the *Esket.*"

"And you still object to that."

"Certainly, for exactly the same reasons as before —which Barlennan, I admit, accepted that time. It's not entirely that we have other specific plans for those two cruisers, but that's part of it. Whatever you may think, Easy, I don't dismiss life as unimportant merely because it isn't human life. I do object, though, to wasting time and resources. Changing policy in the middle of an operation generally does both."

"But if you claim that Mesklinite lives mean as much to you as human ones, how can you talk about waste?"

"You're not thinking, Easy. I understand and don't really blame you, but you're ignoring the fact that the *Kwembly* is something like ten thousand miles airline from the Settlement, and more like thirteen thousand by the route they took. A rescue vehicle could not possibly cover that track in less than two hundred or two hundred and fifty hours. The last part of it, which the *Kwembly* traversed by being washed down a river, might not be findable and the last four thousand miles across the snow field may no longer be passable."

"We could give them directions with satellite fixes."

"We could, no doubt. The fact remains that unless Dondragmer can get himself, his crew, and his vehicle out of their present trouble, nothing Barlennan can send out for him is likely to be of the slightest help; *if* the *Kwembly* is in real and immediate danger. If she is not, if it's just a matter of being frozen in like a nineteenth century whaler, they have indefinite supplies with their closed-cycle life system and fusion converters and we and Barlennan can plan a nice, leisurely rescue."

"Like Destigmet's *Esket*," retorted the woman with some bitterness. "It's been over seven months, and you squelched all rescue talk then and ever since!"

"That was a very different situation. The *Esket* is still standing there, unchanged as far as her vision sets can tell us, but her crew has dropped out of sight. We haven't the faintest idea what has happened to them but since they're not on board and haven't been for all this time it's impossible to believe they're still alive. Even with all their abilities and physical toughness, Mesklinites couldn't live on Dhrawn for seven months without a good deal more equipment than their air-suits."

Easy had no answer. On pure logic, Aucoin was perfectly right; but Easy could not accept the idea that the situation was purely logical. Ib knew how she felt and decided that the time had come to change course again. He shared the planner's opinion, up to a point, on basic policy; he also knew why his wife could not possibly share it.

"The real, immediate problem, as I see it," Hoffman interjected, "is the one Don has with the men who are still outside. As I get it, two are under the ice, as far as anyone can tell; and no one seems to know whether that puddle is frozen to the bottom. In any case, judging by the work they were supposed to be doing, they're in among the *Kwembly's* trucks somewhere. I suppose that means a straight icepick-and-search job. I can't guess what the chances are of an air-suited Mesklinite's living through that sort of thing. The temperature won't bother them that far below melting water-ice, but I don't know what other physiological limitations they may have.

"Don's first officer is also missing, overdue from a helicopter flight. We can't help directly, since he didn't take a communicator with him, but there is another flier available. Has Dondragmer asked us to assist while a search is made with the other machine and a vision set?"

"He hadn't up to half an hour ago," replied Mersereau.

"Then I strongly advise that we suggest it to him."

Aucoin nodded agreement, and glanced at the woman. "Your job, I'd say, Easy."

"If someone hasn't beaten me to it." She rose, pinched Ib's ear in passing, and left the room.

"Next point," Hoffman went on. "Granting that you may be right in opposing a rescue expedition from the Settlement, I think it's time Barlennan was brought up to date about the *Kwembly*."

"Why ask for more troubles than we need?" retorted Aucoin. "I don't like to argue with anyone, especially when he doesn't really have to listen to me."

"I don't think you'll have to argue. Remember, he agreed with us the other time."

"You were saying a few minutes ago that you weren't sure how sincere his agreements have been."

"I'm not but if he had been strongly against us that time he'd have done just what he wanted and sent a crew out to help the *Esket*. He did, remember, on a couple of other occasions when there was a cruiser in trouble."

"That was much closer to the settlement, and we finally approved the action," retorted Aucoin.

"And you know as well as I do that we approved it because we could see that he was going to do it anyway."

"We approved it, Ib, because your wife was on Barlennan's side both times and out-talked us. Your argument, incidentally, is a point against telling him about the present situation."

"Whose side was she on during the *Esket* argument? I still think we should tell Barlennan the present situation pronto. Plain honesty aside, the longer we wait the more certain he is to find out, sooner or later, that we've been censoring expedition reports on him."

"I wouldn't call it censoring. We've never changed a thing."

"But you have delayed the relay plenty of times while you decided what he ought to know, and as I've said before I don't think that's the game as we agreed to play it with him. Pardon my reactionary sentiments, but on purely selfish grounds we'd be well advised to keep his confidence as long as possible."

Several of the others, who had listened in silence

up to this point, spoke up almost at once when Hoffman expressed this sentiment. It took Aucoin several seconds to untangle their words, but it eventually became clear that the feeling of the group was with Ib. The chairman yielded gracefully; his technique did not involve standing in front of the bull.

"All right, we pass on the complete report to Barlennan as soon as we adjourn." He glanced at the winner. "That is, if Mrs. Hoffman hasn't sent it already. What's the next point?"

One of the men who had done little but listen up to this point asked a question. "Forgive me if I didn't follow you too clearly a few minutes ago. Ib, you and Alan both claim that Barlennan agreed with Project policy in limiting to an absolute minimum the amount of sophisticated equipment his expedition was to use. That was my understanding also; but you, Ib, just mentioned having doubts about Barlennan's sincerity. Do any of those doubts stem from his accepting the helicopters?"

Hoffman shook his head. "No. The arguments we used for their necessity were good, and the only surprising thing to me was that Barlennan didn't anticipate them and take the equipment without argument."

"But Mesklinites are acrophobic by nature. The thought of flying, to anyone from a world like that, must be just unimaginable."

Ib smiled grimly. "True. But one of the first things Barlennan did after he made his deal with the Gravity people and started learning basic science was to design, build and fly, on Mesklin, in the polar zone where gravity is at its highest, a hot air balloon. Whatever is motivating Barlennan, it isn't acrophobia. I don't exactly doubt him; I'm just not sure of his thinking, if you'll forgive a rather crude quibble."

"I agree," Aucoin interjected. "And I think we're running dry. I suggest we break up for, say, six hours.

We can think, or go down to Comm and listen to the Mesklinites or talk with them; anything that will keep your thoughts on Dhrawn questions. You know my ideas about that."

"That's where mine have been." It was the same speaker. "I keep wondering about the *Esket,* every time one of the cruisers runs into trouble, even when the trouble is obviously natural."

"So do we all, I imagine," rejoined Aucoin.

"The more I think of it, the more I feel that her crew must have run into intelligent opposition. After all, we know there is life on Dhrawn, more than the bushes and pseudo-algae the Mesklinites have found. They wouldn't account quantitatively for that atmosphere; there must be a complete ecological complex somewhere. I'd guess in the higher-temperature regions."

"Such as Low Alpha." Hoffman completed the thought. "Yes, you don't have ammonia and free oxygen in the same environment for very long, on the time scale of a planet. I can believe the possibility of an intelligent species here. We haven't found any sign of it from space and the Mesklinite ground parties haven't met it, unless the *Esket* did, but seventeen billion square miles of planet make a lot of good reasons for that. The idea is plausible and you're not the first to get it but I don't know where it leaves us. Barlennan thought of it too, according to Easy and debated sending another cruiser to the area of the *Esket's* loss specifically to seek and contact any intelligence that may be there; but even Barlennan was doubtful about undertaking a search. We certainly haven't pushed it."

"Why not?" cut in Mersereau. "If we could get in touch with natives as we did on Mesklin the project could really get going! We wouldn't have to depend so completely on—oh."

Aucoin smiled grimly.

"Precisely," he said. "Now you *have* found a good reason for wondering about Barlennan's frankness. I'm not saying that he's an ice-hearted politician who would give up the lives of his men just to keep a hammerlock on the Dhrawn operation but the *Esket's* crew was pretty certainly already beyond rescue when he finally agreed not to send the *Kalliff* in the same direction."

"There is another point, though," Hoffman said thoughtfully.

"What?"

"I'm not sure it's worth mentioning, since we can't evaluate it; but the *Kwembly* is commanded by Dondragmer, who is a long-time associate of Barlennan's and should by ordinary reasoning be an extremely close friend. Is there any chance that his being involved would influence Barl's judgement about a rescue trip or even make him order one against his better judgement? Like you, I don't think that caterpillar is just an administrative machine. His cold-bloodedness is purely physical."

"I've wondered about that, too," the chief planner admitted. "It supprised me greatly months ago when he let Dondragmer go out at all. I'd gotten the impression that he didn't want him to take major chances. I didn't worry too much about it—certainly no one knows enough about Mesklinite psychology in general or Barlennan's in particular to base any serious planning on. If anyone does, Ib, it's your wife, and she can't or won't put what she understands about them into words. As you say, we can't assign weight to the friendship-influence possibility. We just add it to the list of questions. Let me hear any ideas about those crewmen who are presumably frozen under the *Kwembly* and then we really must break up."

"A fusion converter would keep a good, large heating coil going, and resistors aren't very complex equipment," Mersereau pointed out. "Heaters aren't a very unreasonable piece of equipment on Dhrawn, either. If only—"

"But we didn't," interrupted Aucoin.

"But we did, if you'd let me finish. There are enough converters with the *Kwembly* to lift her off the planet if their energy could be applied to such a job. There must be some metal aboard which could be jury-rigged into resistors or arcs. Whether the Mesklinites could operate such gadgets I don't know. There must be a limit even to their temperature tolerance but we might at least ask if they've thought of such a thing."

"You're wrong on one point. I know there is very little metal either in their equipment or the supplies on those land-cruisers and I'd be startled if Mesklinite rope turned out to be a conductor. I'm no chemist, but anything bonded as firmly as that stuff must have its electrons pretty well latched in place. By all means check with Dondragmer, though. Easy is presumably still in Comm; she can help you if there are no linguistically broad Mesklinites on duty at the other end. We're adjourned."

Mersereau nodded, already heading toward the door, and the meeting broke up. Aucoin followed Mersereau through one door; most of the others went other ways. Only Hoffman remained seated at the table.

His eyes were focussed nowhere in particular, and there was a frown on his face which made him look older than his forty years.

He liked Barlennan. He liked Dondragmer even better, as did his wife. He had no grounds for the slightest complaint about the progress of the Dhrawn research, considering the policies he himself had helped set up, nor did the rest of the planners. There was no concrete reason whatever, except a trick of half a century before, to distrust the Mesklinite commander. That he might want to keep hypothetical natives of

Dhrawn out of the picture could hardly be given credence. No, certainly not. After all, the problems of transferring responsibility to such beings, even if they existed, for the Dhrawn research project, would cause even more delay, as Barlennan would surely realize.

The occasional case of disagreement between explorers and planners was minor. It was the sort of thing which happened ten times as often with, say, Drommians. No, there was no reason to suppose the Mesklinites were already going off on independent plans of their own.

Still, Barlennan had not wanted helicopters, though he had finally been persuaded to accept them. He was the same Barlennan who had built and flown in a hot-air balloon as his first exercise in applied science.

He had not sent relief to the *Esket,* although all the giant land-cruisers were necessary for the Project and despite the fact that a hundred or so of his people were aboard.

He had refused local-range radios, useful as they would obviously be. The argument against them was the sort that a firm-minded teacher might use in a classroom situation, but this was real life and deadly earnest.

He had, fifty years before, not only jumped at the chance to acquire alien knowledge; he had maneuvered deliberately to force his non-Mesklinite sponsors to give it to him.

Ib Hoffman could not rid himself of the notion that Barlennan was up to something underhanded again.

He wondered what Easy thought about it.

VII
ICED WAGON

Beetchermarlf and Takoorch, like the rest of the *Kwembly's* crew, were taken by surprise when the lake froze. Neither had had any occasion for several hours to look around, since the maze of fine cords on which their attention was focussed was considerably more complicated than, say, the rigging of a clipper ship. Both knew exactly what to do, and there was little need for conversation. Even had their eyes wandered from the job, there was little else to see. They were under the immense hulk of their vehicle, roofed by the pneumatic "mattress" which distributed its weight among the trucks, walled partly by the trucks themselves and partly by the blackness of Dhrawn's night which swallowed everything beyond the range of their little portable lights.

So they had not seen, any more than the sailors inside the *Kwembly,* the tiny crystals which began to form at the surface of the lake and settle to the bottom, glinting and sparkling in the *Kwembly's* floods.

They had completed reconnecting on the port row, Number 1, all the way from bow to stern and were working their way forward on Row 2 when they discovered that they were trapped.

Takoorch's battery light was fading a trifle, and he took it over to the nearest fusion converter, which hap-

pened to be on a Row 1 truck, for recharging. He was
quite startled to find that he couldn't get at or even see
the converter; after a few seconds of fumbling and
looking he called Beetchermarlf. It took nearly ten
minutes for them to establish that they were completely
enclosed by an opaque white wall, impenetrable even
to their strength. It had welded all the outer trucks
together and filled all the spaces between them from
mattress above to cobbles below, nearly three feet of
height, on the average. Inside the wall they were still
free to move about.

Their tools were edged rather than pointed, and too
small to make appreciable way against the ice, though
it took fully an hour of scraping to convince them both
of that. Neither was greatly concerned as yet; obviously
the ice was immobilizing the *Kwembly,* and the rest of
the crew would have to dig down to them in the interest
of freeing the vehicle if not for the prime purpose of
rescue. Of course their supply of life hydrogen was
limited, but this meant less to them than a corresponding oxygen shortage would have to a human being.
They had at least ten or twelve hours yet of full activity,
and when the hydrogen partial pressure dropped below
a certain value they would simply lose consciousness.
Their body chemistry would slow down more and more,
but fifty and perhaps a hundred hours would pass before anything irreversible occurred. One of the reasons
for Mesklinite durability, though human biologists had
had no chance to find it out, was the remarkable
simplicity of their biochemistry.

The two were calm enough, in fact, to go back to
their assigned work; and they were almost to the front
of Row 2 before another discovery was made. This one
did perturb them.

The ice was creeping inward. It was not coming
rapidly, but it was coming. As it happened, neither of
them knew any better than Ib Hoffman what being

frozen into a block of the stuff was likely to do to them. Neither had the slightest desire to learn.

At least there was still light. Not all the power units were on outside trucks, and Takoorch had been able to recharge his battery. This made it possible to make another, very careful search of the boundaries of their prison. Beetchermarlf was hoping to find unfrozen space either near the bottom or, preferably, near the top of the walls around them. He did not know whether the freezing would have started from the top or the bottom of the pond. He was not familiar, as any human being would have been, with the fact that ice floats on liquid water. This was just as well, since it would have led him to an erroneous conclusion in this instance. The crystals had indeed formed at the top, but they had been denser than the surrounding liquid and had settled, only to redissolve as they reached levels richer in ammonia. This pseudo-convection effect had had the result of robbing the lake rather uniformly of ammonia until it had reached a composition able to freeze almost simultaneously throughout. As a result, the search turned up no open spaces.

For some time the two lay between two of the trucks, thinking and occasionally checking to see how far the freezing had progressed. They had no time measuring equipment, and therefore no basis for estimating the speed of the process. Takoorch guessed that it was slowing down: Beetchermarlf was less sure.

Occasionally an idea would strike one of them but the other usually managed to find a flaw in it.

"We can move some of these stones, the smaller ones," Takoorch remarked at one point. "Why can't we dig our way under the ice?"

"Where to?" countered his companion. "The nearest edge of the lake is forty or fifty cables away, or was the last I knew. We couldn't begin to dig that far in these rocks before our air gave out, even if there was any reason to suppose the freezing didn't include the water between the rocks underneath. Coming up before the edge wouldn't get us anywhere."

Takoorch admitted the justice of this with an acquiescent gesture and silence fell while the ice grew a fraction of an inch nearer.

Beetchermarlf had the next constructive thought.

"These lights must give off some heat, even if we can't feel it through the suits," he suddenly exclaimed. "Why shouldn't they keep the ice from forming near them, and even let us melt our way to the outside?"

"Worth trying," was Takoorch's laconic answer.

Together they approached the frosty barrier. Beetchermarlf built a small cairn of stones leaning against the ice, and set the light, adjusted for full brightness, at its top. Then both crowded close, their front ends part way up the heap of pebbles, and watched the space between the lamp and the ice.

"Come to think of it," Takoorch remarked as they waited, "Our bodies give off some heat, don't they? Shouldn't our just being here help melt this stuff?"

"I suppose so." Beetchermarlf was dubious. "We'd better watch to make sure that it doesn't freeze at each side and around behind us while we're waiting here."

"What will that matter? If it does, it means that we and the light together are enough to fight the freezing and we should be able to melt our way out."

"That's true. Watch, though, so we'll know if that's happening." Takoorch gestured agreement. They fell silent again.

The older helmsman, however, was not one to endure silence indefinitely, and presently he gave utterance to another idea.

"I know our knives didn't make much impression on the ice, but shouldn't it help if we did some scraping right here where it's nearest the light?" He unclipped one of the blades they carried for general use and reached toward the ice.

"Wait a minute!" exclaimed Beetchermarlf. "If you start working there, how are we ever going to know whether the heat is having any effect?"

"If my knife gets us anywhere, who cares whether it's the heat or the work?" retorted Takoorch. Beetchermarlf found no good answer ready, so he subsided, muttering something about "controlled experiments" while the other Mesklinite went to work with his tiny blade.

As it happened, his interference did not spoil the experiment, though it may have delayed slightly the appearance of observable results. Body heat, lamp heat, and knife all together proved unequal to the job; the ice continued to gain. They had to remove the lamps from the cairn at last, and watch it slowly become enveloped in the crystalline wall.

"It won't be long now," Takoorch remarked as he swung the lights around them. "Only two of the power units are free, now. Should we charge up the lights again before they go, or isn't it worth the trouble?"

"We might as well," answered Beetchermarlf. "It seems a pity that that's the only use we can get out of all that power. Four of those things can push the *Kwembly* around on level ground and I once heard a human being say that one could do it if it could get traction. That certainly could chip ice for us if we could find a way to apply it."

"We can take the power box out easily enough, but what we'd do afterward beats me. The units put out electric current as one choice, but I don't see how we could shock the ice away. The mechanical torque you can get from them works only on the motor shafts."

"We'd be more likely to shock ourselves away if we used the current. I don't know very much about electricity, it was mostly plain mechanics I got in the little time I was at the College, but I know enough of it can kill. Think of something else."

Takoorch endeavored to comply. Like his young companion, he had had only a short period of exposure to alien knowledge; both had volunteered for the Dhrawn project in preference to further classwork. Their knowledge of general physics might have compared fairly well with that of Benj Hoffman when he was ten or twelve years old. Neither was really comfortable in thinking about matters for which no easily visualized model could be furnished.

They were not, however, lacking in the ability to think abstractly. Both had heard of heat as representing a lowest common denominator of energy, even if they didn't picture it as random particle motion.

It was Beetchermarlf who first thought of another effect of electricity.

"Tak! Remember the explanations we got about not putting too much power into the trucks until the cruiser got moving? The humans said it was possible to snap the treads or damage the motors if we tried to accelerate too fast."

"That's right. Quarter power is the limit below a hundred cables per hour."

"Well, we have the power controls here where we can get at them, and those motors certainly aren't going to turn. Why not just power this truck and let the motor get as hot as it wants to?"

"What makes you think it will get hot? You don't know what makes those motors go any more than I do. They didn't say it would make them hot, just that it was bad for them."

"I know, but what else could it be? You know that any sort of energy that isn't used up some other way turns into heat."

"That doesn't sound quite right, somehow," returned the older sailor. "Still, I guess anything is worth trying now. They didn't say anything about the motor's wrecking the rest of the ship too; if it ruins us, well, we won't be much worse off."

Beetchermarlf paused; the thought that he might be endangering the *Kwembly* hadn't crossed his mind. The more he thought of it, the less he felt justified in taking the chance. He looked at the relatively tiny power unit nestling between the treads of the nearby truck, and wondered whether such a minute thing could really be a danger to the huge bulk above them. Then he remembered the vastly greater size of the machine which had brought him and his fellows to Dhrawn and realized that the sort of power which could hurl such immense masses through the sky was not to be handled casually. He would never be afraid to *use* such engines, since he had been given a chance to become familiar with their normal and proper handling; but deliberately *misusing* one of them was a different story.

"You're right," he admitted somewhat inaccurately, Takoorch had been, after all, willing to take the chance. "We'll have to work it differently. Look, if the tracks are free to turn, then we can't damage the motor or the power box and just stirring up water will warm it."

"You think so? I remember hearing something like that, but if I can't break up this ice with my own strength it's hard to see how simply stirring water is going to do it. Besides, the trucks aren't free; they're on the bottom with the *Kwembly's* weight on them."

"Right. You wanted to dig. Start moving rocks; that ice is getting close."

Beetchermarlf set the example and began prying the rounded cobbles from the edges of the treads. It was a hard job even for Mesklinite muscles. Smooth as they were, the stones were tightly packed; furthermore when one was moved, there was not too much room in which to put it. The stones under the treads, which were the ones which really had to be shifted, could not even be reached until those at the sides were out of the way. The two labored furiously to clear a ditch around the truck. They were frightened at the time it took.

When the ditch was deep enough, they tried to pry stones from under the treads and this was even more discouraging.

The *Kwembly* had a mass of about two hundred tons. On Dhrawn, this meant a weight of sixteen million pounds to distribute among the fifty-six remaining trucks: the mattress did a good job of distributing. Three hundred thousand pounds, even if it is a rather short three hundred thousand, is too much even for a Mesklinite, whose weight, even at Mesklin's pole, is little over three hundred. It is a great deal even for some eight square feet of caterpillar tread. If Dhrawn's gravity had not done an equally impressive job of packing its surface materials, the *Kwembly* and her sister vehicles would probably have sunk to their mattresses before travelling a yard.

In other words, the rocks under the tread were held quite firmly. Nothing the two sailors could do would move one of them at all. There was nothing to use as a lever; their ample supplies of spare rope were useless without pulleys; their unaided muscles were pitifully inadequate—a situation still less familiar to them than to races whose mechanical revolution lay a few centuries in the past.

The approaching ice, however, was a stimulus to thought. It could also have been a stimulus to panic but neither of the sailors was prone to that form of disintegration. Again, it was Beetchermarlf who led.

"Tak, get out from under. We can move those pebbles. Get forward; they're going to go the other way." The youngster was climbing the truck as he spoke, and Takoorch grasped the idea at once. He vanished beyond the next-forward truck without a word. Beetchermarlf stretched out along the main body of the drive unit, between the treads. In this foot-wide space, beneath and in front of him, was the recess which held the power converter. This was a rectangular object about the same size as the communicators, with ring-tipped control rods projecting from its surface and guide loops equipped with tiny pulleys at the edges. Lines for remote handling from the bridge were threaded through some of the guides and attached to the rings but the helmsman ignored them. He could see little, since the lights were still on the bottom several feet away and the top of the truck was in shadow, however, he did not need sight. Even clad in an airsuit he could handle these levers by touch.

Carefully he eased the master reactor control to the "operate" position; then, even more gingerly, started the motors forward. They responded properly; the treads on either side of him moved forward, and a clattering of small, hard objects against each other became audible for a moment. Then this ceased, and the treads began to race. Beetchermarlf instantly cut off the power, and crawled off the truck to see what had happened.

The plan had worked, just as a computer program with a logic error works: there is an answer forthcoming but not the one desired. As the helmsman had planned, the treads had scuffed the rocks under them backward; but he had forgotten the effect of the pneumatic mattress above. The truck had settled under its own weight and the downward thrust of the gas pressure until the chassis between the treads had met the bottom. Looking up, Beetchermarlf could see the bulge in the mattress where the entire drive unit had been let down some four inches.

Takoorch appeared from his shelter and looked the situation over, but said nothing. There was nothing useful to say.

Neither of them could guess how much more give there was to the mattress, and how much further the truck would have to be let down before it would really hang free, though they knew the details of the *Kwembly's* construction. The mattress was not a single gas bag but was divided into thirty separate cells, having two trucks in tandem attached to each. The helmsmen knew the details of the attachment—both had just spent many hours repairing the assemblies—but even the recent display of the *Kwembly's* underside with the weight off nearly all the trucks left them very doubtful about how far any one truck could extend by itself.

"Well, back to stone lugging," remarked Takoorch as he worked his nippers under a pebble. "Maybe these have been jarred loose now; otherwise it's going to be awkward, getting at them only from the ends."

"There isn't enough time for the job. The ice is still growing toward us. We might have to get the treads a whole body-length deeper before they'll run free. Leave the trucks alone, Tak. We'll have to try something else."

"All I want to know is what."

Beetchermarlf showed him. Taking a light with him this time, he climbed once more to the top of the truck. Takoorch followed, mystified. The younger sailor reared up against the shaft which formed the swivelling support of the truck, and attacked the mattress with his knife.

"But you can't hurt the ship!" Takoorch objected.

"We can fix it later. I don't like it any better than you do, and I'd gladly let the air out by the regular bleeder valve if we could only reach it; but we can't, and if we don't get the load off this truck very soon we won't do it at all." He continued slashing as he spoke.

It was little easier than moving the stones. The mattress fabric was extremely thick and tough; to support

the *Kwembly* it had to hold in a pressure more than
a hundred pounds per square inch above the ground.
One of the nuisances of the long trips was the need
to pump the cells up manually or to bleed off excess
pressure, when the height of the ground they were
traversing changed more than a few feet. At the moment the mattress was a little flat, since no pumping
had been done after the run down the river but the
inner pressure was that much higher.

Again and again Beetchermarlf sliced at the same
point on the taut-stretched surface. Each time the blade
went just a little deeper. Takoorch, convinced at last of
the necessity, joined him. The second blade's path
crossed that of the first, the two flashing alternately in
a rhythm almost too fast for a human eye to follow.
A human witness, had one been possible, would have
expected them to sever each other's nippers at any moment.

Even so, it took many minutes to get through. The
first warning of success was a fine stream of bubbles
which spread in all directions up the slope of the
bulging gas cell. A few more slashes and the cross-
shaped hole with its inch-long arms was gushing Dhraw-
nian air in a flood of bubbles that made the work
invisible. The prisoners ceased their efforts.

Slowly but visibly the stretched fabric was collaps-
ing. The bubbles fled more slowly across its surface,
gathering at the high point near the wall of ice. For a
few moments Beetchermarlf thought the fabric would
go entirely flat, but the weight of the suspended truck
prevented that. The center of the cell or the point at
which the truck was attached (neither of them knew
just where the cell boundaries were) was straining
downward: it was now pull instead of push.

"I'll start the engine again and see what happens,"
said Beetchermarlf. "Get forward again for a minute."
Takoorch obeyed. The younger helmsman deliberate-

ly wedged a number of pebbles under the front ends
of the treads, climbed the truck once more and settled
down. He had kept the light with him this time, not to
help him with handling controls but to make it easier
to tell how and whether the unit moved. He looked at
the point of attachment a few inches above him as he
started the engine once more.

The pebbles had provided some traction; the fabric
wrinkled and the swivel tilted slightly as the truck
strained forward. An upper socket, inaccessible inside
the cell, into which the shaft telescoped, prevented the
tilt from exceeding a few degrees. The trucks, of course,
could not be allowed to touch each other but the strain
could be seen. As the motion reached its limit the
tracks continued moving, but this time they did not
race free. Sound and tactile vibrations both indicated
that they were slipping on the pebbles and after a few
seconds the feel of swirling, eddying water became per-
ceptible against Beetchermarlf's air-suit. He started to
climb down from the truck and was nearly swept under
one of the treads as he shifted grips. He barely stopped
the motor in time with a hasty snatch at the control.
He needed several seconds to regain his composure after that; even his resilient physique could hardly have
survived being worked through the space between
treads and rocks. At the very least, his air-suit would
have been ruined.

Then he took time to trace very carefully the control cords leading from the reactor to the upper guides
along the bottom of the mattress, following them by
eye to the point above the next truck forward where
he could reach them. A few seconds later he was
on top of the other truck, starting the motor up again
from a safe distance and mentally kicking himself for
not having done it that way from the beginning.

Takoorch reappeared beside him and remarked.

"Well, we'll soon know whether stirring water up does any warming."

"It will," replied Beetchermarlf. "Besides, the treads are rubbing against the stones on the bottom instead of kicking them out of the way this time. Whether or not you believe that stirring makes heat, you certainly know that friction does. Watch the ice, or tell me if the neighborhood is getting too hot. I'm at the lowest power setting, but that's still a lot of energy."

Takoorch rather pessimistically went over to a point where the cairn should be visible if it were ever freed of ice. He settled down to wait. The currents weren't too bad here, though he could feel them tugging at his not-too-well-ballasted body. He anchored himself to a couple of medium-sized rocks and stopped worrying about being washed under the treads.

He did not really see how merely stirring water could heat anything but Beetchermarlf's point about friction was comforting. Also, while he would not have admitted it in so many words, he tended to give more weight to the younger sailor's opinion than to his own and he fully expected to see the ice yielding very shortly.

He was not disappointed; within five minutes he thought that more of the stony bottom was becoming visible between him and the barrier. In ten he was sure, and a hoot of glee appraised Beetchermarlf of the fact. The latter took the risk of leaving the control lines untended to come to see for himself and agreed. The ice was retreating. Immediately he began to plan.

"All right, Tak. Let's get the other units going as fast as they melt free and we can get at their controls. We should be able to melt the *Kwembly* loose from this thing, besides getting ourselves out from under."

Takoorch asked a question.

"Are you going to puncture the cells under all the powered units? That will let the air out of a third of the mattress."

Beetchermarlf was taken slightly aback.

"I'd forgotten that. No, well, we could patch them all, but—no, that's not so good. Let's see. When we get another power unit clear we can mount it on the other truck that's on this cell we've drained already; that will give us twice as much heat. After that I don't know. We could see about digging under the others—no, that didn't work so well—I don't know. Well, we can set one more driver going, anyway. Maybe that will be enough."

"We can hope," said Takoorch dubiously. The youngster's uncertainty had rather disappointed him, and he wasn't too impressed with the toned-down substitute for a plan; but he had nothing better himself to offer. "What do I do first?" he asked.

"I'd better go back and stand by those ropes, though I suppose everything's safe enough," replied Beetchermarlf indirectly. "Why don't you keep checking around the edges of the ice, and get hold of another converter as soon as one is unfrozen? We can put it into that truck," he indicated the other one attached to the deflated cell, "and start it up as soon as possible. All right?"

Takoorch gestured agreement and started surveying of the ice barrier. Beetchermarlf returned to the control lines, waiting passively. Takoorch made several circuits of the boundary, watching happily as the ice retreated in all directions. He was a little bothered by the discovery that the process was slowing down as the cleared space increased but even he was not too surprised. He made up his mind eventually which of the frozen-in power boxes would be the first to be released and settled down near it to wait.

His attitude, like that of his companion waiting at the controls, cannot be described exactly to a human being. He was neither patient nor impatient in the human sense. He knew that waiting was unavoidable, and he was quite unaffected emotionally by the inconvenience. He was reasonably intelligent and even imaginative by both human and Mesklinite standards, but he felt no need of anything even remotely resembling daydreaming to occupy his mind during the delay. A half-conscious mental clock caused him to check the progress of the melting at reasonably frequent intervals; this is all a human being can grasp, much less describe, about what went on in his mind.

He was certainly neither asleep nor preoccupied, because he reacted promptly to a sudden loud thud and a scattering of pebbles around him. The spot where he was lying was almost directly aft of the truck which was running, so he knew instantly what must have happened.

So did Beetchermarlf, and the power unit was shut down by a tug on the control line before a man would have perceived any trouble. The two Mesklinites met a second or two later beside the truck which had been running.

It was in a predictable condition, Beetchermarlf had to admit to himself. Mesklinite organics are very, very tough materials and the tread would have lasted for many more months under ordinary travel wear: deliberate friction against unyielding rocks, even with very modest engine power, was a little too much for it.

Perhaps the word "unyielding" does not quite describe the rocks; those which had been under the moving band of fabric had been visibly flattened on top by the wear of the last hour or so. Some of them were more than half gone. The young helmsman decided, after careful examination, that the failure of the tread had been due less to simple wear than to a cut started by a formerly spherical pebble which had worn down to a thin slice with sharp edges. Takoorch agreed, when the evidence was pointed out to him.

There was no question about what to do, and they

annoyed with himself for not having thought of the
same thing earlier. For half an hour the two labored
heaping pebbles between and around the trucks surrounding their heat source. They eventually produced
did it at once. In less than five minutes the power converter had been removed from the damaged truck and
installed in the one aft of it, which had also been un-
loaded by puncturing the pressure cell. Without worrying about the certainty of destroying another set of
treads, Beetchermarlf started this one up promptly.

Takoorch was uneasy now. The reasonable optimism
of an hour before had had the foundation cut from
under it; he was doubtful that the second set of treads
would last long enough to melt a path all the way to
freedom. It occurred to him, after some minutes of
wrestling with the question, that concentrating the
warmed water on one spot might be a good idea and
he suggested this to his companion. Beetchermarlf was
faction of seeing the ice along a two-yard front toward
a fairly solid wall confining some of the water they
the starboard side of the *Kwembly* melting back almost
nearest part of the ice wall. Takoorch had the satis-
visibly.

He was not completely happy, of course. It did not
seem possible to him, any more than it did to Beetchermarlf, that the treads could last very long on the second
were heating to a region between the truck and the
truck either; if they went before the way out was clear,
it was hard to see what else they could do toward their
own salvation. A man in such a situation can sometimes
sit back and hope that his friends will rescue him in
time; he can, in fact, carry that hope to the last moment of consciousness. Few Mesklinites are so constituted, and neither of the helmsmen was among the
number. There was a Stennish word which Easy had
translated as "hope" but this was one of her less successful inferences from context.

Takoorch, driven by this undefinable attitude, stationed himself between the humming truck and the melting ice, hugging the bottom to keep from deflecting the warmed current of water, trying to watch both simultaneously. Beetchermarlf remained at the control lines.

Since no digging had been done under the second truck, the friction was greater and the heating effect stronger. The control was for speed rather than power, in spite of the words the helmsmen had used. Naturally but unfortunately, the wear on the treads was also greater. The heavy thud which announced their failure came annoyingly soon after the completion of the rubble wall. As before, the two bands of fabric gave way almost simultaneously: the jerk imparted to the drive shaft as one let go was enough to take care of the other.

Again the Mesklinites acted instantly, in concert, and without consultation. Beetchermarlf cut the power as he plunged away from his station toward the melting surface; Takoorch got there before him only because he started from halfway there. Both had blades out when they reached the barrier, and both began scraping frantically at the frosty surface. They knew they were fairly close to the *Kwembly's* side; less than a body length of ice remained to be penetrated, at least horizontally. Perhaps before freezing took over once more sheer muscle could get them through . . .

Takoorch's knife broke in the first minute. Several of the human beings above would have been interested in the sounds he made, though not even Easy Hoffman would have understood them. Beetchermarlf cut them off with a suggestion.

"Get behind me and move around as much as you can, so that the water cooled by the ice is moved away and mixed with the rest. I'll keep scraping, you keep stirring." The older sailor obeyed, and several more minutes passed with no sound exept that of the knife.

Progress continued, but both could see that its rate was decreasing. The heat in the water around them was giving out. Though neither knew it, the only reason that their environment had stayed liquid for so long was that the freezing around them had cut off the escape of the ammonia. The theoreticians, both human and Mesklinite, had been perfectly correct, though they had been no help to Dondragmer. The freezing *under* the *Kwembly* had been more a matter of ammonia slowly diffusing into the ice through the still-liquid boundaries between the solid crystals.

The captain, even with this information, could have done no more about it than his two men now trapped under his ship. Of course, if the information had come as a prediction instead of an inspired afterthought, he might have driven the *Kwembly* onto dry land, if she had been able to move in time.

Even if Beetchermarlf had had all this information at the time, he would not have been considering it consciously. He was far too busy. His knife flashed in the lamplight as rapidly and as hard as he dared. His conscious mind was concerned solely with getting the most out of the tool with the least risk of breaking it.

But break it he did. He never cared to discuss the reason later. He knew that his progress was slowing, with the urge to scrape harder changing in inverse proportion; being the person he was, he disliked the faintest suggestion that he might have been the victim of panic. Being what he was also prevented him, ever, from making any suggestion that the bone of the knife might have been defective. He himself could think of no explanations but those two. Whatever the reason, the knife gripped in his right-forward pair of chelae was suddenly without a blade, and the sliver of material lying in front of him was no more practical to handle for his nippers than it would have been for human fingers. He flung the handle down in annoyance and since he was under water didn't even have the satisfaction of hearing it strike the bottom violently.

Takoorch grasped the situation immediately. His comment would have been considered cynical if it had been heard six million miles above, but Beetchermarlf took it at face value.

"Do you think it would be better to stay here and freeze up near the side or get back toward the middle? The time won't make much difference, I'd say."

"I don't know. Near the side they *might* find us sooner; it would depend on where they come through first, if they manage to do it at all. If they don't, I can't see that it will make any difference at all. I wish I knew what being frozen into a block of ice would do to a person."

"Well, someone will know before long," said Takoorch.

"Maybe. Remember the *Esket*."

"What has that to do with it? This is a genuine emergency."

"Just that there are a lot of people who don't know what happened there."

"Oh, I see. Well, personally I'm going back to the middle and think while I can."

Beetchermarlf was surprised. "What's there to think about? We're here to stay unless someone gets us out or the weather warms and we thaw out naturally. Settle down."

"Not here. Do you suppose that running the drivers, with no treads on them, would make enough friction with anything to keep the water nearby from—"

"Try it if you like. I wouldn't expect it, with no real load on them even at their fastest. Besides, I'd be afraid to get close to them if they're really turning up speed. Face it, Tak, we're under water, water, not regular ocean, and when it freezes we're going to be inside it. There's just nowhere else to—oh!"

"What?"

"You win. We should never stop thinking. I'm sorry. Come on."

Ninety seconds later the two Mesklinites, after some trouble in wriggling through the knife slits, were up inside the punctured air cell, safely out of the water.

VIII
FINGERS IN THE BROTH

Dondragmer, dismissing as negligible the chance that one of his missing helmsmen might be directly underneath, had ordered his scientists to set up the test drill near the main lock and get a sample of the ice. This established that the puddle in which the *Kwembly* was standing had frozen all the way to the bottom in at least one spot. It might be hoped that this would not apply directly under the hull, where neither heat nor ammonia could escape so rapidly; but the captain vetoed the suggestion of a slanting bore into this region. That did seem to be the most likely whereabouts of the missing helmsmen. They had been at work there and it was hard to imagine how they could have failed to see the freeze coming if they had been anywhere else.

There was no obvious way to get in touch with them, however. The *Kwembly's* plastic hull would transmit sound, of course; rapping would have solved the problem if it had not been for the mattress. On the off chance that hull sounds might be heard even through its bulk, Dondragmer ordered a crewman to go from bow to stern on the lowest deck, tapping with a pry bar every few feet. The results were negative, which meant inconclusive. There was no way to tell whether there was no one alive below to hear or no penetration of the sound or simply no way for those below to reply.

Another group was outside working at the ice but the captain had already learned that progress would be slow. Even with Mesklinite muscular strength little was being accomplished. Tools about the size of a human machinist's center punch, wielded by eighteen-inch, twenty-pound caterpillars, would take a long time to get around some two hundred and fifty feet of hull circumference to an unknown depth. They would take even longer if detailed chipping around drivers, trucks, and control lines were to be necessary, as seemed likely.

Besides all this, the second helicopter was aloft again with Reffel again at its controls. The communicator was still aboard and the human beings were examining as carefully as Reffel himself the landscape revealed by the little machine's lights. They were also cursing as heartily as the pilot the length of Dhrawn's nights. This one had well over six hundred hours yet to go and, until the sun rose, really quick and effective searching would be impossible.

To be helpful to either Mesklinite eyes or the video pick-up of the communicator, the lights had to be held to a rather narrow beam, covering a circle only a few hundred feet across. Reffel was flying a slow zigzag course which swept this circle back and forth across the valley as he moved slowly westward. At the station far above, the televised image on his screen was being recorded and reproduced for the benefit of topographers. These were already working happily on the structure of an intermittent stream valley under forty Earth gravities. Of the search for the missing Kervenser, little could be expected for some time; but pure information was coming in so no one was complaining, not even the Mesklinites.

Dondragmer was not exactly *worried* about his first

officer and helmsmen, since he couldn't really worry. It would be fair to say that he was concerned: but he had done all he could about the missing crewmen and having done it, his attention had turned elsewhere. He had two principal things on his mind. He would have liked information about how soon the ice was likely to melt, compared with how soon another flood might arrive. He would also have given even more for a workable suggestion on how to get rid of the ice quickly and safely. He had expressed both wishes to the human beings as well as to his own scientists, though he had made it clear to the latter that he was not demanding a crash program. The search for ideas could be combined with, or even subordinated to, the basic research they were carrying on. Dondragmer was not exactly cold-blooded, but his sense of values included the notion that even his final act should be a useful one.

The human reaction to this remarkably objective and inhumanly calm behavior was mixed. The weather men and planetologists took it for granted. Most of them probably weren't even aware of the *Kwembly's* predicament, much less of the missing Mesklinites. Easy Hoffman, who had stayed on watch after bringing Barlennan up to date as Aucoin had directed, was not surprised. If she had any emotional reaction so far, it was one of respect for the captain's ability to avoid panic in a personally dangerous situation.

Her son felt very differently about it. He had been released temporarily from duty in the aerology lab by McDevitt, who, as a tactful and sympathetic person, had been aware of the friendship developing between the boy and Beetchermarlf. Benj had become a fixture in the communication room as a result.

He had watched quietly while arrangements were being made by Dondragmer to dispatch the helicopter and the ice-chipping crews. He had even been somewhat interested in the exchange between the human

and Mesklinite scientists. McDevitt had been a little
reluctant to risk more weather predictions, feeling that
his professional reputation had taken jolts enough recently but he promised to do his best. When all these
matters had been settled and Dondragmer seemed willing to do nothing but lie on his bridge and wait on
events, the boy grew uneasy. Patience, the closest human equivalent to the Mesklinite reaction now being
displayed, was not yet one of his strong points. For
some minutes he shifted uneasily in his seat before
the screens, waiting for something to happen. Finally,
he could restrain himself no longer.

"If no one has any immediate material to send, is
it all right for me to talk to Don and his scientists?"
he asked.

Easy glanced at him, and then at the others. The
men shrugged or otherwise gestured indifference, so she
nodded. "Go ahead. I don't know whether any of
them are in a mood for casual chatter, but the worst
they'll do is tell you they aren't."

Benj didn't waste time explaining that he was not
going to indulge in chatter, casual or otherwise. He
switched his microphone to Dondragmer's bridge set
and began to talk.

"Don, this is Benj Hoffman. You have nothing but
a bunch of sailors chipping away the ice at the
Kwembly's bow. There is a lot of energy in your
power units, more than a planetful of Mesklinites could
put out by muscle in a year. Have your scientists
thought of using converter output either to run that
test drill for moving ice, or in some sort of heater?

"Second, are your sailors just removing ice, or are
they specifically trying to get down underneath to find
Beetchermarlf and Takoorch? I know it's important to
get the *Kwembly* loose, but the same ice will have to
be taken out sometime anyway. It seems to me there's
a good chance that some of the water under the ship

hasn't frozen yet, and that your two men are still alive in it. Are you tunneling, or just ditching?"

Some of the human listeners frowned slightly at the boy's choice of words, but no one saw fit to interrupt or even comment. Most of those who heard glanced at Easy and decided against saying anything which might be interpreted as criticism of her son. Some, as it happened, did not feel critical anyway; they had wanted to ask similar questions but had not quite wanted to be heard at it.

As usual in conversations between the station and Dhrawn, Benj had plenty of time while waiting for the answer to think of other things he might have asked or said, and of better ways in which he might have put the things he did say. Most of the adults knew from experience what was going on in his mind at this point; some were amused; all were to some degree sympathetic. Several bet that he would not be able to resist the temptation to send a reworded version of his message before the answer came back. When Dondragmer's response came from the speaker with Benj still silent no one actually cheered, but those who knew Easy best could read and understand the satisfaction in her expression. She had not dared to bet, even with herself.

"Hello, Benj. We're doing all we can, both for the helmsmen and my first officer. I'm afraid there is no way to apply ship's power to any of the tools. The converters produce electric current and also supply rotating torque fields to the truck motors, as I am sure you know, but none of our ordinary equipment can use this, just the helicopters, some of the research equipment in the laboratory, and the lights. Even if we could work out a way to apply the drive motors to digging, we can't get at them; they're all under the ice. You must remember, Benj, that we deliberately chose to remain as independent as possible of really complex equipment. Just about everything we have on the planet which we couldn't make ourselves is directly concerned with your research project." Ib Hoffman was not present to hear that sentence, which was unfortunate; later he spent a long time trying to make sure of its exact wording from his son's memory.

"I know that, but—" Benj fell silent; none of the words he wanted to say seemed to have ideas under them. The lights, he knew, could not be used as heaters; they were solid state electroluminescent devices, not arcs or resistance bulbs. They had, after all, been designed not only to last indefinitely but to operate in Dhrawn's atmosphere, with its free oxygen and enormous pressure range, without killing the Mesklinites. If Beetchermarlf had realized this he might have wasted less time, though he might not have accomplished any more. "Can't you, can't you just run the current from a converter through some heavy wires, and melt the ice with the heat? Or even run it straight through the water? There must be plenty of ammonia left: it would surely conduct."

Again there was a pause, while Benj hunted for flaws in his own suggestions and the message flashed its way across emptiness.

"I'm not sure I know enough about that sort of physics, though I suppose Borndender and his men would," Dondragmer replied doubtfully. "More to the point, I don't know what we'd use for wires and I don't know what current would flow. I know that when the power units are connected to regular equipment like lights or motors there is automatic safety control but I have no idea of how that works or whether it would work on a simple, direct, series circuit. If you'll find out from your engineers what sort of risk we'd be running, I'll be glad of the information but I still don't know what we'd use to carry the current. There just isn't much metal in the *Kwembly*. Most of our maintenance supplies are things like rope and fabric and lumber. Certainly there's nothing that's *meant* to carry heavy electrical current. You may be right about using the ice itself as a conductor, but do you think it would be a good idea with Beetchermarlf and Takoorch somewhere under it? Although I can see they wouldn't be right in the circuit, I'm still a little uncertain that they'd be safe. There again one of you people could probably help out. If you can, if we can get enough detailed information from you to plan something really promising, I'll be glad to try it. Until that happens, I can only say we're doing all we can. I'm as concerned about the *Kwembly,* and Kervenser, and Beetchermarlf, and Takoorch as you can possibly be."

The captain's closing sentence was not entirely true, though the error was not intentional. He did not really grasp how a friendship could become at all close in a short time and without direct contact between the parties; his cultural background included neither an efficient mail service nor amateur radio. The concept of a microphone relationship developing emotional weight may not have been completely strange to him: he had, after all, been with Barlennan years before when Charles Lackland had accompanied the *Bree* by radio across thousands of miles of Mesklin's oceans; still, real friendship was, to him, in a different category. He had been only conventionally regretful at the news of Lackland's death years later. Dondragmer knew that Benj and the younger helmsman had been talking to each other a great deal, but he had not overheard much of their conversation and would probably not have fully understood the feelings involved even if he had.

Fortunately Benj did not realize this, so he had no reason to doubt the captain's sincerity. However, he was not satisfied with either the answer or the situation. It seemed to him that far too little was being done specifically for Beetchermarlf; he had only been *told* about this. He could not participate in the help. He could not even see very much of it happening. He had to sit and wait for verbal reports. Many human beings both more mature and more sedate by nature than Benj Hoffman would have had trouble enduring that situation.

His feelings showed clearly enough in his next words, as far as the human hearers were concerned. Easy made a half-completed gesture of protest. Then she controlled herself; it was too late, and there was always the chance that the Mesklinite would not read as much into the words and tone as the speaker's mother had.

"But you can't just sprawl there and do nothing!" Benj exclaimed. "Your men could be drowning this very second. Do you know how much air they had in their suits?"

This time temptation won. Realization of what he had said caught up with him within seconds, and in less than half a minute he had what he hoped were better chosen words on their way to Dhrawn.

"I know you're not doing *nothing* but I just don't see how you can simply wait around for results. I'd have to go outside myself and chip ice or something, but I can't, up here."

"I have done all that can be done in the way of starting rescue action," Dondragmer's response to the first part of the message finally arrived. "There is no need to worry about the air for many hours yet. We don't respond to its lack as I understand you human beings do. Even if the hydrogen concentration goes too low for them to stay conscious, their body machinery will just slow down more and more for several eights of hours. No one knows just how long and it probably isn't the same for everyone. You needn't worry about their—drowning—I think was the word you used, if I have guessed its meaning correctly.

"All the tools we have are in use. There would be no way for me to help outside if I did go, and it would take me longer to get reports from Reffel through your people. Perhaps you can tell me how his search for Kervenser is coming on. I assume that nothing meaningful has turned up, since the light from his flier is still visible from here and his flight pattern has not changed. Perhaps there is description you could pass on to me. I'd like to know as much about this region as possible."

Easy once again stifled an exclamation before it could be noticed by Benj. As the boy shifted his attention to the screen carrying the helicopter's signal, she wondered whether Dondragmer were merely trying to keep her son out of his figurative hair or whether he had some real grasp of the human need to be busy and feel useful. The latter seemed unlikely but even Easy Hoffman, who probably knew Mesklinite nature better than any other human being then alive, was not sure.

Benj had not been watching the other screen at all and had to ask whether anything had been happening. One of the observers replied briefly that all anyone had seen had been a surface of pea-to-house-sized cobbles, interrupted by frozen pools similar to the one holding the *Kwembly*. There had been no sign of the other helicopter or its pilot. No one really expected any for some time. The search had to be slow to be complete. If Kervenser had actually crashed this close to his starting point the accident would probably have been seen from the cruiser. The little fliers did carry lights and Kervenser had certainly been using his.

Benj relayed this information to Dhrawn, then threw in an obvious question of his own.

"Why is Reffel making such a slow and careful search so close to you? Wasn't Kervenser at least watched out of sight?"

The delayed response provided a little relief for the boy's feeling of helplessness.

"He was, Benj. It seemed more reasonable to make a complete coverage centering here and starting outward, which would also have the advantage of providing more complete data for your scientists. If they can wait for the information, please tell Reffel I said to fly straight west along the valley until he can just see my bridge light, then resume the search pattern at that point."

"Sure thing, Captain." The conversation had been in Stennish, so none of the watching scientists had understood it. Benj did not bother to ask their approval before passing on the order in the same language. Reffel seemed to have no trouble understanding Benj's accent and in due course his little machine headed west.

"And what's happening to our map?" growled a topographer.

"You heard the captain," replied Benj.

"I heard something. If I'd understood it I'd have entered an objection but I suppose it's too late now. Do you suppose when they return they'll fill in the gap they're leaving now?"

"I'll ask Dondragmer," the boy replied obligingly, but with an uneasy glance toward his mother. She had put on the unreadable expression which he could read all too well. Fortunately, the scientist was already leaving the communication room growling under his breath; and fortunately Benj turned his attention back to Reffel's screen before Easy lost her gravity. Several other nearby adults who had gleaned the substance of the conversation with Dondragmer were also having trouble keeping their faces straight. For some reason they all enjoyed putting one over on the scientific group. But Benj failed to notice. He was still worried about Beetchermarlf.

Dondragmer's assurance that lack of hydrogen would

not be an immediate problem had helped but the idea of the crewmen being frozen solidly into the ice was still bothersome. Even if this took longer to happen under the *Kwembly's* hull, it would happen at last. It might even have happened already. It should be possible to do *something*.

Heat melts ice. Heat is energy. The *Kwembly* carried enough energy to lift her out of Dhrawn's gravity well, though there was no way to apply it to that task. Didn't the huge vehicle have any sort of heaters in its life-support equipment which could be disassembled and used outside?

No. The Mesklinites were unlikely ever to need heat on Dhrawn. Even the parts of the planet where internal heat seemed to be lacking were kept close to fifty degrees absolute by the sun. The regions they would have most to do with for many years yet, such as Low Alpha's center, were too hot rather than too cold for them. The *Kwembly* did have refrigeration equipment powered from its fusion converters but as far as Benj knew, it had never been used since the original testing. It was expected to be useful during penetration of the central part of Low Alpha, not scheduled for at least an Earth year yet, possibly even later. The fate of the *Esket* had made some of the original plans rather shaky.

But a refrigerator is a heat pump. Even Benj knew that and at least in theory, most pumps are reversible. This one must have, somewhere *outside* the cruiser's hull, a high-temperature section for dumping heat. Where was it? Was it removable? At what temperature did it run? Dondragmer must know. But wouldn't he have thought of this already? Maybe not. He was far from stupid, but his background wasn't human. What physics he knew had been picked up from non-Mesklinites long after he was adult. It would not, presumably, be part of the basic stock of knowledge which most intelligent beings lump under the concept of "common sense." Benj nodded at this thought, spent another second or two reminding himself that even if he made himself look silly this might be worth it and reached for his microphone switch.

This time there was no amusement among the surrounding adults as the message pulsed toward Dhrawn. None of those present knew enough about the engineering details of the land-cruisers to answer the questions about the refrigerator heat-dump, but all knew enough physics to be annoyed with themselves for not having thought of the question earlier. They waited for Dondragmer's answer with as much impatience as Benj.

"The refrigerator is one of your solid-state electronic devices which I don't pretend to understand in detail," the captain's words finally reached the station. He was still using his own language, to the annoyance of some of the listeners. "We haven't had to use it since the acceptance tests; the weather here has sometimes been pretty warm, but not really unbearable. It's a simple thing to describe; there are metal plates in all the rooms which get cold when we turn the power on in the system. There is a metal bar, a sort of loop, running along each side of the hull up at the top. It starts near the stern, runs forward about half a body-length to the port side of the center-line, crosses over about four body-lengths back of the bridge and goes back along the other side to a point even with its start. It runs through the hull at start and finish, one of the few things that does. I assume that bar must be the heat radiator. I see, as you imply I should, that there must be such a part to the system and that it must be outside. Nothing else seems to qualify. Unfortunately, it couldn't be further from the ice than it is, even if it runs hot enough to melt it, which I don't know, offhand. I realize that it could be made as hot as you please by running enough electricity through it but I'm not sure I like the idea of trying to take if off the hull for such a purpose."

"I suppose it would wreck your refrigeration system, especially if you couldn't get it back," agreed Benj. "Still, maybe it's not that bad. Let me find an engineer who really knows that system. I have an idea. I'll call you back later." The boy slid out of his seat without waiting for Dondragmer's reply, and left the communication room on the run.

The moment he was gone, the observers who had not understood the language asked Easy for a summary of the conversation, which she gladly supplied. When Benj returned with an engineer in tow, those in hearing frankly abandoned their jobs to listen. Several heartfelt prayers of thanksgiving must have ascended when it was noted that the newcomer was not a linguist, and the boy was interpreting for him. The two settled into seats before the screens, and Benj made sure he knew what to say before energizing his microphone.

"I should tell the captain that most of the fastenings holding the radiator bar to the *Kwembly's* skin are sort of nails; they only go a little way into the skin and can be pried out without damaging the hull. It might be necessary to use cement to fasten them back in afterward but the supplies are there. The connections at the rear will have to be cut, though. The alloy isn't very hard and saws will be able to handle it. Once detached, the bar can be used as a resistance heater simply by pushing its ends into the D. C. holes in a power box. I can tell the captain that there is no danger from a short circuit, since the converters have internal safeties. Is that right, Mr. Katini?"

"That's it," the small, grizzled engineer replied with a nod. He was one of those who had helped design and build the land-cruisers and one of the very few human beings actually to spend much time at Mesklin's three-gravity equator. "I don't think you'll have any trouble making it clear to Dondragmer, even without translation; I'll tell him directly if you wish. He and I always got along easily enough in my own language."

Benj nodded acknowledgement of this, but started speaking into his microphone in Stennish. Easy suspected that he was showing off and hoped that it wouldn't backfire on him too badly but saw no real need to interfere. She had to admit that he was doing a good job of the translation. He must have picked up a great deal from his friend Beetchermarlf. In some ways he was doing better than she would have herself; he was using analogies which should be meaningful to the captain but which would not have occurred to her.

When the captain's answer came back it was in the human tongue. Dondragmer had seen the most probable reason why Benj, rather than the engineer who had provided the information, should be doing the talking. The boy looked a little startled, and confirmed his mother's suspicions by glancing quickly at her. She carefully kept her eyes on Dondragmer's screen.

"I have the picture," the Mesklinite's slightly accented voice came through. He was not always perfectly successful in confining his voice to the human audibility range. "We can detach the refrigerator bar and use it, with a power box, as a heater to melt the ice around the ship. There will be plenty of power in the converter and no danger of blowing it up. Please clear up two points, however.

"First, how can we be sure that we can reconnect the bar electrically afterward? I know enough to doubt that cement is the right method. I don't want to lose the refrigerator system permanently, since Dhrawn is approaching its sun and the weather will be getting warmer.

"Second, with the metal carrying a current touching

the ice, or dipping into the melted water, will there be any danger to people on, in, or under that water? Will the air-suits be protection enough? I suppose they must be pretty good electrical insulators, since they are transparent."

The engineer began to answer at once, leaving Benj to wonder what connection there might be between transparency and electrical conductivity and how Dondragmer, with his background, happened to be acquainted with it.

"You can make the connection easily enough. Simply have the metal ends pressed tightly together and use the adhesive to fasten a wrapping of fabric around the joint. You're right about the glue's conductance; make sure it doesn't get between the metal surfaces.

"Also, you needn't worry about electrocuting anyone in an air-suit. They'll be adequate protection. I suspect that it would take a lot of voltage to hurt you people anyway, since your body fluids are non-polar but I have no experimental proof and I don't suppose you want any. It occurred to me that you might do better by striking an arc at the surface of the ice, which should have enough ammonia to be a fair conductor. If it works at all, it should work very well. Only it may be too hot for any of your men to stay in the neighborhood and it *would* have to be controlled carefully. Come to think of it, the procedure would destroy too much of the bar to let you get the system together again afterward. We'd better stick to simple resistance heating, and be satisfied with melting the ice rather than boiling it." Katini fell silent, and waited for Dondragmer's answer. Benj was still thinking, and all the others within hearing had their eyes fixed on the captain's screen. His shift of language had attracted even those who might otherwise have waited patiently for a translation.

This was unfortunate from the human viewpoint. Barlennan, later, wrote it off as a stroke of luck.

"All right," Dondragmer's answer finally came. "We will take off the metal bar and try to use it as a heater. I am now ordering men outside to start detaching the small brackets. I will have one of the communicators set up outside so that you can watch as we cut through the conductors, and check everything before we turn on power. We will work slowly, so that you can tell us if we are doing something wrong before it has gone too far. I don't like this situation—I don't like doing anything when I am so unsure of what is happening and what is likely to happen. I'm supposed to be in command here and I can only wish I had learned more of your science and technology. I may have an accurate picture as far as it goes and I'm sure I can trust your knowledge and judgement for the rest but it's the first time in years I've been so uncertain of myself."

It was Benj who answered, beating his mother by a fraction of a second.

"I heard you were the first Mesklinite to grasp the general idea of real science and that you were the one who did most to get the College going. What do you mean, you wish you had learned more?"

Easy cut in; like Benj, she used Dondragmer's own language.

"You know far more than I do, Don, and you *are* in command. If you hadn't been convinced by what Katini told you, you wouldn't have given those orders. You'll have to get used to that feeling you don't like; you've just collided with something new again. It's like that time fifty years ago, long before I was born, when you suddenly realized that the science we aliens were using was just knowledge carried on past the common-sense level. Now you have bumped into the fact that no one, not even a commander, can know everything, and that you sometimes have to take professional advice. Live with it, Don, and calm down!"

Easy leaned back and looked at her son, who was the only one in the room to have followed her speech completely. The boy looked startled, almost awe-struck. Whatever impression she had made on Dondragmer or would, when her words got to him, she had certainly gotten home to Benjamin Ibson Hoffman. It was an intoxicating sensation for a parent; she had to fight the urge to say more. She was assisted by an interruption in a human voice.

"Hey! What happened to the helicopter?"

All eyes went to Reffel's screen. There was a full second of silence. Then Easy snapped, "Benj, report to Dondragmer while I call Barlennan!"

IX
CROSSED PURPOSES

The weather had long since cleared at the Settlement, the ammonia fog had blown into the unknown central regions of Low Alpha and the wind had dropped to a gentle breeze from the northwest. Stars twinkled violently, catching the attention of occasional Mesklinites who were outside or in the corridors but going unnoticed by those in the better lighted rooms under the transparent roof.

Because Barlennan was in the laboratory area at the west side of the Settlement when Easy called, her message did not reach him at once. It arrived in written form, borne by one of Guzmeen's messengers who, in accordance with standing orders, paid no attention to the fact that Barlennan was in conference. He thrust the note in front of his commander, who broke off his own words in mid-sentence to read it. Bendivence and Deeslenver, the scientists with whom he was speaking, waited in silence for him to finish, though their body attitudes betrayed curiosity.

Barlennan read the message twice, seemed to be trying to recall something, and then turned to the messenger.

"All this just came in, I take it."

"Yes, Sir."

"And how long has it been since the preceding report from Dondragmer?"

"Not long, sir, less than an hour, I'd say. The log would show; shall I check?"

"It's not that urgent, as long as you know. The last I heard was that the *Kwembly* had grounded after drifting down a river for a couple of hours and that was a long time ago. I assumed that everything was all right, since Guz didn't pass any more on to me about it. I assume now that he either heard interim reports at the usual intervals or asked the humans about it?"

"I don't know, sir. I haven't been on duty the whole time. Shall I check?"

"No. I'll be there in a little while myself. Tell Guz not to send anything out after me; just hold any calls." The runner vanished, and Barlennan turned back to the scientists.

"Sometimes I wonder whether we shouldn't have more electrical communication in this place. I'd like to know how long it's taken Don to get into this mess, but I want to learn some other things before I walk all the way to Guzmeen's place."

Bendivence gestured the equivalent of a shrug. "We can do it if you say the word. There are telephones here in the lab which work fairly well and we can wire the whole Settlement if you want the metal used that way."

"I don't yet. We'll keep to the original priorities. Here, read this. The *Kwembly* has gotten herself stuck in frozen water or something and both her helicopters have disappeared. One had a communicator to the human beings aboard and it was in use at the time."

Deeslenver indicated his emotion by a soft buzz, and reached for the message in turn. Bendivence passed it over silently. The former read it silently, twice, as Barlennan had done, before he spoke.

"You'd think the humans would have a little more

information if they were watching at all carefully. All this says is that Kervenser failed to come back from a flight and that a flier searching for him with a communicator on board suddenly stopped sending; the screen just went blank all of a sudden."

"I can see one possible reason for that," remarked Bendivence.

"I thought you would," returned the commander. "The question is not what blanked the screen but why it should have happened there and then. We can assume that Reffel used the shutter on his set. It would have been nice if you'd thought of that trick before the *Esket* went out; it would have simplified that operation a lot. Something must have come into his field of view which wouldn't have fit in with the *Esket* story. But what could it have been? The *Kwembly* is five or six million cables from the *Esket*. I suppose one of the dirigibles *could* be down that way, but why *should* it be?"

"We won't know until another flight gets back from Destigmet's place," replied the scientist practically. "What interests me is why we didn't hear about Kervenser's disappearance earlier. Why was there time for Reffel's mission to be flown and for him to disappear too before we were told about it? Was Dondragmer late in reporting to the human observers?"

"I doubt that very much," replied Barlennan. "Actually, they may have told us about Kervenser when it happened. Remember, the runner said that other messages had been coming in. Guzmeen might not have thought the disappearance worth sending a runner for until Kerv had been gone for a while. We can check up on that in a few minutes but I imagine there's nothing funny this time.

"On the other hand, I have been wondering lately whether the people up there have always been relaying information completely and promptly. Once or twice

I've had the impression that, well, things were being saved up and sent in one package. It may be just sloppiness, or it may not really be happening—"

"Or they may be deliberately organizing what we hear," said Bendivence. "Half our crew could be lost at this point without our knowing it, if the human beings chose to play it that way. I can see their being afraid we'd quit the job and demand to be taken home, according to contract, if risks proved too high."

"I suppose that's possible," admitted Barlennan. "It hadn't occurred to me just that way. I don't think that particular notion is very likely, but the more I consider the situation, the more I'd like to think of a way of checking things; at least, to make sure they're not taking time to hold conferences on just how much to tell us every time something does go wrong with an exploring cruiser."

"Do you really think there's much likelihood of that?" asked Deeslenver.

"It's hard to tell. Certainly we've been a bit less than completely frank with them and we have what we consider some very good reasons for it. I'm not really bothered either way. We know some of these people are good at business, and if we can't keep even with them it's our fault. All I really would like to be sure of is whether it's business or carelessness. I can think of one way to check up, but I'd rather not use it yet. If anyone can suggest an alternative, it will be very welcome."

"What's the one you have?" both scientists asked together, Deeslenver perhaps half a syllable ahead.

"The *Esket,* of course. It's the only place where we can get an independent check on what they tell us. At least, I haven't thought of any other so far. Of course, even that would take a long time; there won't be another flight from there until sunrise and that's twelve hundred hours or so away. Of course, we *could* send the Deedee even at night—"

"If we'd set up that light relay I suggested—" began Deeslenver.

"Too risky. It would have much too big a chance of being seen. We just don't know how good the human instruments are. I know most of them stay way up at that station overhead, but I don't know what they can see from it. The casual way they distribute these picture-senders for us to carry around here on this planet suggests that they don't regard them as very fancy equipment, as does the fact that they used them twelve years ago on Mesklin. There's just too much chance that they'd spot any light on the night side of this planet. That's why I overrode your idea, Dee; otherwise, I admit it was a very good one."

"Well, there's nothing like enough metal yet for electrical contact that far," added Bendivence. "I don't have any other ideas at the moment. Come to think of it, you might make a simple test on how well the humans can pick up lights."

"How?" the question came in body attitudes, not verbally.

"We could ask them innocently if there were any way of their hunting for the running lights or the floods of the missing fliers."

Barlennan pondered the suggestion briefly.

"Good. Excellent. Let's go. However, if they say they can't, we won't be sure that they aren't just keeping it from us. You might be thinking of a further check for *that*." He led the way out of the map room where the discussion had been held, along the corridors of the Settlement toward the communication room. Most of the passageways were relatively dark. The sponsors of the expedition had not stinted on the supply of artificial lights but Barlennan himself had been rather close-nippered with their distribution. Rooms were adequately lit; hallways had a bare minimum of illumination.

This gave the Mesklinites the comforting feeling that there was nothing overhead, by letting them see the stars without too much trouble. No native of that planet was really happy to face the fact that there was anything in a position to fall on him. Even the scientists glanced up occasionally as they went, taking comfort from the sight of stars not even their own. Mesklin's sun, which men called 61 Cygni, was below the horizon at the moment.

Barlennan looked upward more than he looked ahead; he was trying to get a glimpse of the human station. This carried a beacon light visible from Dhrawn, bright as a fourth magnitude star. Its barely visible crawl against the celestial background was the best long-term clock the Mesklinites had. They used it to reset the pendulum-type instruments which they had made, which seldom agreed with each other for more than a few score hours at a time.

Stars and station alike faded from view as the trio entered the brightly lighted communication room. Guzmeen saw Barlennan and instantly reported, "No further news of either flier."

"What reports have you had from Dondragmer between the time the Kwembly ran aground and now; the last hundred and thirty hours or so? Do you know how long ago Don's first officer disappeared?"

"Only roughly, sir. The incident was reported, but nothing specific was said about how recently it had happened. I took for granted it had just occurred, but didn't ask. The two disappearances were reported quite close together: less than an hour apart."

"And you didn't wonder when the second one came in why we heard about both disappearances so nearly simultaneously, even though they must have occurred some time apart?"

"Yes, Sir. I started wondering about a quarter of an hour before you did, when the last message came in. I don't have any explanation, but I thought I'd leave it to you to ask the humans if you think one is needed."

Bendivence cut in. "Do you suppose Don failed to report the first disappearance because it resulted from a mistake, and he hoped to be able to minimize it by reporting disappearance and recovery at the same time, as minor incidents?"

Barlennan looked at the speaker speculatively but lost no time in answering.

"No, I don't suppose that. Dondragmer and I don't always agree on everything but there are some things that neither of us would do."

"Even if an immediate report couldn't really make a difference? After all, neither we nor the human beings could really help even after we'd heard the news."

"Even then."

"I don't see why."

"I do. Take my word for it; I haven't time for a detailed explanation and I doubt that I could compose one anyway. If Dondragmer failed to make that initial report, he had a very good reason. Personally I doubt very much that the failure was his. Guz, which humans gave you the reports? Was it always the same one?"

"No, Sir. I didn't recognize all their voices, and they often didn't bother to identify themselves. About half the time nowadays the reports come in human language. Most of the rest come from the Hoffman humans. There are others who speak our language but those two seem the only ones who do it comfortably. With the young one particularly, I got the impression that he'd been talking a lot with the *Kwembly* and I assumed that if there were casual chatter going on, nothing much serious could be happening."

"All right. I'd probably have done the same. I'll

use the set; I have a couple of questions to put to the humans." Barlennan took his place in front of the pickup, the speaker on watch making way for him without being ordered. The screen was blank. The captain squeezed the "attention" control and waited patiently for the minute to pass. He could have started talking at once, since it was a safe bet that whoever was at the other end would lose no time readying his receiver but Barlennan wanted to see who was there. If the delay made anyone suspicious, he'd have to live with it.

The face which did appear was unfamiliar to him. Even fifty Earth years of acquaintance with human beings had not sufficed to educate him in such matters as family resemblance, though no human being would have failed to guess that Benj was Easy's son. Actually, the fifty years had not supplied many different people for comparison; fewer than two score men, and no women, had ever landed on Mesklin. Guzmeen recognized the boy but was spared the need to tell Barlennan by Benj himself.

"Benj Hoffman here," the image spoke. "Nothing has come from the *Kwembly* since Mother called you about twenty minutes ago and there are no engineers or scientists in this room at the moment. If you have questions which need technical answers, tell me so I can call the right one. If it's just a matter of detail as to what's been happening, I've been here in the comm room most of the last seven hours and can probably tell you. I'm waiting."

"I have two questions," Barlennan responded. "One of them you can probably answer, the other perhaps not. The first has to do with the second disappearance. I am wondering how far from the *Kwembly* the second helicopter was when it ceased communicating. If you don't know the distance, perhaps you can tell me how long its pilot had been searching."

"The second does depend on a bit of your technology which I don't know but you may. Is there any possibility of your seeing lights such as those on the helicopters from where you are? I suppose it couldn't be done by your unaided eyes any more than it could be done by mine but you have many optical devices which I know little about, probably some which I've never heard of. I'm standing by."

Benj's screened image held up one finger and nodded just as Barlennan finished speaking but the boy waited for the other question to reach him before he spoke.

"I can answer your first question, and Mr. Cavanaugh has gone to find someone who can take care of the second," were his opening words. "Kervenser started out on his scouting flight about eleven hours ago. It wasn't realized that he must be in trouble until about eight hours later, when everything popped at once: Kervenser and his flier gone, the *Kwembly* frozen in and Beetchermarlf and Takoorch somewhere under the ice; at least, no one knows that's where they are but they were working under the hull and there's no other place anyone can think of for them to be. One of the sailors, Reffel, took up the other flier with a vision set to look for Kervenser, and searched very close to the *Kwembly* for a while. Then we suggested that he move out to where an accident to Kervenser wouldn't have been seen or heard from the cruiser, which he did; of course Dondragmer lost sight of him from the bridge. Then we got into a discussion with the captain; everyone up here got interested and it turned out that no one was watching Reffel's screen for several minutes. Then someone noticed that the screen had gone completely blank: not no-signal-*blank* but no-light *black;* that was that."

Barlennan glanced at Guzmeen and the scientists. None of them spoke, but none of them needed to. No one had been watching the screen when Reffel used the shutter! It was not the sort of luck one counted on.

Benj was still speaking.

"The sound wasn't on, of course, since no one had been talking with Reffel, and no one has any idea what happened. This was just before my mother called you, less than half an hour ago. That would make something like two and a half hours between the two disappearances. We'll have to wait for your other answer, since Mr. Cavanaugh isn't back yet."

Barlennan was a little bewildered by the arithmetic, since the boy had used Mesklinite number-words with human number-background. He got it straight after a few seconds of thought.

"I'm not complaining," he returned, "but I gather from what you say that over two hours passed between the *Kwembly's* freezing in and Kervenser's disappearance, and our being told about it. Do you know why that might have happened? I realize, of course, that there was nothing I could have done but there was some understanding about keeping me up to date with the land-cruisers. I don't know just what your job is at the station; you may not have that information; but I hear from my communications man that you have been talking a lot to the *Kwembly,* so you may be able to help. I'm waiting."

Barlennan had several motives behind his closing remark. One was obvious enough; he wanted to learn more about Benj Hoffman, especially since the latter was good with the Mesklinite language and if Guz were right, seemed to want to talk to Mesklinites. Maybe he would be like the other Hoffman, a second sympathy-center in the station. If so, it would be important to know just how much weight he could swing.

Also, the commander wanted to check unobtrusively on Guzmeen's notion that Ben had been chattering with *Kwembly* crew members. Finally, even Barlennan could tell that Benj was young for a human being doing serious work: his selection of words and general narrative style had been a give-away. That fact might well be put to good use *if* a reasonably close relationship could be established.

The boy's answer, when it finally came, was inconclusive in one way but promising in another.

"I don't know why you weren't told about Kervenser and the freeze-up right away," he said. "Personally, I thought you had been. I'd been talking a lot with Beetchermarlf; I guess you know him; one of Don's helmsmen; the one you can talk with and not just listen to. When I heard he'd disappeared I was concentrating on what could be done about it. I wasn't here in the comm room quite all the time; it's not my duty station. I just come when I can to talk with Beetch. I admit someone should have told you sooner. If you'd like I'll try to find out who should have and why he didn't. My mother ought to know, or Mr. Mersereau.

"I don't know how much explaining I'd better supply about the background to my job here. On Earth, when someone finishes basic education (the sort of thing everyone has to get, like reading and physics and sociology) he has to work at unskilled labor on some essential job for two to three of our years before he is eligible for either specialized or general higher education. Nobody says it right out, but everyone knows that the people you work for have the main say in what you can do afterward. Nominally I'm assigned to the aerology lab here as a sort of picker-upper and hey-you; actually anyone in the station who yells first and loudest gets me. I must admit they don't make my life very hard. I've been able to spend a lot of time talking to Beetch the last few days." Barlennan was able, with fifty years experience, to translate without effort the thought behind a human being's use of the word *day*. "Of course," the boy went on, "knowing your language helps. My mother's a language nut, and I picked it up from her. She started on yours ten years ago when Dad was first connected with the Dhrawn project. I'll probably be doing comm work semi-official-ly a good deal of the time from now on. Here comes Mr. Cavanaugh with one of the astronomers whose name I think is Tebbetts. They'll answer your question about seeing lights, and I'll try to find out about the other business."

Benj's face was replaced on the screen by that of the astronomer, a set of broad, dark features which rather surprised Barlennan. He had never seen a bearded human being, though he was used to wide variations in cranial hair. Tebbetts' was a small Van Dyke adornment quite compatible with a space helmet but it made a drastic difference to the Mesklinite's eye. Barlennan decided that asking the astronomer about it would be tactless. It might be better to get the information from Benj later. There was nothing to be gained by embarrassing anyone.

The facial extension, to the commander's relief, did not interfere with its owner's diction. Tebbetts had evidently been given the question already. He started to talk at once, using the human tongue.

"We can detect from here any of the artificial lights you have, including the portables, though we might have trouble with beamed ones not pointed our way. We'd use regular equipment: photomultiplier mosaics behind an appropriate objective; anything you're likely to need could be set up in a few minutes. What do you want us to do?"

This question caught Barlennan by surprise. He had, in the few minutes since discussing the matter with his scientists, been growing more and more certain that the men would deny being able to detect such lights. Certainly if the commander had been a little more foresighted he would not have answered as he had. In fact, he was regretting what he said well before the words reached the station.

"You should have no trouble spotting our land-cruiser *Kwembly;* you already know its location better than I do, and its bridge lights would be on. Its two helicopters have just disappeared, and they normally carry lights. I'd like to have you scan the area within, say, two hundred miles of the *Kwembly* as carefully as you can for other lights, then tell both me and Dondragmer the positions of any you find. Would that take long?"

The message lag was quite long enough to let Barlennan realize how he had slipped. There was nothing to be done about it now but to hope, though that word is a bad translation of the nearest possible Mesklinite attitude. The answer did cause him to brighten up a little; maybe the slip hadn't been too serious: as long as the human beings didn't find more than two other lights near the *Kwembly!*

"I'm afraid I was thinking merely of detecting lights," said Tebbetts. "Pinpointing the sources will be harder, especially from here. I'm pretty sure we can solve your problem if your missing helis are shining their lights. If you think they may have crashed, I shouldn't think there'd be much chance of light, but I'll get right to it."

"How about their power plants?" asked Barlennan, determined to learn the worst now that he had started. "Aren't there other radiations than light given off in nu-clear reactions?"

By the time this question reached the station Tebbetts had left, according to his promise; fortunately Benj was able to supply the answer. The information happened to be basic to the Project, which had been carefully explained to him right after his arrival.

"The fusion converters give off neutrinos which we can detect, but we can't spot their source exactly," he told the commander. "That's what the shadow satellites are for. They detect neutrinos, which are practically all coming from the sun. The power plants on Dhrawn and up here don't count for much against that, even if it isn't much of a sun. The computers keep track of where the satellites are and especially whether the planet is between a given one and the sun, so there's a measure of the neutrino absorption through different parts of the planet. In a few years we hope to have a statistical x-ray of Dhrawn. Maybe that isn't a good analogy for you: I mean a good idea of the density and composition of the planet's insides. They're still arguing, you know, whether Dhrawn should be called a planet or a star or whether the extra heat is from hydrogen fusion in the middle or radioactivity near the surface.

"But I'm sure as can be that they couldn't find your missing fliers from their neutrino emission, even if their converters are still on."

Barlennan managed to conceal his glee at this news; he merely answered, "Thanks. We can't have everything. I take it you'll tell me when your astronomer finds anything, or when he is sure he'll find nothing; I'd like to know if I have to stop counting on that. I'm through talking for now, Benj, but call here if anything comes up on either the fliers or those friends of yours. After all, I'm concerned about them, though perhaps not the way you are about Beetchermarlf. Takoorch is the one I remember." Barlennan, having had more direct contact with human beings and more selfish reasons to develop such skills, had been able to read more accurately between the lines of Benj's talk and obtain a more nearly correct picture of the boy's feelings than Dondragmer had. It would, he was sure, be useful; but he put it from his mind as he turned away from the communicator.

"That could be both better and worse," he remarked

to the two scientists. "It's certainly just as well we didn't set up that blinker system for night communication; they'd have seen us certainly."

"Not certainly," objected Deeslenver. "The human said they *could* spot such lights but there was no suggestion that they made a habit of looking for them. If it takes instruments, I'd bet the instruments are busy on more important things."

"So would I, if the stakes weren't so high," returned Barlennan. "Anyway, we wouldn't dare use it now because we know they'll be looking this way with the best machines they have. We just asked them to."

"But they won't be looking here. They'll be searching the neighborhood of the *Kwembly,* millions of cables from here."

"Think of yourself back home looking up at Toorey. If you were supposed to examine one part of it closely with a telescope, how much of a slip would it take to make you glance at another?"

Deeslenver conceded the point with a gesture.

"Then we either wait for sunrise, or fly a special if we want to use the *Esket* as you suggested. I admit I haven't thought of anything else. I haven't even thought of what we might do there which would make a good test."

"It shouldn't matter too much. The real question would be how soon and how accurately and completely, the human beings do report whatever we set up for them to see. I'll think of something in the next couple of hours. Aren't you researchers setting up for a flight to leave soon, anyway?"

"Not that soon," said Bendivence. "Also, I don't agree with you that details don't matter. You don't want them to get the idea that *we* could possibly have anything to do with what they see happen at the *Esket.* They certainly aren't stupid."

"Of course. I didn't mean that they should. It will

be something natural, making full allowance for the fact that the human beings know even less than we do about what's natural on this world. You get back to the labs and tell everyone who has equipment to get onto the *Deedee* that departure time has been moved ahead. I'll have a written message for Destigmet in two hours."

"All right." The scientists vanished through the door, and Barlennan followed them more slowly. He was just beginning to realize how valid Bendivence's point was. What could be made to happen, in range of one of the *Esket's* vision transmitters, which would not suggest that there were Mesklinites in the neighborhood but which would attract human interest *and* tempt the big creatures to edit their reports? Could he think of such a thing without knowing why the reports were being held up? Or, for that matter, without being quite sure that they were? It was still possible that the delay on the *Kwembly* matter had been a genuine oversight; as the young human had suggested, each person might have thought that someone else had attended to the matter. To Barlennan's sailor's viewpoint this smacked of gross incompetence and inexcusable disorganization; but it would not be the first time he had suspected these qualities in human beings; not as a species, of course, but on an individual basis.

The test certainly had to be made, and the *Esket's* transmitters might surely be tools for the purpose. As far as Barlennan knew, the transmitters were still active. Naturally, care had been taken that no one enter their field of view since the "loss" of the cruiser, and it had been long since any human being had made mention of them. They would have been shuttered rather than avoided, since this would obviously have left the Mesklinites at the place much greater freedom of action; but the idea of the shutters had not occurred until after Destigmet had departed with his instructions to set up a second Settlement unknown to the human beings.

As Barlennan remembered, one of the transmitters had been at the usual spot on the bridge, one in the laboratory, one in the hangar where the helicopters were kept, these had been carefully arranged to be out on routine flights when the "catastrophe" occurred; and the fourth was in the life-support section, though not covering the entrance. It had been necessary to take much of the equipment from this chamber, of course.

With all the planning, the situation was still inconvenient; having the lab and life rooms out of bounds or at best accessible only with the greatest care, had caused Destigmet and his first officer, Kabremm, much annoyance. They had more than once requested permission to shutter the sets, since the technique had been invented. Barlennan had refused, not wanting to call human attention back to the *Esket;* now, well, maybe the same net could take two fish. The sudden blanking of one or perhaps of all four of those screens would certainly be noticed from above. Whether the humans would feel any inclination to hide the event from the Settlement there was no way of telling; one could only try.

The more he thought it over the better the plan sounded. Barlennan felt the glow familiar to every intelligent being, regardless of species, who has solved a major problem unassisted. He enjoyed it for fully half a minute. At the end of that time, another of Guzmeen's runners caught up with him.

"Commander!" The messenger fell into step beside him in the nearly dark corridor. "Guzmeen says that you should come back to Communications at once. One of the human beings, the one called Mersereau, is on the screen. Guz says he ought to be excited, but isn't, because he's reporting something going on at the *Esket*—something is moving in the laboratory!"

X
WEIGHTED DATA

Keeping in phase with Barlennan as he switched directions took some doing but the messenger managed it. The commander took his continued presence for granted.

"Any further details? When, or what was moving?"

"None, sir. The man simply appeared on the screen without any warning. He said, 'Something is happening at the *Esket*. Tell the commander.' Guzmeen ordered me to bring you back on hurricane priority, so I didn't hear any more."

"Those were his exact words? He used our language?"

"No, it was the human speech. His words were—" the runner repeated the phrase, this time in the original tongue. Barlennan could read no more into the words than had been implicit in the translation.

"Then we don't know whether someone slipped up and was seen, or dropped something into the field of the lens, or—"

"I doubt the first, sir. The human could hardly have failed to recognize a person."

"I suppose not. Well, some sort of detail should be in by the time we get back there."

There wasn't, however. Boyd Mersereau was not even on the screen by the time Barlennan reached

Communications. More surprising, neither was anyone else. The commander looked at Guzmeen suspiciously; the communication officer gave the equivalent of a shrug. "He just went, sir, after that one sentence about the lab."

Barlennan, mystified, squeezed the "attention" control.

But Boyd Mersereau had other concerns on his mind. Most, but not quite all, involved events on Dhrawn, not the *Esket*. There were a few matters much closer to home than the giant star-planet.

The chief of these was the cooling down of Aucoin. Aucoin was annoyed at not having been brought into the exchanges between Dondragmer and Katini, and the captain and Tebbetts. He was inclined to blame young Hoffman for going ahead with policy-disturbing matters without official approval. However, he did not want to say anything which would annoy Easy. He regarded her, with some justification, as the most nearly indispensable member of the communications group. In consequence, Mersereau and others suffered fallout from the administrator's deflected ire.

This was not too serious, as far as Boyd was concerned. He had years ago classified the pacifying of administrators along with shaving as something which took time but did not demand full attention; it was worth doing at all only because it was usually less trouble in the long run. The real attention-getter, the thing which kept even news from the *Esket* in the background, was the state of affairs at the *Kwembly*.

Left alone Boyd might have been moderately concerned, but only moderately. The missing Mesklinites weren't close personal friends of his. He was civilized enough to be bothered by their loss as much as if they had been human, though they were not his brothers or sons.

The *Kwembly* herself was a problem, but a fairly

routine one. Land-cruisers had been in trouble before; so far they had always been extricated sooner or later. All in all, Mersereau would have been merely absorbed, not bothered, if left to himself.

He was not left to himself. Benj Hoffman felt strongly about the whole matter and had a way of making his feelings clear, not entirely by talking, though he was perfectly willing to talk. Even when silent he radiated sympathy. Boyd would find himself discussing with Dondragmer the progress of the melting-out plan or the chances of another flood in terms of their effect on the missing helmsmen, rather than with reasonable and proper professional detachment. It was annoying. Beetchermarlf and Takoorch, even Kervenser, just weren't that central to the work; the real question was the survival of the crew. Benj, whether sitting silently beside him or interjecting a few remarks, somehow managed to make objectivity seem callous. Mersereau had no defense against that particular effect. Easy knew perfectly well what was going on, but she did not interfere because she almost entirely shared her son's feelings. Partly because of her sex and partly because of her own background she felt a very intense sympathy for Beetchermarlf and his companion, and even for Takoorch. She had been caught in a rather similar situation some twenty-five years before, when a concatenation of errors had stranded her in an unmanned research vessel on a high-temperature, high-pressure planet.

In fact, she went further than Benj would have dared. Dondragmer might and probably would have sent a ground party to the site of Reffel's disappearance, since the location was fairly well known; it was unlikely that he would have risked sending one of his three remaining communicators along. Yet Easy, partly by straightforward arguments of her own and partly by using her son's techniques to swing Mersereau to her view, convinced the captain that the risk of *not* taking the communicator along would be even greater. This discussion, among many others, was conducted in Aucoin's absence; even as he argued with Dondragmer, Mersereau was wondering how he would justify this step to planner Aucoin. Nevertheless, he argued on Easy's side, as Benj suppressed a grin in the background.

With this claim on his attention, Boyd scarcely noticed the call from another observer that a couple of objects were moving across the screen which showed the *Esket's* laboratory. He switched channels briefly and passed the word on to the Settlement, cutting back to the *Kwembly* without waiting for the end of the communication cycle. Later he claimed that he had never been really conscious of the *Esket's* name in the report; he had thought of the message as a routine report from some observer or other; his principal feeling had been one of irritation at being distracted. Some people would have snapped at the observer; Boyd, being the person he was, had taken what seemed to him the quickest and simplest way of disposing of the interruption. He had then quite genuinely forgotten the incident.

Benj had paid even less attention. The stranding of the *Esket* had occurred long before his arrival at the station, and the name meant nothing in particular to him, although his mother had once mentioned her friends Destigmet and Kabremm to him.

It was Easy, of course, who had really reacted to the call. She scarcely noticed what Mersereau did or said, and never thought of telling Barlennan herself until more details came in. She moved immediately to a chair commanding a view of the "lost" cruiser's screens and relegated the rest of the universe to the background.

Barlennan's return call therefore brought him very

little information. Easy, to whom it was passed, had seen nothing herself; by the time she had reached her new station all motion had ceased. The original observer was only able to say that he had seen two objects, a reel of cable or rope and a short length of pipe, roll across the *Esket's* laboratory floor. It was possible that something might have pushed them, though there had been no sign of life around the vehicle for several terrestrial months; it was equally possible, and perhaps more probable, that something had tilted the *Esket* to start them rolling. So said the observer, though he could not suggest what specifically might have tipped the monstrous machine.

This left Barlennan in a quandary. It was possible that one of Destigmet's crew had become careless. It was possible that natural causes might be operating, as the humans seemed to prefer to believe. It was also possible, considering what Barlennan himself had just been planning to do, that the whole thing was a piece of human fiction. The commander's conscience made him attach more weight to this possibility than he might have done in other circumstances.

It was hard to see just what they could expect to accomplish by such a fiction. It could hardly be a trap of any sort; there could be no wrong reaction to the story. Complete mystification was the only possible response. If there were something deeper and more subtle involved, Barlennan had to admit to himself that he couldn't guess what it was.

He didn't like guessing anyway. It was much easier to take reports at face value, allowing only for the capabilities of the speaker without worrying about possible motives. At times, the commander reflected, Dondragmer's annoying directness which had made him disapprove of the whole *Esket* trick had something to be said for it.

Yes, he had to assume that the report was truthful.

By so doing, he would turn any human trick against its planners. Well then, there was nothing to do except check with Destigmet. That was simply another message to send on the *Deedee.*

Come to think of it, that was another way to check the veracity of the human reports. This report, whatever else could be said for or against its truth, showed signs of having come through quickly. And Mrs. Hoffman must be involved.

The thought that Easy's involvement made the situation a special one was the only idea on the incident Barlennan and Aucoin would have had in common. Of course, the latter hadn't heard anything about the new *Esket* incident so far; even Mersereau hadn't really thought about it. He was still otherwise engaged.

"Easy!" Boyd turned from his microphone and called across to her new station. "We seem to have convinced Don. He's sending a vision set with his six-man search party. He wants to check his own estimate of the distance at which Reffel vanished. He thinks we can pinpoint where his transmitter was. We might have estimated it at the time, but I'm not sure it was recorded. Do you want to take over here while I check up with the mappers, or would you rather go yourself?"

"I want to watch here a little longer. Benj can go up, if he can stand leaving the screens for a minute." She looked half-questioningly at the boy; he nodded and disappeared at once. He was gone longer than she expected and returned somewhat crestfallen.

"They said they'd gladly give me the map recorded from the first part of Reffel's flight, before I had told him to go on until he could barely see the *Kwembly.* All they could say about where he disappeared was that it must be off that map; the map covers the valley for about a mile westward of the cruiser."

Mersereau grunted in annoyance. "I'd forgotten about

that." He turned back to his microphone to relay this not very helpful information to Dondragmer.

The captain was neither particularly surprised nor greatly disturbed. He had already discussed his own estimate of the distance and direction involved with Stakendee, who was leading the search party.

"I suppose the human beings were right about having you take the set along," the captain had remarked. "It will be a nuisance to carry and I don't much like risking its loss, but having it will cut down the risk of losing you. I'm still concerned about a repetition of the flood that brought us here, and the people up above can't give us any definite prediction. They do agree that there should indeed be a flood season coming. With the set, they'll be able to warn you directly if they get any definite information, and you'll be able to reach me through them if you do find anything."

"I'm not sure in my own mind what's best to do if a flood does come," said Stakendee. "Of course if we're close to the *Kwembly* we'll do our best to get back aboard, and I suppose if we're really distant we'd make for the north side of the valley, which seems to be nearer. In a borderline case, though, I'm not sure which would be best; surviving the flood would do us little good if the ship got washed a year's walk further downstream."

"I've been thinking about that, too," replied the captain, "and I still don't have an answer. If we're washed away again there's a very large chance the ship will be ruined. I can't decide whether we should take time to get life-support equipment out and set up on the valley side before we get on with trying to melt her out. Your own point is a good one, and maybe I should have the set there for your sake as well as ours. Well, I'll solve it. Get on your way. The sooner the search is done, the less we'll have to worry about floods."

Stakendee gestured agreement, and five minutes later

Dondragmer saw him and his group emerge from the main lock. The communicator gave the party a grotesque appearance; the block of plastic, four inches high and wide and twelve in length, was being carried litter fashion by two of the searchers. The three-foot poles were only two inches apart, supported on yokes at the mid-point of the eighteen-inch-long bodies of the bearers. The poles and yokes had been fashioned from ship's stores; the Mesklinite equivalent of lumber. There were tons of the stuff in the store compartments: another of the incongruities with which the nuclear-powered cruiser was loaded in such profusion.

The search party rounded the bow of the *Kwembly*, which was facing northwest, and proceeded straight west. Dondragmer watched its lights for a few minutes as they wound around and over the boulders but had to turn to other matters long before they were out of sight.

Elongated figures swarmed over the hull working the radiator bar loose. Dondragmer had not liked to give the order for such destructive activity; but he had weighed as best he could the relative risks of doing it or of leaving it undone; having reached a decision it was not in his nature to keep on worrying about its rightness. Just as most human beings thought of Drommians as typically paranoid, most Mesklinites who knew them at all thought of human beings as typically vacillating. Dondragmer, the decision made and the order given, simply watched to make sure that minimal damage was done to the hull. From the bridge he was unable to see over its curve to the point, far astern, where the conductors came through; he would have to go outside a little later to oversee that part of the work. Maybe it would be even better to take a vision set outside and let the human engineers supervise it. Of course, with the communication delay it would be difficult for them to stop a serious error in time.

For the moment the job could be left in Praffen's nippers. The problem the captain had mentioned to Stakendee needed more thought. The life-support equipment was easy to dismount and he could spare the men to transport it without cutting into the ice-removal project too badly; but if a flood came while it was ashore and carried the *Kwembly* a long distance, things might become awkward. The system was a closed-cycle one using Mesklinite plants, depending on the fusion converters for its prime energy. By its nature, it had just about the right amount of vegetation to take care of the crew; had there been much more, there would not have been enough Mesklinites to take care of the plants! It might be possible to carry part of the system away and leave the rest, then expand each part to take care of the whole crew should circumstances force a decision between ship and shore. It would be easy enough to make more tanks but making either culture large enough to supply hydrogen for the whole crew could take more time than they might have.

In a way, it was too bad that all the communication went through the human station. One of the major and primary tasks of the *Esket* crew was to modify the old life system or to produce a new one capable of supporting a larger population. For all Dondragmer knew, this might already have been accomplished months ago.

His musings were interrupted by the communicator.

"Captain! Benj Hoffman here. Would it be too much trouble to set up one of the viewers so that we could watch your men work on the melting project? Maybe the one on the bridge would do if you just slid it out to starboard and faced it aft."

"That will be easy enough," replied the captain. "I was thinking perhaps it would be well for some of you people to watch the work." Since the set weighed less than five hundred pounds in Dhrawn's gravity, it was only its rather awkward dimensions which gave him trouble; he went about the same problem like a man trying to move an empty refrigerator carton. By pushing it along the deck rather than trying to pick it up, he worked it into a good position in a few seconds. In due course, the boy's acknowledgement came back.

"Thanks, Captain; that's good. I can see the ground to starboard and what I suppose is the main lock and some of your people working along the sides. It's a little hard to judge distances, but I know how big the *Kwembly* is and about how far back the main lock is and of course I know how big your people are, so I'd guess your lights let me see the ice for fifty or sixty yards on past the lock."

Dondragmer was surprised. "I can see fully three times that far—no, wait; you're using your twelve-based numbers so it's not that much: but I do see farther. Eyes must be better than the pickup cells in your set. I hope that you are not just watching what goes on here. Are the other screens for the *Kwembly* sets all where you can see them? Or are there other people watching them? I want to be kept in as close touch as I possibly can with the search party that has just left on foot. After what happened to Reffel, I'm uneasy about both them and their set."

Dondragmer was debating with his own conscience as he sent this message. On the one hand, he was pretty certain that Reffel had shuttered his set deliberately, though it was even less clear to him than to Barlennan why this should have been necessary. On the other hand he disapproved of the secrecy of the whole *Esket* maneuver. While he would not deliberately ruin Barlennan's plans by any act of his own, he would not be too disappointed if everything came out in the open. There certainly was a good chance that Reffel was in real trouble; if, as seemed likely, whatever had happened to him had happened only a few miles away, he would have had time to get back and explain, even on foot.

In short, Dondragmer had a good excuse, but disliked the thought that he needed one. After all, there was Kervenser, too.

"All four screens are right in front of me," Benj's assurance came back. "Just now I'm alone at this station, though there are other people in the room. Mother is about ten feet away, at the *Esket's* screens. Did anyone tell you that something had moved on one of those? Mr. Mersereau has just gone off for another argument with Dr. Aucoin." (Barlennan would have given a great deal to hear that sentence.) "There are about ten other observers in the room watching the other sets, but I don't know any of them very well. Reffel's screen is still blank; five people are working in whatever room in the *Kwembly* your other set is in but I can't tell just what they're doing. Your foot party is just walking along. I can see only a few feet around them, and only in one direction, of course. The lights they're carrying aren't nearly as strong as the ones around the *Kwembly*. If anything does come after them or some trouble develops, I may not even get as much warning as they do; and of course there'd be a delay before I could tell them anyway."

"Will you remind them of that?" asked Dondragmer. "The leader is named Stakendee. He doesn't have enough of the human language to do any good. He may very well be depending too heavily on you and your equipment for warning. I'm afraid I took for granted, without saying much about it, that your set would help warn him when we were planning the search. Please tell him that it is strictly an indirect communicator between him and me."

The boy's response was considerably longer in coming than light-lag alone would explain. Presumably he was carrying out the request without bothering to acknowledge its receipt. The captain decided not to make a point of the matter; Hoffman was very young. There was plenty else to keep Dondragmer busy, and he occupied himself with this, filing the unfinished conversation until Benj's voice once more reached the bridge.

"I've been in touch with Stak and told him what you asked. He promised to take care, but he's not very far from the *Kwembly* yet, still among the stones; they give out a little way upstream, you remember. He's still on the map, I think, though I can't really tell one square yard of that rock garden from another. It's either smooth ice or ice with cobblestones sticking up through it, or occasionally cobblestones with no ice between them. I don't see how they're going to search it very effectively. Even if you climb on the highest rock in the neighborhood, there are a lot of others you can't see beyond. The helicopters aren't very big, and you Mesklinites are a lot smaller."

"We realized that when we sent out the party," Dondragmer answered. "A really effective search will be nearly impossible among the stones if the missing are dead or even helpless. However, as you said, the stones give way to bare rock a short distance from here; in any case, it is possible that Kerv or Reffel could answer calls, or call for help themselves. Certainly at night one can be heard much farther than he can be seen. Also, whatever is responsible for their disappearance may be bigger or easier to spot." The captain had a pretty good idea how Benj would answer the last sentence. He was right.

"Finding whatever is responsible by having another group disappear wouldn't put us much farther ahead."

"It would if we actually learned what had happened. Keep in close touch with Stakendee's party, please, Benj. My time is going to be taken up with other matters and you'll learn whatever happens half a minute before I could anyway. I don't know that those seconds will make much real difference but at least you're closer to Stak in time than I am."

"Also, I have to go outside now. We're getting to a ticklish point in taking this metal bar off the hull. I'd bring one of the sets outside to keep in closer touch with you but I wouldn't be able to hear you very well through a suit. The volume of these communicators of yours isn't very impressive. I'll give you a call when I'm back in touch; there's no one handy to leave on watch here. In the meantime please keep a running log, in any way you find convenient, on what happens to Stakendee."

The captain waited just long enough to receive Benj's acknowledgement, which did arrive this time, before making his way down to the lock and donning his air-suit. Preferring an inside climb to an outside one, he took the ramps back to the bridge and made use of the small lock which gave onto the top of the hull: a U-shaped pipe of liquid ammonia just about large enough for a Mesklinite body. Dondragmer unsealed and lifted the inner lid and entered the three-gallon pool of liquid, the cover closing by its own weight above him. He followed the curve down and up again and emerged through a similar lid outside the bridge.

With the smooth plastic of the hull curving down on all sides of him except aft he felt a little tense but he had long ago learned to control himself even in high places. His nippers flashed from one holdfast to another as he made his way aft to the point where the few remaining refrigerator attachments were still intact. Two of these were the ones which extended entirely through the hull as electrical contacts, and were therefore the ones which caused Dondragmer the most concern. The others, as he had hoped, were coming out of the cruiser's skin like nails; but these last would have to be severed, but severed so that they could be reconnected later on. Welding and soldering were arts which Dondragmer knew only in theory; he did know whatever procedure was to be used, it would certainly need stubs projecting from the hull as a starting point. The captain wanted to make particularly sure that the cutting would allow for this.

The cutting itself, as he had been told, would be no trouble with Mesklinite saws. He carefully selected the points where the cuts were to be made and had two of his sailors get started on the task. He warned the rest to get out of the way when the bar was free. This meant not only down to the surface but well away from the hull. The idea was to lower the metal on the lock side, once it was detached, but Dondragmer was cautious about weights and knew that the bar might possibly not wait to be lowered. Even a Mesklinite would regret being underneath when it descended from the top of the hull, feeble as Dhrawn's gravity seemed to them.

All this had taken the best part of an hour. The captain was wondering about the progress of the foot party but there was another part of the melting project to check first. He reentered the ship and sought the laboratory, where Borndender was readying a power unit to fit the makeshift resistor. Actually there was little to be done; polarized sockets, one at one end of the block and one at the other, would provide direct current if the bar could be gotten into the holes and any changes needed to make a fit possible would have to be made on the bar rather than the power box. It took only a moment to make this clear to the captain, who looked for himself, decided the scientist was obviously right and made his way hastily back to the bridge. Only when he got there and tried to call Benj did he realize that he had never removed his air-suit; talking to Borndender through his suit was one thing, talking to a human over the radio quite another. He stripped enough to get his speaking-siphon into the open and spoke again.

"I'm back, Benj. Has anything happened to Staken-dee?" He finished removing the suit while waiting for the answer, smoothed it, and stowed it close to the center hatchway. It didn't belong there, but there wouldn't be time to get it down to the rack by the main lock and return before Benj's words.

"Nothing really important, as far as I can tell, Captain," came the boy's voice. "They've walked a long way, though I can't tell just how far; maybe three miles since you went, but that's a guess. There has been no sign of either flier, and the only thing they or I have seen which might possibly have affected either of them has been an occasional patch of cloud a few hundred feet up; at least that's what Stak guesses, I can't see well enough myself, drifting back toward the *Kwembly.* I suppose if you accidentally flew into a big cloud you might get disoriented and if it was low enough you'd crash before you could straighten out; there aren't any blind flying instruments on those things, are there? It's hard to believe they'd do such a thing. Of course, if they were keeping their eyes on the ground instead of their flying . . . but none of the clouds we've seen so far is anywhere near big enough to give them time to lose their way, Stak says."

Dondragmer was inclined to share this doubt about clouds being responsible; he would have doubted it even had he not had reason for another opinion. An upward glance showed that no clouds had yet reached the *Kwembly;* the stars twinkled everywhere. Since Benj had said clouds were coming toward the cruiser, the ones Stakendee had seen must have been at the edge of the pattern and much farther to the west when the fliers were up. This might mean nothing as far as Kervenser was concerned, he could have been a long, long way from the *Kwembly.* Also Reffel had probably not encountered them. Dondragmer brought his attention back to Benj, who had not paused for a reply.

"Stak says the stream bed is going uphill noticeably, but he didn't tell me how he knew; just that they'd gone up several feet since leaving the *Kwembly*." Pressure change, Dondragmer assumed; it was always more noticeable in the suits. Just climbing around on the hull made a difference in suit tightness which could be felt. Besides, the stream which had carried the cruiser here had been flowing fairly fast; even allowing for Dhrawn's gravity, it's fall must be fairly great. "The only other real change is the nature of the bottom. They're well away from the cobbles. It's mostly bare rock, with patches of ice in the hollows."

"Good. Thank you, Benj. Have your weather men come up with anything at all about the likelihood of another flood?"

The boy chuckled, though the sound meant little to the Mesklinite. "Nothing, I'm afraid. Dr. McDevitt just can't be sure. Dr. Aucoin was complaining about it a little while ago, and my boss just cut loose. He said that it had taken men a couple of centuries before they could make reliable ten-day forecasts on Earth, with only one phase-varying component, water, and the whole planet accessible for measurement. Anyone who expects forecasting perfected in a couple of years for a world as big as Dhrawn, when we know an area the size of a large backyard and that with two phase-variables and a temperature range from fifty to over a thousand degrees Kelvin, must still believe in magic. He said we were lucky the weather hadn't produced ice fields that turned into swamps when the temperature dropped and rain storms six feet deep with clear air underneath but icing up the cruiser bridges and forty other things that his computer keeps coming up with every time he changes another variable. It was funny watching Dr. Aucoin try to calm him down. Usually it's the other way around."

"I'm sorry I wasn't there to hear it. You seem amused," replied the captain. "Did you tell your chief about the clouds which Stakendee has reported?"

"Oh, certainly. I told everyone. That was only a few minutes ago, though, and they haven't come back with anything yet. I really wouldn't expect them to, Captain; there just isn't enough detailed information from the surface for interpretation, let alone prognosis. There *was* one thing though; Dr. McDevitt was very interested in finding out how many feet Stak's group had climbed and he said that if the clouds they reported hadn't reached the *Kwembly* yet he wanted to know as exactly as possible the time they do. I'm sorry; I should have reported that earlier."

"It doesn't matter," replied Dondragmer. "The sky is still clear here. I'll let you know the moment I see any clouds. Does this mean that he thinks another fog is coming, like the one which preceded the last flood?" In spite of his innate defenses against worry, the captain waited out the next minute with some uneasiness.

"He didn't say, and he wouldn't. He's been caught too wrong too many times. He won't take the chance again, if I know him, unless its a matter of warning you against some very probable danger. Wait! There's something on Stak's screen." Dondragmer's many legs tensed under him. "Let me check. Yes, all of Stak's men but one are in sight, and he must be carrying the back end of the set because it's still moving. There's another light ahead. It's brighter than the ones we're carrying, at least, I think so, but I can't really tell its distance. I'm not sure whether Stak's people have seen it yet, but they should have; you said your eyes are better than the pickups. Mother, do you want to get in on this? And should we call Barlennan? I'm keeping Don posted. Yes, Stak has seen it and his party has stopped moving. The light isn't moving either. Stak has the sound volume up, but I can't hear anything that means anything to me. They've put the transmitter down, and are fanning out in front of it; I can see all six of them now. The ground is nearly bare, only an occasional patch of ice. No rocks. Now Stak's men have put out their lights, and I can't see anything except the new one. It's getting brighter, but I guess it's just the pickup cells reacting to the darker field. I can't see anything around it; it looks a little foggy, if anything. Something has blocked it for a moment; no, it's on again. I could see enough of a silhouette to be pretty sure it was one of the search party; he must have reared up to get a better look ahead. Now I can hear some hooting, but it's not any words I know. I don't see why . . . wait. Now Stak's people are turning their lights back on. Two of them are coming back toward the set; they're picking it up and bringing it forward toward the rest of the group. All the lights are up in front with them, so I can see pretty well now. There's mist blowing past only a few feet, maybe a few inches up; the new light *is* up in it a little way. I can't judge its distance yet at all. The ground has no marks to help; just bare stone, with six Mesklinites flattened down against it and their lights and a dark line beyond them which might be different colored rock or maybe a narrow stream slanting toward them from the far left and going out of sight to my right. Now I get a vague impression of motion around the new light. Maybe it's the running light of a helicopter. I don't know how they're arranged or how high off the ground they are when the machine is parked or how bright they are.

"Now it's clearer, yes, there's something moving. It's coming toward us, just a dark blob in the mist. It's not carrying any light. If my guess at distance means anything, which it probably doesn't, it's about the same size as the Mesklinites. Maybe it's Kervenser or Reffel.

"Yes. I'm almost sure it's a Mesklinite, but still too far away for me to recognize. I'm not sure I'd know either of those two anyway. He's crossing that line; it must be a stream; some liquid splashed up for a split second into the path of the light; now he's only a few yards away, and the others are converging on him. They're talking, but not loudly enough for me to make any of it out. The group is milling around, and I can't recognize anyone. If they'd come a little closer I'd ask them who's there, but I suppose they'll report pretty soon anyway and I can't make them hear through the air-suits unless they're right beside the set. Now they're all coming this way and the bunch is opening out; two of them are right in front of the set; I suppose it's Stakendee and the one who's just—"

He was interrupted by a voice which originated beside him. It reached not only his ear, but three open microphones, and through them three different receivers on Dhrawn, where it produced three very different results.

"Kabremm! Where have you been all these months?" cried Easy.

XI
PLAYING WITH WIRE

It really wasn't quite Kabremm's fault, though Barlennan was a long time forgiving him. The transmitter had been away from the lights. When the newcomer had first joined Stakendee's group he had not been able to see it; later he had failed to notice it; not until he was within a foot or two did he recognize it. Even then he wasn't worried greatly; human beings all looked alike to him, he assumed that his own people looked at least as indistinguishable to the humans, and while he would not have put himself deliberately in view, a sudden withdrawal or any attempt to hide would have been far more suspicious than staying calmly where he was.

When Easy's voice erupted from the speaker with his name, it was obviously sixty-four seconds too late to do anything. Stakendee, whose reflex response to the sound was to reach for the shutter on top of the vision set, realized in time that this would only make matters worse.

What they should do was far from obvious to either of them. Neither was an expert in intrigue, though Mesklin was no more innocent of political deceit than it was of the commercial variety. Neither was particularly quick-witted. Both, unlike Dondragmer, were enthusiastic proponents of the *Esket* deception.

178

And both realized that whatever they did, or failed to do, about this mistake was likely to conflict with whatever Barlennan or Dondragmer might do. Coordination was impossible. Stakendee thought, after some seconds, of trying to address Kabremm as though he were the missing Reffel or Kervenser, but he doubted that he could get away with it. Mrs. Hoffman's recognition must have been pretty firm to let her speak as emphatically as she had, and Kabremm's response was unlikely to be helpful. He didn't, presumably, know the status of either of the missing men.

The human being had said no more, after the one question; she must be waiting for an answer. What had she seen between speaking and that time delay!

Barlennan had also heard Easy's cry, and was in exactly the same spot. He could only guess why Kabremm might be anywhere near the *Kwembly,* though the incident of Reffel's communication cutoff had prepared him for something of the sort. Only one of the three dirigibles was employed on the regular shuttle run between the *Esket* site and the Settlement; the others were under Destigmet's control and were usually exploring. Still, Dhrawn was large enough to make the presence of one of them in the *Kwembly's* neighborhood a distinct surprise.

However, it seemed to have happened. It was simply bad luck, Barlennan assumed, compounded by the fact that the only human being in the universe who could possibly have recognized Kabremm by sight had been in a position to see him when the slip occurred.

So the human beings now knew that the *Esket's* crew had not been obliterated. No provision had been made for such a discovery; no planned, rehearsed story existed which Barlennan could count on Kabremm's using. Maybe Dondragmer would fill in; he could be counted on to do his best, no matter what he thought of the whole matter but it was hard to see what he *could* do. The trouble was that Barlennan himself would have no idea what Dondragmer had said and would not know what to say himself when questions came, as they surely would, toward the Settlement. Probably the safest tactic was to claim utter ignorance, and ask honestly for as complete a report as possible from Dondragmer. The captain would at least keep Kabremm, who had obviously been playing the fool, from leaking the whole cask.

It was fortunate for Barlennan's peace of mind that he did not realize where Kabremm had been met. Easy, a few seconds before her cry of recognition, had told him that Benj was reporting something from a *Kwembly* screen, or he would have assumed that Kabremm had inadvertently stepped into the field of view of an *Esket* communicator. He knew no details about the search party of Stakendee and assumed the incident was occurring *at* the *Kwembly* and not five miles away. The five miles was just as bad as five thousand, under the circumstances; communication between Mesklinites not within hooting range of each other had to go through the human linkage, and Dondragmer was in no better position to cover the slip than was Barlennan himself. However, the *Kwembly's* captain managed to do it, quite unintentionally.

He, too, had heard Easy's exclamation, much more loudly than Barlennan in view of the woman's position among the microphones. However, it had been little more than a distraction to him, for his mind was wholly taken up with some words Benj had uttered a few seconds before. In fact, he was so disturbed by them as to do something which everyone at all experienced in Dhrawn-satellite communication had long ago learned not to do. He had interrupted, sending an urgent call of his own pulsing upward to the station while Benj was still talking.

"Please! Before you do anything else, tell me more

about that liquid. I get the impression from what you've said that there is a stream flowing in the river-bed in view of Stakendee's vision pickup. If that is the case, please send these orders immediately: Stak, with two men to carry the communicator, is to follow that stream upward immediately, keeping you and through you, me, informed of its nature; particularly, is it growing any larger? The other three are to follow it down to find how close it comes to the *Kwembly;* when they have ascertained this, they are to come in with the information at once. I'll worry about whom you've found later on; I'm glad one of them has turned up. If this trickle is the beginning of the next flood, we'll have to stop everything else and get life-support equipment out of the ship and out of the valley. Please check, and get those orders to Stakendee at once!"

This request began to come in just as Easy finished her sentence and long before either Kabremm or Barlennan could have gotten a reply back to it. Mersereau and Aucoin were still gone, so Benj had no hesitation about passing Dondragmer's orders along. Easy, after a second or two of thought, shelved the Kabremm question and reported the same information to Barlennan. If Don saw the situation as an emergency, she was willing to go along with his opinion; he was on the scene. She did not take her eyes from the screen which showed Kabremm's image, however; his presence still needed explanation. She, too, helped Barlennan unwittingly at this point.

After completing the relay of Dondragmer's orders, she added a report of her own which clarified much for the commander.

"I don't know how up to date you are, Barl; things have been happening rather suddenly. Don sent out a foot party with a communicator to look for Kervenser and Reffel. This was the group which found the running stream which is bothering Don so much, and at the same time ran into Kabremm. I don't know how he got there, thousands of miles from the *Esket,* but we'll get his story and relay it to you as soon as we can. I've sometimes wondered whether he and any of the others were alive, but I never really hoped for it. I know the life-support equipment in the cruisers is supposed to be removable in case the vehicles had to be abandoned; but there was never any sign of anything's being taken from the *Esket.* This will be useful news as well as pleasant; there must be some way for you people to live on at least some parts of Dhrawn without human equipment."

Barlennan's answer was a conventional acknowledgement-plus-thanks, given with very little of his attention. Easy's closing sentence had started a new train of thought in his mind.

Benj had paid little attention to his mother's words, having a conversation of his own to maintain. He relayed Dondragmer's command to the foot party, saw the group break up accordingly, though he failed to interpret the confusion caused by Kabremm's telling Stakendee how he had reached the spot, then reported the start of the new mission to the captain. He followed the report, however, with comments of his own.

"Captain, I hope this isn't going to take all your men. I know there's a lot of work in getting your life equipment to the bank but surely you can keep on with the job of melting the *Kwembly* loose. You're not just giving up in the ship, are you? You still have Beetch and his friend underneath; you can't just abandon them. It won't take many men to get the heater going, it seems to me."

Dondragmer had formed by now a pretty clear basic picture of Benj's personality, though some detailed aspects of it were fundamentally beyond his grasp. He answered as tactfully as he could.

"I'm certainly not giving up the *Kwembly* while

there's any reasonable chance of saving her," he said, "but the presence of liquid only a few miles away forces me to assume that the risk of another flood is now very high. My crew, as a group, comes first. The metal bar we have cut from the hull will be lowered to the ground in a few more minutes. Once that is done, only Borndender and one other man will be left on the heater detail. Everyone else, except of course Stakendee's crew, will start immediately carrying plant tanks and lights to the side of the valley. I do not want to abandon my helmsmen, but if I get certain news that high water is on the way we are all going to head for higher ground whether or not any are still missing. I gather you don't like the idea, but I am sure you see why there is no other possible course." The captain fell silent, neither knowing nor greatly caring whether Benj had an answer for this; there was too much else to consider.

He stood watching as the heavy length of metal, which was to be a heater if everyone's ideas worked out, was eased toward the *Kwembly's* starboard side. Lines were attached to it, snubbed around the climbing holdfasts, and held by men on the ice who were carefully giving length under the orders of Praffen. Perched on the helicopter lock panel with his front end reared four inches higher, Praffen watched and gestured commands as the starboard part of the long strip of metal slid slowly away from him and the other side approached. Dondragmer flinched slightly as the sailor seemed about to be brushed off the hull by the silvery length of alloy, but Praffen let it pass under him with plenty of legs still on the plastic and at least three pairs of pincers gripping the holdfasts. With this personal risk ended he let the rope-men work a little faster; it took less than five more minutes to get the bar down to the ice.

Dondragmer had redonned his air-suit during the last

part of the operation and gone out on the hull again, where he hooted a number of orders. Everyone else outside obediently headed for the main lock to start transferring the life-support equipment; the captain himself reentered the bridge to get back in radio contact with Benj and Stakendee.

The boy had said nothing during the lowering-away, which had been carried out in view of the bridge communicator. What he could see required no explanation. He was a little unhappy at the disappearance of the crew afterward, for Dondragmer had been right. Benj did not like the idea of the entire group's being diverted to the abandon-ship operation. The emergence of two Mesklinites with a power box gave him something to watch besides Stakendee's upstream crawl on the adjacent screen.

Benj did not know which of the two was Borndender. However, their actions were of more interest than their identity, especially their troubles with the radiator.

The wire was rigid enough to hold its shape fairly well as it was moved; it now lay flat on the ice in much the same shape it had had when attached to the hull, rather like a long, narrow hairpin with a set of right-angle bends near the center where it had outlined the helicopter lock, the cut ends being some two feet apart. The original vertical component of its curvature, formerly impressed by the shape of the hull, had now flattened out under gravity. The unit had been turned over during the lowering so that the prongs which had attached it to the plastic were now pointing upward; hence there was good contact with the ice for its entire length.

The Mesklinites spent a few minutes trying to straighten it out; Benj got the impression that they wanted to run it around the side of the hull as closely as possible. However, it finally dawned on them that the free ends would have to be close together anyway in order to go into the same power box, so they left the wire alone and dragged the power unit aft. One of them examined the holes in the box and the ends of the wire carefully, while the other stood by.

Benj could not see the box very well, since its image on the screen was very small, but he was familiar with similar machines. It was a standard piece of equipment which had needed very little modification to render it usable on Dhrawn. There were several kinds of power takeoff on it besides the rotating field used for mechanical drive. The direct electrical current which Borndender wanted could be drawn from any of several places; there were contact plates on opposite sides of the box which could be energized; several different sizes of jack-type bipolar sockets and simple unipolar sockets at opposite ends of the box. The plates would have been easiest to use, but the Mesklinites, as Benj learned later, had dismissed them as too dangerous; they chose to use the end sockets. This meant that one end of the "hairpin" had to go into one end of the unit, and the other into the other end. Borndender already knew that the wire was a little large for these holes and would have to be filed down, and had brought the appropriate tools out with him; this was no problem. Bending the ends, however, so that short lengths of them pointed toward each other, was a different matter. While he was still working on this problem, the rest of the crew emerged from the main lock with their burden of hydroponic tanks, pumps, lights, and power units, and headed northward toward the side of the valley. Borndender ignored them, except for a brief glance, wondering, at the same time, whether he could commandeer some assistance.

The two ninety-degree bends he had to make were not entirely a matter of strength. The metal was of semicircular cross section, about a quarter of an inch in radius, Benj thought of it as heavy wire, while to the

Mesklinites it was bar stock. The alloy was reasonably tough even at a hundred and seventy degrees Kelvin, so there was no risk of breaking it. Mesklinite strength was certainly equal to the task. What the two scientists lacked, which made the bending an operation instead of a procedure, was traction. The ice under them was fairly pure water with a modest percentage of ammonia, not so far below its melting point or removed from the ideal ice crystal structure, as to have lost its slipperiness. The small area of the Mesklinite extremities caused them to dig in in normal walking, which combined with their low structure and multiplicity of legs, prevented slipping during ordinary walking around the frozen-in *Kwembly*. Now, however, Borndender and his assistant were trying to apply a strong sidewise force, and their twenty pounds of weight simply did not give enough dig for their claws. The metal refused to bend, and the long bodies lashed about on the ice with Newton's Third Law in complete control of the situation. The sight was enough to make Benj chuckle in spite of his worry, a reaction which was shared by Seumas McDevitt, who had just come down from the weather lab.

Borndender finally solved his engineering problem by going back into the *Kwembly* and bringing out the drilling equipment. With this he sank half a dozen foot-deep holes in the ice. By standing lengths of drill-tower support rod in these he was able to provide anchorage for the Mesklinite muscles. The rod was finally changed from a hairpin to a caliper shape.

Fitting the ends into the appropriate holes was comparatively easy after the filing was finished. It involved a modest lifting job to get the wire up to the two-inch height of the socket holes but this was no problem of strength or traction and was done in half a minute. With some hesitation, visible even to the human watchers, Borndender approached the controls of the power unit. The watchers were at least as tense; Dondragmer was not entirely sure that the operation was safe for his ship, having only the words of the human beings about this particular situation. Benj and McDevitt also had doubts about the efficacy of the jury-rigged heater.

Their doubts were speedily settled. The safety devices built into the unit acted properly as far as the machine's own protection was concerned; they were not, however, capable of analyzing the exterior load in detail. They permitted the unit to deliver a current, not a voltage, up to a limit determined by the manual control setting. Borndender had of course set this at the lowest available value. The resistor lasted for several seconds, and might have held up indefinitely if the ends had not been off the ice.

For most of the length of the loop, all went well. A cloud of microscopic ice crystals began to rise the moment the power came on, as water boiled away from around the wire and froze again in the dense, frigid air. It hid the sight of the wire sinking into the surface ice, but no one doubted that this was happening.

The last foot or so at each end of the loop, however, was not protected by the high specific and latent heats of water. Those inches of metal showed no sign of the load they were carrying for perhaps three seconds; then they began to glow. The resistance of the wire naturally increased with its temperature, and in the effort to maintain constant current the power box applied more voltage. The additional heat developed was concentrated almost entirely in the already overheated sections. For a long moment a red, and then a white, glow illuminated the rising cloud, causing Dondragmer to retreat involuntarily to the other end of the bridge while Borndender and his companion flattened themselves against the ice.

The human watchers cried out, Benj wordlessly, McDevitt protestingly, "It can't blow!" Their reactions were of course far too late to be meaningful. By the time the picture reached the station, one end of the wire loop had melted through and the unit had shut down automatically. Borndender, rather surprised to find himself alive, supplemented the automatic control with the manual one, and without taking time to report to the captain set about figuring what had happened.

This did not take him long; he was an orderly thinker, and had absorbed a great deal more alien knowledge than had the helmsmen, still hoping for rescue a few yards away. He understood the theory and construction of the power units about as well as a high school student understands the theory and construction of a television set; he could not have built one himself, but he could make a reasonable deduction as to the cause of a gross malfunction. He was more of a chemist than a physicist, as far as specific training went.

While the human beings watched in surprise and Dondragmer in some uneasiness, the two scientists repeated the bending operation until what was left of the resistor was once again usable. With the drilling equipment they made a pit large enough to hold the power box at the end of the deep groove boiled in the ice by the first few seconds of power. They set the box in the hole, connected the ends once more, and covered everything with chips of ice removed in the digging, leaving only the controls exposed. Then Borndender switched on the power again, this time retreating much more hastily than before.

The white cloud reappeared at once, but this time grew and spread. It enveloped the near side of the Kwembly, including the bridge, blocking the view for Dondragmer and the communicator lens. Illuminated by the outside flood lamps, it caught the attention of the crew, now nearing the edge of the valley, and of Stakendee and his men miles to the west. This time the entire length of the wire was submerged in melted ice, which bubbled away from around it as hot vapor, condensed to liquid a fraction of a millimeter away, evaporated again much less violently from the surface of the widening pool, and again condensed, this time to ice, in the air above. The steaming pool, some three quarters of the *Kwembly's* length and originally some six feet in width, began to sink below the surrounding ice, its contents borne away as ice dust by the gentle wind faster than they were replenished by melting.

One side of it reached the cruiser, and Dondragmer, catching a glimpse of it through a momentary break in the swirling fog, suddenly had a frightening thought. He donned his air-suit hurriedly and rushed to the inner door of the main lock. Here he hesitated; with the suit's protection he could not tell by feel whether the ship was heating dangerously, and there were no internal thermometers except in the lab. For a moment he thought of getting one; then he decided that the time needed might be risky, and opened the upper safety valves in the outer lock, which were handled by pull-cords from inside reaching down through the liquid trap. He did not know whether the heat from outside would last long enough to boil ammonia in the lock itself—the *Kwembly's* hull was well insulated, and leakage would be slow, but he had no desire to have boiling ammonia confined aboard his command. It was an example of a little knowledge causing superfluous worry; the temperature needed to bring ammonia's vapor pressure anywhere near the ambient values would have made an explosion the least of any Mesklinite's concerns. However, no real harm was done by opening the valves, and the captain felt better as a result of the action. He returned hastily to the bridge to see what was going on.

A gentle breeze from the west was providing occasional glimpses as it swept the ice fog aside and he could see that the level of the molten pool was lower. Its area had increased greatly, but as the minutes passed he decided that some limit had been reached. His two men were visible at times, crawling here and there trying to find a good viewpoint. They finally settled down almost under the bridge, with the breeze behind them.

For some time the liquid level seemed to reach a steady state, though none of the watchers could understand why. Later they decided that the spreading pool had melted its way into the still-liquid reservoir under the *Kwembly*, which took fully fifteen minutes to evaporate. By the end of that time, cobbles from the river bottom began to show their tops above the simmering water, and the problem of turning the power unit off before another length of wire was destroyed suddenly occurred to Dondragmer.

He knew now that there was no danger of the power unit's blowing up; however, several inches of the wire had already melted away, and there was going to be trouble restoring the refrigerator to service. This situation should not be allowed to get any worse, which it would if more metal were lost. Now, as the water level reached the cobbles and the wire ceased to follow the melting ice downward, the captain suddenly wondered whether he could get out to the controls fast enough to prevent the sort of shut-off which had occurred before. He wasted no time mentally blasting the scientists for not attaching a cord to the appropriate controls; he hadn't thought of it in time either.

He donned his suit again and went out through the bridge lock. Here the curve of the hull hid the pool from view, and he began to make his way down the holdfasts as rapidly as he could in the poor visibility. As he went, he hooted urgently to Borndender, "Don't let the wire melt again! Turn off the power!"

An answering but wordless hoot told him that he had been heard, but no other information came through the white blankness. He continued to grope his way downward, finally reaching the bottom of the hull curve. Below him, separated from his level by the thickness of the mattress and two thirds the height of the trucks, was the gently steaming surface of the water. It was not, of course, actively boiling at this pressure; but it was hot even by human standards and the captain had no illusions about the ability of an air-suit to protect him from it. It occurred to him, rather late, that there was an excellent chance that he had just cooked his two missing helmsmen to death. This was only a passing thought; there was work to be done.

The power box lay well aft of his present position, but the nearest surface on which he could walk had to be forward. Either way there was going to be trouble reaching the unit, now presumably surrounded by hot water; but if jumping were going to be necessary, the hull holdfasts were about the poorest possible takeoff point. Dondragmer went forward.

This brought him into clear air almost at once, and he saw that his two men were gone. Presumably they had started around the far side of the pool in the hope of carrying out his order. The captain continued forward, and in another yard or two found it possible to descend to solid ice. He did so, and hastened on what he hoped was the trail of his men.

He had to slow down almost at once, however, as his course brought him back into the ice fog. He was too close to the edge of the pool to take chances. As he went he called repeatedly, and was reassured to hear each hoot answered by another. His men had not yet fallen in.

He caught up with them almost under the cruiser's stern, having walked entirely around the part of the pool not bounded by the hull. None of them had accomplished anything; the power unit was not only out of reach but out of sight. Jumping would have been utter lunacy, even if Mesklinites normally tended to think of such a thing. Borndender and his assistant had not, and the idea had only occurred to Dondragmer because of his unusual experiences in Mesklin's low-gravity equatorial zone so long ago.

But there could not be much more time. Looking over the edge of the ice, the three could catch glimpses of the rounded tops of the rooks, separated by water surfaces which narrowed as they watched. The wire must be practically out of water by now; chance alone would not have let it settle between the stones to a point much lower than their average height, and the protecting water was already there. The captain had been weighing the various risks for minutes; without further hesitation, and without issuing any orders, he slipped over the edge and dropped two feet to the top of one of the boulders.

It was the energy equivalent of an eight-story fall on Earth, and even the Mesklinite was jolted. However, he retained his self command. A single hoot told those above that he had survived without serious injury, and warned them against following in case pride might have furnished an impulse which intelligence certainly would not. The captain, with that order issued, relegated the scientists to the back of his mind and concentrated on the next step.

The nearest rock with enough exposed area to accommodate him was two feet, well over a body length, away, but it was at least visible. Better still, another one only slightly off the line to it exposed a square inch or so of its surface. Two seconds after analyzing this situation, Dondragmer was two feet closer to the power box and looking for another stopping point. The lone square inch of the stepping stone had been touched by perhaps a dozen feet as the red-and-black length of his body had ricochetted from it to the second rock.

The next stage was more difficult. It was harder to be sure which way to go, since the hull which had furnished orientation was now barely visible; also, there were no more large surfaces as close as the one from which he had come. He hesitated, looking and planning; before he reached a decision the question was resolved for him. The grumbling sound which had gone on for so many minutes as water exploded into steam against the hot wire and almost instantly collapsed again under Dhrawn's atmospheric pressure abruptly ceased, and Dondragmer knew that he was too late to save the metal. He relaxed immediately and waited where he was while the water cooled, the evaporation slowed, and the fog of ice crystals cleared away. He himself grew uncomfortably warm, and was more than once tempted to return the way he had come; but the two-foot climb up an ice overhang with hot water at its foot, which would form part of the journey, made the temptation easy to resist. He waited.

He was still alive when the air cleared and crystals of ice began to grow around the edges of the rocks. He was some six feet from the power unit, and was able to reach it by a rather zigzag course over the cobbles once the way could be seen. He shut off the power controls, and only when that was done did he look around.

His two men had already made their way along the ice cliff to a point about level with the original front bend of the wire; Dondragmer guessed that this must be where the metal had again melted through.

In the other direction, under the bulk of the hull, was a black cavern which the *Kwembly's* lights did not illuminate. The captain had no real wish to enter it; it was very likely that he would find the bodies of his two helmsmen there. His hesitation was observed from above.

"What's he waiting there at the power box for?" muttered McDevitt. "Oh, I suppose the ice isn't thick enough for him yet."

"That's not all of it, I'd guess." Benj's tone made the meteorologist look sharply away from the screen.

"What's the matter?" he asked.

"You must know what's the matter. Beetch and his friend were under there. They must have been. How could they have gotten away from that hot water? I bet the captain only just thought of it; he'd never have let them use that way if he'd seen what would happen, any more than I would have. Can you imagine what happened to Beetch?"

McDevitt thought rapidly; the boy wouldn't be convinced, or even comforted, by anything but sound reasoning, and McDevitt's soundest reasoning suggested that Benj's conclusion was probably right. However, he tried.

"It looks bad, but don't give up. It doesn't look as though this thing melted its way all the way across under the ship, but it might have; and either way there's some hope. If it did, they could have gotten out the other side, which we can't see; if it didn't, they could have stayed right at the edge of the liquid zone, where the ice could have saved them. Also, they may not have been under there."

"Water ice save them? I thought you said that this stuff froze because it lost its ammonia, not because the temperature went down. Water ice at its melting point, zero centigrade, would give heat-stroke to a Mesklinite."

"That was my guess," admitted the meteorologist, "but I'm certainly not sure of it. I don't have enough measurements of any sort. I admit your little friend may have been killed; but we know so little of what has happened down there that it would be silly to give up hope. Just wait, there's nothing else to do at this distance anyway. Even Dondragmer is staying put. You can trust him to check as soon as it's possible."

Benj restrained himself, and did his best to look for bright possibilities; but the eye he was supposed to be keeping on Stakendee remained fixed on the captain's image.

Several times Dondragmer extended part of his length onto the ice, but each time he drew back again, to the boy's intense annoyance. At last, however, he seemed satisfied that the ice would hold his weight, and inch by inch extended himself entirely onto the newly frozen surface. Once off the power box he waited for a moment as though expecting something to happen; the ice held, and he resumed his way toward the side of the *Kwembly*. The human beings watched, Benj's fists were clenched tightly and even the man was more tense than usual.

They could hear nothing. Not even the hoot which suddenly echoed across the ice penetrated the bridge to affect their communicator. They could not even guess why Dondragmer suddenly turned back from the hull as he was about to disappear under it. They could only watch as he raced back across the ice to a point just below his two men and waved excitedly at them, apparently indifferent to whatever there was to be learned about the fate of his helmsman and Benj's friend.

XII
GUIDED EXTRAPOLATION

Dondragmer was far from indifferent, but by his standards it was normal to focus attention on a new matter likely to require action rather than to clear up an old one where action was unlikely to help. He had not forgotten the fate of his men but when a distant hoot bore the words "Here's the end of the stream," his program changed abruptly and drastically.

He could not see where the voice was coming from, since he was two feet below the general surface, but Borndender reported glimpses of a light perhaps half a mile away. At the captain's order, the scientist climbed the hull part way to get a better view, while his assistant went in search of a rope to get the captain out of the ice pit. This took time. The sailors had, with proper professional care, returned the lines used in lowering the radiator bar to their proper places inside the cruiser; and when Skendra, Borndender's assistant, tried to get through the main lock he found it sealed by a layer of clear ice which had frozen a quarter of an inch thick on the starboard side of the hull, evidently from the vapor emited by the hot pool. Fortunately most of the holdfasts were projecting far enough through this to be usable, so he was able to climb on up to the bridge lock.

Meanwhile, Borndender called down that there were two lights approaching across the river bed. At the captain's order, he howled questions across the thousand-yard gap, and the two listened carefully for answers: even Mesklinite voices had trouble carrying distinct words for such a distance and through two layers of air-suit fabric. By the time Dondragmer was out of the hole, they knew that the approaching men were the part of Stakendee's command which had been ordered downstream: they had reached its end less than a mile from the ship, but until the group actually reached them, no further details could be obtained.

When they were, the officers could not entirely understand them; the description did not match anything familiar.

"The river stayed about the same size all the way down," the sailors reported. "It wasn't being fed from anywhere, and didn't seem to be evaporating. It wound among the stones a lot, when it got down to where they were. Then we began to run into the funniest obstructions. There would be a sort of dam of ice, with the stream running around one end or the other of it. Half a cable or so farther on there'd be another dam, with just the same thing happening. It was as though some of it froze when it met the ice among the stones, but only the lead part. The water that followed stayed liquid and went on around the dam until *it* found some ice. The dams would build up to maybe half a body length high before the following water would find its way around. We reached the last one, where it was still happening, just a few minutes ago. We'd seen the bright cloud rising over the ship before that, and wondered whether we ought to come back in case something was wrong but we decided to carry out orders at least until the river started to lead us away from the *Kwembly* again."

"Good," said the captain. "You're sure the stream wasn't getting any bigger?"

"As nearly as we could judge, no."

"All right. Maybe we have more time than I thought, and what's happening isn't a prelude to what brought us here. I wish I understood why the liquid was freezing in that funny way, though."

"We'd better check with the human beings," suggested Borndender, who had no ideas on the matter either but preferred not to put the fact too bluntly.

"Right. And they'll want measurements and analyses. I suppose you didn't bring a sample of that river," he said, rather than asked, the newcomers.

"No, Sir. We had nothing to carry it in."

"All right. Born, get containers and bring some back; analyze it as well and as quickly as you can. One of these men will guide you. I'll go back to the bridge and bring the humans up to date. The rest of you get tools and start chipping ice so we can use the main lock." Dondragmer closed the conversation by starting to climb the ice-crusted hull. He waved toward the bridge as he went, assuming that he was being watched and perhaps even recognized.

Benj and McDevitt had managed to keep track of him, though neither found it easy to tell Mesklinites apart. They were waiting eagerly when he reached the bridge to hear what he had to say. Benj in particular had grown ever more tense since the search under the cruiser had been interrupted; perhaps the helmsmen had not been there after all; perhaps they had been among the newcomers who had arrived to interrupt the search, perhaps, perhaps.

Although McDevitt was a quiet man by nature, even he was getting impatient by the time Dondragmer's voice reached the station.

The report fascinated the meteorologist, though it was no consolation to his young companion. Benj wanted to interrupt with a question about Beetchermarlf, but knew that it would be futile; and when the captain's account ended, McDevitt immediately began to talk.

"This is not much more than a guess, Captain," he began, "though perhaps your scientist will be able to stiffen it when he analyzes those samples. It seems possible that the pool around you was originally an ammonia-water solution (we had evidence of that before) which froze, not because the temperature went down but because it lost much of its ammonia and its freezing point went up. The fog around you just before this whole trouble started, back on the snow field, was ammonia, your scientists reported. I'm guessing that it came from the colder areas far to the west. Its droplets began to react with the water ice, and melted it partly by forming a eutectic and partly by releasing heat; you were afraid of something of that sort even before it happened, as I remember. That started your first flood. When the ammonia cloud passed on into Low Alpha, the solution around you began to lose ammonia by evaporation, and finally the mixture which was left was below its freezing point. I'm guessing that the fog encountered by Stakendee is more ammonia, and has provided the material for the rivulet he has found. As the fog meets the water ice near you they mix until the mixture is too dilute in ammonia to be liquid any more (this forms the dam your men described) and the liquid ammonia still coming has to find a way around. I would suggest that if you can find a way to divert that stream over to your ship and if there proves to be enough of it, your melting-out problem would be solved." Benj, listening in spite of his mood, thought of wax flowing from a guttering candle and freezing first on one front and then another. He wondered whether the computers would handle the two situations alike, if ammonia and heat were handled the same way in the two problems.

"You mean I shouldn't worry about a possible flood?" Dondragmer's voice finally returned.

"I'm guessing not," replied McDevitt. "If I'm right about this picture, and we've been talking it over a lot up here, the fog that Stakendee met should have passed over the snow plain you came from, or what's left of it, and if it were going to cause another flood that should have reached you by now. I suspect the snow which was high enough to spill into the pass you were washed through was all used up on the first flood, and that's why you were finally left stranded where you are. If the new fog hasn't reached you yet, by the way, I think I know the reason. The place where Stakendee met it is a few feet higher than you are and air flowing from the west is coming downhill. With Dhrawn's gravity and that air composition there'd be a terrific foehn effect (adiabatic heating as the pressure rises) and the stuff is probably evaporating just as it gets to the place where Stakendee met it."

Dondragmer took a while to digest this. For a few seconds after the normal delay time, McDevitt wondered whether he had made himself clear; then another question came through.

"But if the ammonia fog were simply evaporating, the gas would still be there, and must be in the air around us now. Why isn't it melting the ice just as effectively as though it were in liquid drops? Is some physical law operating which I missed in the College?"

"I'm not sure whether state and concentration would make all that difference, just from memory," admitted the meteorologist. "When Borndender gets the new data up here I'll feed the whole works into the machine to see whether this guess of ours is ignoring too many facts. On the basis of what I have now, I still think it's a reasonable one, but I admit it has its fuzzy aspects. There are just too many variables; with only water they are practically infinite, if you'll forgive a loose use of the word; with water and ammonia together the number is infinity squared.

"To shift from abstract to concrete, I can see Stakendee's screen and he's still going along beside that streamlet in the fog; he hasn't reached the source but I haven't seen any other watercourses feeding in from either side. It's only a couple of your body-lengths wide, and has stayed about the same all along."

"That's a relief," came the eventual response. "I suppose if a real flood were coming, that river would give some indication. Very well, I'll report again as soon as Borndender has his information. Please keep watching Stakendee. I'm going outside again to check under the hull; I was interrupted before." The meteorologist had wanted to say more, but was silenced by the realization that Dondragmer would not be there to hear his words by the time they arrived. He may also have been feeling some sympathy for Benj. They watched eagerly, the man almost as concerned as his companion, for the red-and-black inchworm to appear on the side of the hull within range of the pickup. It was not visible all the way to the ground, since Dondragmer had to go forward directly under the bridge and out of the field of view; but they saw him again near where the rope which had been used to get him out a few minutes earlier was still snubbed around one of Borndender's bending posts.

They watched him swarm down the line into the pit. A Mesklinite hanging on a rope about the thickness of a six-pound nylon fishline, and free to swing pendulum-style in forty Earth gravities, is quite a sight even when the distance he has to climb is not much greater than his own body length. Even Benj stopped thinking about Beetchermarlf for a moment.

The captain was no longer worried about the ice; it was presumably frozen all the way to the bottom by now, and he went straight toward the cruiser without bothering to stay on the stones. He slowed a trifle as he drew near, eyeing the cavity in front of him thoughtfully.

Practically, the *Kwembly* was still frozen in, of course. The melted area had reached her trucks some sixty feet fore and aft, but the ice was still above the mattress beyond those limits and on the port side. Even within that range, the lower part of the treads had still been an inch or two under water when the heater had given out. Beetchermarlf's control cables had been largely freed, but of the helmsman himself there was no sign whatever. Dondragmer had no hope of finding the two alive under the *Kwembly;* they would obviously have emerged long ago had this been the case. The captain would not have offered large odds on the chance of finding bodies, either. Like McDevitt, he knew that there was a possibility that the crewmen had not been under the hull at all when the freeze-up occurred. There had, after all, been two other unexplained disappearances; Dondragmer's educated guess at the whereabouts of Kervenser and Reffel was far from a certainty even in his own mind.

It was dark underneath, out of range of the floods. Dondragmer could still see (a response to abrupt changes of illumination was a normal adaptation to Mesklin's eighteen-minute rotation period) but some details escaped him. He saw the condition of the two trucks whose treads had been ruined by the helmsmen's escape efforts, and he saw the piles of stones they had made in the attempt to confine the hot water in a small area; but he missed the slash in the mattress where the two had taken final refuge.

What he saw made it obvious, however, that at least one of the missing men had been there for a while. Since the volume which had evidently not frozen at all was small, the most likely guess seemed to be that they had been caught in the encroaching ice after doing

the work which could be seen; though it was certainly
hard to see just how this could have happened. The
captain made a rapid check the full length of the ice-
walled cavern, examining every exposed truck fore and
aft, top and sides. It never occurred to him to look
higher. He had, after all, taken part in the building of
the huge vehicle; he knew there was nowhere higher
to go.

He emerged at last into the light and the field of view
of the communicator. His appearance alone was something of a relief to Benj; the boy had concluded, just
as the captain had, that the helmsmen could not be
under the hull alive, and he had rather expected to see
Dondragmer pulling bodies after him. The relief was
short, and the burning question remained: where was
Beetchermarlf? The captain was climbing out of the
pit and leaving the field of view. Maybe he was coming
back to the bridge to make a detailed report. Benj,
now showing clearly the symptoms of sleeplessness,
waited silently with his fists clenched.

But Dondragmer's voice did not come. The captain
had planned to tell the human observers what he had
found, but on the way up the side of the hull, visible
but unrecognized, he paused to talk to one of the men
who was chipping ice from the lock exit.

"I only know what the human, Hoffman, told me
you found when your party reached that stream," he
said. "Are there more details I should know? I know
that you met someone at the point where the ground
reached up into the fog, but I never heard from Hoffman whether it was Reffel or Kervenser. Which was it?
And are the helicopters all right? There was an interruption just then; someone up above apparently caught
sight of Kabremm back at the *Esket;* then I broke in
myself because the stream you had found worried me.
That's why I split your party. Who was it you found?"

"It was Kabremm."

Dondragmer almost lost his grip on the holdfasts.

"Kabremm? Destigmet's first officer? Here? And a human being recognized him; it was *your* screen he was seen on?"

"It sounded that way, sir. He didn't see our communicator until it was too late, and none of us thought for an instant that there was a chance of a human being telling one of us from another; at least, not between the time we recognized him ourselves and the time it was too late."

"But what is he doing here? This planet has three times the area of Mesklin; there are plenty of other places to be. I knew the commander was going to hit shoals sooner or later playing this *Esket* trick on the human beings, but I certainly never thought he'd ground on such silly bad luck as this."

"It's not entirely chance, sir. Kabremm didn't have time to tell us much. We took advantage of your order about exploring the stream to break up and get him out of sight of the communicator, but I understand this river has been giving trouble most of the night. There's a buildup of ice five million or so cables downstream, not very far from the *Esket,* and a sort of ice river is flowing slowly into the hot lands. The *Esket* and the mines and the farms are right in its way."

"Farms?"

"That's what Destigmet calls them. Actually a Settlement with hydroponic tanks; a sort of oversized life-support rig that doesn't have to balance as closely as the cruiser rigs do. Anyway, Destigmet sent out the *Gwelf* under Kabremm to explore upstream in the hope of finding out how bad the ice river was likely to get. They had grounded where we met them because of the fog; they could have flown over it easily enough, but they couldn't have seen the river bed through it."

"Then they must have arrived since the flood that brought us here; if they were examining the river bed they flew right over us. How could they possibly have missed our lights?"

"I don't know, sir. If Kabremm told Stakendee, I didn't hear him."

Dondragmer gave the rippling equivalent of a shrug. "Probably he did, and made it a point to stay out of reach of our human eyes. I suppose Kervenser and Reffel ran into the *Gwelf,* and Reffel used his vision shutter to keep the dirigible from human sight; but I still don't see why Kervenser, at least, didn't come back to report."

"I'm afraid I don't know about any of that, either," replied the sailor.

"Then the river we've washed into must bend north, if it leads to the *Esket* area." The other judged correctly that Dondragmer was merely thinking out loud, and made no comment. The captain pondered silently for another minute or two. "The big question is whether the commander heard it, too, when the human . . . I suppose it was Mrs. Hoffman; she is about the only one that familiar with us—called out Kabremm's name. If he did, he probably thought that someone had been careless back at the *Esket,* as I did. You heard her on your set and I heard her on mine, but that's reasonable. They're both *Kwembly* communicators, and probably all in one place up at the station. We don't know, though, about their links with the Settlement. I've heard that all their communication gear is in one room, but it must be a big room and the different sets may not be very close together. Barl may or may not have heard her.

"What it all shapes up to is that one human being has recognized an *Esket* crew member, not only alive long after they were supposed to be dead but five or six million cables from the place where they supposedly died. We don't know how certain this human being was of the identification; certain enough to call Kabremm's name aloud, perhaps not certain enough to spread the word among other humans without further checking. I gather they don't like looking silly any more than we do. We don't know whether Barlennan knows of the slip; worst of all, we can't tell what he's likely to answer when questions about it come his way. His safest and most probable line would be complete ignorance seasoned with shocked amazement, and I suppose he'll realize that, but I certainly wish I could talk to him without having human beings along the corridor."

"Wouldn't your best line be ignorance, too?" queried the sailor.

"It would be," the captain answered, "but I can't get away with it. I've already told the humans your party was back, and I couldn't convince them that nothing at all had happened on your trip. I'd like to make Mrs. Hoffman believe she made a mistake in identity and that you had met Reffel or Kervenser; but until we find at least one of them even that would be hard to organize. How did she recognize Kabremm? How does she recognize any of us? Color pattern and habitual leg stance, as you'd expect? Or what?

"And furthermore, what did become of that pair? I suppose Reffel came on the *Gwelf* unexpectedly, and had to shutter his set to keep the humans from seeing it; in that case we should be back in touch before long. I wish he looked more like Kabremm. I might take a chance on claiming that it was Ref she'd seen. After all, the light was pretty bad, even for those seeing machines, as I picture the situation, only I don't know what Barl is going to do. I don't even know whether he heard her or not. That's the sort of thing that's been worrying me ever since this *Esket* trick was started; with all our long-distance communication going through the human station, coordination was bound to be difficult. If something like this happened, as it was always likely to, before we got our own communication systems developed and working, we wind up on a raft with no center-boards and breakers downwind." He paused and thought briefly. "Did Kabremm make any arrangements with your group about further communication when we got the talking-box out of the way?"

"Not that I know of, sir. Your orders to break up and go different ways came before much was said."

"All right. You carry on, and I'll think of something."

"All that ever worried me," replied the sailor as he resumed chipping at the ice, "was what would happen when they *did* learn about what we were doing. I keep telling myself they wouldn't really abandon us here; they don't seem to be quite that firm, even on business deals; but they *could* as long as we don't have space craft of our own."

"It was something like that fear which caused the commander to start the whole project, as you know," returned Dondragmer. "They seem to be well-intentioned beings, as dependable as their life-spans allow; personally I'd trust them as far as I would anyone. Still, they *are* different, and one is never quite sure what they will consider an adequate motive or excuse for some strange action. That's why Barlennan wanted to get us self-supporting on this world as soon as possible and without their knowledge; some of them might have preferred to keep us dependent on them."

"I know."

"The mines were a long step, and the dirigibles were a triumph, but we're a long, long way from being able to make do without the human energy-boxes; and I sometimes wonder if the commander realizes just how far beyond us those things really are.

"But this talk isn't solving problems. I have to talk to the humans again. I hope that not mentioning Kabremm at all won't make them suspicious, at least it would be consistent with the mistaken-identity line, if we have to use it. Carry on, and give me a wave on the bridge when the main lock is clear."

The sailor gestured understanding-and-compliance, and Dondragmer at last got to the bridge.

There was plenty to say to the human beings without mentioning Kabremm, and the captain began saying it as soon as he had doffed his air-suit.

"At least one of the helmsmen was under the hull for a while, and probably they both were, but I couldn't find any trace of either one just now except work they had done trying to get out; at least, I can't see any other reason for the work; it certainly wasn't an assigned job. They wrecked, or nearly wrecked, two of the trucks in the process. Much of the space under there is still frozen up, and I'm afraid they're probably in the ice. We'll search more carefully, with lights, when the crew comes back and I can spare the men. The water, or whatever it was, that was boiled away by our heater coated an ice layer on the hull which has sealed the main lock; we must get that back into service as quickly as possible. There is much equipment which can't now be moved out if we have to abandon the *Kwembly,* and much which can't be moved back inside if we don't, because it won't go through any other lock.

"Also, the use of that heater caused the melting of about a body length of the radiator wire, and I don't see how we are going to restore the refrigerator to service if we do get the *Kwembly* free. This may not be of immediate importance, but if we do get back into service we'd have to think twice about going very far into Low Alpha without refrigeration. One of the few things you people seem really sure of is that the low-pressure area is caused by high temperature, presumably from internal heat, and I know you set a very high priority on finding out about it. There is virtually no metal in the ship, and one of the few things I understand about that refrigerator is that its outside radiator must be an electrical conductor. Right?"

The captain waited for his reply with some interest. He hoped that the technical problem would divert human interest from the whole question of Kabremm and the *Esket;* but he knew that this would not have worked if he himself were on the other end of the conversation. Of course, Benj Hoffman was young; but he was probably not the only person there.

Benj answered; he didn't seem much interested in technology.

"If you think they're in the ice, shouldn't people get down there right away and look? They might still be alive in those suits, mightn't they? You said a while ago that no one had ever found out, but that at least they wouldn't suffocate. It seems to me that the longer you put off finding them, the less chance they have of living. Isn't that the most important problem right now?"

Easy's voice broke in before Dondragmer could frame an answer; she seemed to be talking to her son as well as to the captain.

"It's not quite the most important. The *Kwembly* is synonymous with the lives of its entire crew, Benj. The captain is not being callous about his men. I know how you feel about your friend and it's perfectly proper; but a person with responsibility has to think as well as feel."

"I thought you were on my side."

"I feel with you very strongly; but that doesn't keep me from knowing the captain is right."

"I suppose Barlennan would react the same way. Have you asked him what Dondragmer should do?"

"I haven't asked him, but he knows the situation; if you don't think so, there's the microphone; give your side of it to him. Personally I don't think he'd dream of overriding Dondragmer or any other cruiser captain in such a matter, when he himself isn't on the scene."

There was a pause while Benj hunted for words to re-
fute this claim; he was still young enough to think that
there was something fundamentally inhuman about
thinking more than one step ahead at a time. After ten
seconds or so of silence, Dondragmer assumed that the
station transmission was over and a reply was in order.

"Mrs. Hoffman, I believe I recognized her voice, is
quite right, Benj. I have not forgotten Beetchermarlf,
any more than you have forgotten Takoorch, although
it is obvious even to me that you are thinking less of
him. It is simply that I have more lives to consider
than theirs. I'm afraid I'll have to leave any more discussion of it to her, right now. Would you please get
some of your engineers thinking about the problem of
my refrigerator? And you probably see Borndender
climbing the hull with his sample; the report about the
stream should come up in a few minutes. If Mr. McDevitt is still there, please have him stand by; if he has
left for any reason, will you please have him come
back?"

The watchers had seen a climbing Mesklinite as the
captain had said, though not even Easy had recognized
Borndender. Before Benj could say anything, McDevitt
answered, "I'm still here, Captain. We'll wait, and as
soon as the analysis is here I'll take it to the computer.
If Borndender has any temperature and pressure readings to send along with his chemical information, they
will be useful."

Benj was still unhappy, but even he could see that
this was not the time for further interruption. Besides,
his father had just entered the communication room,
accompanied by Aucoin and Mersereau. Benj tactfully
slid out of the seat in front of the bridge screen to make
room for the planner, though he was too angry and
upset to hope that his badly chosen words of the last
few minutes would go unmentioned. He was not even
relieved when Easy, in bringing the newcomers up to

date, left the question of the missing helmsmen unmentioned.

Her account was interrupted by Dondragmer's voice.

"Borndender says that he has checked the density and boiling temperature of the liquid in the stream: it is about three eighths ammonia and five eighths water. He also says that the outside temperature is 71, the pressure 26.6 standard atmospheres, our standard, of course, and the wind a little north of west, 21 degrees to be more precise, at 120 cables per hour. A very light breeze. Will that suffice for your computer?"

"It will all help. I'm on my way," replied McDevitt as he slid from his seat and headed toward the door. As he reached the exit he looked back thoughtfully, paused, and called, "Benj, I hate to pull you from the screens right now, but I think you'd better come with me for a while. You can check me on the input, then you can bring the preliminary run back to report to Dondragmer while I do the recheck."

Easy kept her approval to herself as Benj silently followed his superior. The approval was divided between McDevitt, for turning the youngster's attention in a safer direction, and her son for showing more self-control than she had really expected.

Aucoin paid no attention to the exchange; he was still trying to clarify his picture of the current state of affairs.

"I take it that none of the missing personnel have turned up," he said. "All right, I've been thinking it over. I assume that Barlennan has been brought up to date, as we agreed a few hours ago. Is there anything else which has happened, which he has been told about but I haven't?" Easy looked up quickly, trying to catch evidence of resentment on the administrator's face, but he seemed unaware that his words could possibly be interpreted as criticism. She thought quickly before answering.

"Yes. Roughly three hours ago, Cavanaugh reported action on one of the *Esket* screens. He saw a couple of objects sliding or rolling across the floor of the laboratory from one side of the screen to the other. I started watching, but nothing has happened there since.

"Then an hour or so later, the search party Don had out for the missing helicopters met a Mesklinite which we of course assumed at first to be one of the pilots; when he got close to the transmitter I recognized Kabremm, the first officer of the *Esket*."

"Six thousand miles from where the *Esket's* crew is supposed to have died?"

"Yes."

"You told this to Barlennan?"

"Yes."

"What was his comment?"

"Nothing specific. He acknowledged the whole report, but didn't offer any theories."

"He didn't even ask you how sure you were of the identification? Or on what you based it?"

"No."

"Well, if you don't mind I'd like to. Just how did you know this Kabremm, and how certain are you that you were right?"

"I knew him, before the loss of the *Esket*, well enough to make it difficult to say what I went by; he's simply distinctive, in color pattern, stance and walk, just as you and Ib and Boyd are."

"The light was good enough for color pattern? It's night down there."

"There were lights near the set, though most of them were in front of it, in the field of view, and Kabremm was mostly back-lighted."

"Do you know the two missing men well enough to be certain it was neither of them; do you know that neither one looks much like Kabremm?"

Easy flushed. "It certainly wasn't Kervenser, Don's

first officer. I'm afraid I don't know Reffel well enough to be sure; that possibility hadn't occurred to me. I just saw the man, and called out his name pretty much by reflex. After that I couldn't do much but make a report; the Settlement microphone was alive at the time, and Barlennan or whoever was on duty could hardly have helped hearing me."

"Then there is a reasonable chance that Barlennan's lack of comment was a polite attempt to avoid embarrassing you, to gloss over what may have seemed to him a silly mistake?"

"I suppose it's possible." Easy could not make herself sound anything but doubtful, but even she knew that her opinion was unlikely to be objective.

"Then I think," Aucoin said slowly and thoughtfully, "that I'd better talk to Barlennan myself. You say nothing more has happened at the *Esket* since Cavanaugh saw those objects rolling?"

"I haven't seen anything. The bridge set, of course, is looking out into darkness, but the other three are lighted perfectly well and have shown no change except that one."

"All right. Barlennan knows our language well enough, in my experience, so that I won't need you to translate."

"Oh, no; he'll understand you. You mean you'd rather I left?"

"No, no, certainly not. In fact, it would be better if you listened and warned me if you thought there might be any misunderstanding developing." Aucoin reached for the Settlement microphone switch, but glanced once more at Easy before closing it. "You don't mind, do you, if I make sure of Barlennan's opinion about your identification of Kabremm? I think our main problem is what to do about the *Kwembly,* but I'd like to settle that point too. After you have brought the matter up with him, I'd hate Barlennan to get the idea that we were trying to, well, censor anything, to phrase it the way Ib did at the meeting." He turned away and sent his call toward Dhrawn.

Barlennan was in the communicator chamber at the Settlement, so no time was lost reaching him. Aucoin identified himself, once he was sure the commander was at the other end, and began his speech.

Easy, Ib, and Boyd found it annoyingly repetitious, but they had to admire the skill with which the planner emphasized his own ideas. Essentially, he was trying to forestall any suggestion that another vehicle be sent to the rescue of the *Kwembly,* without his suggesting such a thing. It was a very difficult piece of language manipulation, even though the matter had been uppermost in Aucoin's mind ever since the conference, so that while it was anything but an impromptu speech, it certainly had merit as a work of art, as Ib remarked later. He did mention Easy's identification of Kabremm to the commander, but so fleetingly that she almost failed to recognize the item. He didn't actually say that she must have been mistaken, but he was obviously attaching no importance to the incident.

It was a pity, as Easy remarked later, that such polished eloquence was so completely wasted. Of course Aucoin had no more way of knowing than did the other human beings that the identification of Kabremm was Barlennan's main current worry, that for two hours he had been concerned with nothing else. Faced with the imminent collapse of his complex scheme and, as he suddenly realized with embarrassment, having no ready alternative, he had employed those hours in furious and cogent thought. By the time Aucoin had called, Barlennan had the first steps of another plan. He was waiting so eagerly for a chance to put it into operation that he paid little attention to the planner's beautifully selected words. When a pause came, Barlennan had his own speech ready, though it had remarkably little to do with what had just been said.

The pause had not actually been meant as time for an answer; Aucoin had taken a moment to review mentally what he had covered and what should come next. Mersereau, however, caught him as he was about to resume talking.

"That break was long enough to let Barlennan assume you had finished and wanted an answer," he said. "Better wait. He'll probably have started talking before whatever you were just going to say gets down there." The administrator obediently waited; a convention was, after all, a convention. He was prepared to be sarcastic if Mersereau were wrong, but the Mesklinite commander's voice came through on the scheduled second—closer to it than they would have been willing to bet, Ib and Easy thought later.

"I've been thinking deeply ever since Mrs. Hoffman told me about Kabremm," he said, "and I've been able to come up with only one theory. As you know, we've always had to carry in mind the possibility that there was an intelligent species here on Dhrawn. Your scientists were certain there was highly organized life even before the landing, because of the oxygen-rich air, they said. I know we haven't run into anything but simple plants and practically microscopic animals, but the *Esket* had ventured farther into Low Alpha than any of the other cruisers, and conditions are different there; certainly the temperature is higher, and we don't know how that may change other factors.

"Until now, the chance that the *Esket* had met intelligent opposition was only one possibility, with no more to support it than any other idea we could dream up. However, as your own people have pointed out repeatedly, none of her crew could have lived this long without the cruiser's support system or something like it. They certainly couldn't have travelled from where the *Esket* still is, as far as we can tell, to Dondragmer's neighborhood. It seems to me that Kabremm's presence there is convincing evidence that Destigmet's crew has encountered and been captured by natives of Dhrawn. I don't know why Kabremm was free enough to meet that search party; maybe he escaped, but it's hard to see how he would have dared to try under the circumstances. More likely they sent him deliberately to make contact. I wish very much that you'd pass this idea along to Dondragmer for his opinion, and have him find out what he can from Kabremm, if *he* is still available. You haven't told me whether he was still with the search party or not. Will you do that?"

Several pieces fell into place in Ib Hoffman's mental jigsaw puzzle. His silent applause went unnoticed, even by Easy.

XIII
FACT IS STRANGE,
FICTION CONVINCING

Barlennan was quite pleased with his speech. He had not told a single falsehood; the worst he could be accused of was fuzzy thinking. Unless some humans were already actively suspicious, there would be no reason for them not to pass on the "theory" to the *Kwembly's* captain, thus telling him the line that Barlennan proposed to follow. Dondragmer could be trusted to play up properly, especially if the hint that Kabremm might not be available for further questioning were transmitted to him. It was too bad, in a way, to spring the "native menace" so long before he had meant to; it would have been much nicer to let the human beings invent it for themselves; but any plan which couldn't be modified to suit new circumstances was a poor plan, Barlennan told himself.

Aucoin was taken very much aback. He had personally had no doubt whatever that Easy was mistaken, since he had long ago written the *Esket* completely off, in his own mind, and Barlennan's taking her opinion seriously had been a bad jolt. The administrator knew that Easy was by far the best qualified person in the station to make such a recognition; he had not, however, expected the Mesklinites themselves to be aware of this. He blamed himself for not paying much more attention to the casual conversation between human observers (especially Easy) and the Mesklinites over the past few months. He had let himself get out of touch, a cardinal administrative sin.

He could see no reason for denying Barlennan's request, however. He glanced at the others. Easy and Mersereau were looking expectantly at him; the woman had her hand on the microphone selector in her chair arm as though about to call Dondragmer. Her husband had a half-smile on his face which puzzled Aucoin slightly for a moment, but as their eyes met Hoffman nodded as though he had been analyzing the Mesklinite's theory and found it reasonable. The planner hesitated a moment longer, then spoke into his microphone.

"We'll do that right away, Commander." He nodded to Easy, who promptly changed her selector switch and began talking. Benj returned just as she started, obviously bursting with information, but he restrained himself when he saw that a conversation with the *Kwembly* was already in progress. His father watched the boy as Easy relayed the Barlennan theory, and had some difficulty in concealing his amusement. It was so obvious that Benj was swallowing the idea whole. Well, he was young, and several of his elders seemed a bit uncritical too.

"Barlennan wants your thoughts on this possibility, and especially any more information you may have obtained from Kabremm," concluded Easy. "That's all— no, wait." Benj had caught her attention. "My son has come back from the aerology lab, and seems to have something for you."

"Mr. McDevitt has made one run with the new measures added to the earlier data and is making a second now," Benj said without preamble. "According to the first, he was right about the reason for the melting and freezing of your lake, and the nature of the clouds which Stakendee has encountered. The chances are better than even that condensation from these will increase, and make the stream near you bigger. He suggests that you check very carefully, as he mentioned before, the time the clouds reach the *Kwembly*. As he guessed, they are evaporating from adiabatic heating as the air carrying them comes down the ground slope. He says that the later they are in getting to you, the worse the flood will be when *it* does. I don't see why myself, but that's what the computer implies. He said to be sure to remind you that this was just another tentative calculation, just as likely to be wrong as any of the earlier ones. He went into a long speech about all the reasons he couldn't be sure, but you've heard it already."

Dondragmer's answer commenced almost on the light-echo; he could not have spent more than a second or two after the end of Benj's report in deciding what to say.

"Very well, Benj. Please tell Barlennan that his idea sounds reasonable, and at least fits in with the disappearance of my two fliers. I have had no opportunity to get information from Kabremm, if it really was he; I haven't seen him. He hasn't come back to the *Kwembly*. You could tell better than I whether he's still with Stakendee and those who went upstream. I will take precautions on the assumption that the commander is right. If the idea had occurred to me earlier, I certainly would not have sent out practically my entire crew to set up the safety base at the side of the valley.

"However, it may be just as well I did. I see no possibility of freeing the cruiser in any reasonable time, and if Mr. McDevitt is even moderately sure that another flood is on the way we'll have to finish moving out shortly. If a current anything like the one that brought us here hits the *Kwembly* while she's fastened down like this, there'll be pieces of hull scattered for a million cables downstream. When my men come back we'll take one more load of necessary equipment and abandon the ship for the time being. We'll set up on the valley rim, and as soon as life-support equipment is running adequately I'll start sending crews back here to work on freeing the *Kwembly*, provided the flood isn't obviously on the way. That's a firm basic plan; I'll work out details for covering the work crews with your assistance, and if Barlennan's theory calls for special action I'll take it, but I haven't time to argue the basic decision. I can see moving lights to the north; I assume it's my crew on the way back. I'll turn the set so that you can see them."

The view on the screen wavered, then panned jerkily as the captain nudged the transmitter box through a third of a circle. The result was no improvement, from the human viewpoint; the lighted region around the *Kwembly* where details could not only be seen but compared and interpreted, was replaced by almost total darkness relieved by a few specks of light. It took close, careful watching to confirm Dondragmer's claim that they were moving. Easy was about to ask that the lens be returned to its former position when Benj began talking.

"You mean you've given up all hope of finding Beetchermarlf and Takoorch and the others, and are just going off and leaving them there? I know you have nearly a hundred other people to worry about, but there are times when that seems a pretty thin excuse for not even trying to rescue someone!"

Easy was startled and rather dismayed at her son's choice of words, and almost cut in with a combined rebuke to the boy and apology to Dondragmer. She hesitated, however, in the effort to find words which would do this without doing violence to her own feelings; these bore a strong resemblance to Benj's. Aucoin and Mersereau had not followed the exchange at all closely, since both were concentrating on Barlennan on

the other screen and Benj had uttered his tirade in
Stennish. Ib Hoffman showed no expression which the
casual observer could have translated, though Easy
might have detected traces of amusement if she had
been looking at him. McDeivtt had just come in,
but was too late to catch anything except Easy's facial
expression.

The pause went overtime, so they waited for Dondragmer's answer. This revealed no annoyance in tone
or choice of words; Easy wished she could see him to
judge his body attitude.

"I haven't given them up, Benj. The equipment we
plan to take includes as many power units as possible,
which means that men will have to go under the hull
with lights to get as many of them as they can from
the unfrozen trucks. Those men will also have orders
to search the ice walls carefully for traces of the helmsmen. If they are found, men will be assigned to chip
them out, and I will leave those men on the job until
the last possible instant. However, I can't justify putting the entire crew to work breaking ice until there is
nothing else to be done to get the cruiser free. After
all, it is perfectly possible that they discovered what
was going on before the pond froze to the bottom,
and were trapped while looking for a hole in the ice
somewhere else in the pond."

Benj nodded, his face somewhat red; Easy spared
him the need of composing a verbal apology.

"Thanks, Captain," she said. "We understand. We
weren't seriously accusing you of desertion; it was an
unfortunate choice of words. Do you suppose you could
aim the communicator back at the lighted space? We
really can't see anything recognizable the way it's
pointed now."

"Also," McDevitt cut in without allowing a pause to
develop at the end of Easy's request, "even though you
are planning to leave the *Kwembly,* do you suppose

you could leave a power unit on board to run the lights, and lash the bridge communicator about where it is so we can see the hull? That would not only let us observe the flood if it comes, which I'm almost certain it will in the next three to fifteen hours, but would also give us a chance to tell you whether there was any use looking for the cruiser afterward, and possibly even *where* to look for it. I know that will leave you with only two communicators, but it seems to me that this would be worth it."

Again, Dondragmer appeared to make up his mind on the spot; his answer emerged from the speaker almost with the sixty-four second bell.

"Yes, we'll do it that way. I would have had to leave light power anyway, since I wanted crews to come back for work; and as I said, I wanted some sort of safety communication with them. Your suggestion fits that perfectly. I've turned the set back to cover the starboard side, as you no doubt see. I must leave the bridge now; the crew will be back in a minute or two, and I want to assign duties to them as they arrive."

Again, Benj began talking without checking with anyone else.

"Captain, if you're still in hearing when this gets to you, will you wave or signal some way, or have Beetch do it, if you find him alive? I won't ask you to make a special trip back to the bridge to give details."

There was no answer. Presumably Dondragmer had suited up and gone outside the moment he finished speaking. There was nothing for the human beings to do but wait.

Aucoin, with Easy's assistance, had relayed Dondragmer's answer to the Settlement, and received Barlennan's acknowledgement. The commander asked that he be kept up to date as completely as possible on *Kwembly* matters, and especially on any ideas which

Dondragmer might have. Aucoin agreed, asked Easy to relay the request to the captain, and was told that this would be done as soon as the latter reestablished contact.

"All right," nodded the planner. "At least, there's been no mention so far of sending a rescue vehicle. We'll leave well enough alone."

"Personally," retorted Easy, "I'd have dispatched the *Kalliff* or the *Hoorsh* hours ago, when they first froze in."

"I know you would. I'm very thankful that your particular brand of ethics won't let you suggest it to Barlennan over my objections. My only hope is that he won't decide to suggest it himself, because every time I've had both of you really against me I've been talked down." Easy looked at Aucoin, and then at the microphone, speculatively. Her husband decided that distraction was in order, and cut into the thickening silence with a question.

"Alan, what do you think of that theory of Barlennan's?"

Aucoin frowned. He and Easy both knew perfectly well why Ib had interrupted, but the question itself was hard to ignore; and Easy, at least, recognized that the interruption itself was a good idea.

"It's a fascinating idea," the planner said slowly, "but I can't say that I think it very probable. Dhrawn is a huge planet, if it can be called a planet, and it seems funny, well, I don't know whether it seems funnier that we'd have met intelligence so quickly or that only one of the cruisers has done so. There certainly isn't a culture using electromagnetic energy; we'd have detected it when we first approached the place. A much lower one, well, how could they have done what seems to have been done to the *Esket's* crew?"

"Not knowing their physical and mental capabilities, quite aside from their cultural level, I couldn't even guess," replied Hoffman. "Didn't some of the first Indians Columbus met wind up in Spain?"

"I think you're stretching resemblances, to put it mildly. There's a practical infinity of things which could have happened to the *Esket* without her running into intelligent opposition. You know that as well as I do; you helped make up some of the lists, until you decided it was pointless speculation. I grant that Barlennan's theory is a little bit more believable than it was, but only a very little."

"You still think I was wrong in my identification of Kabremm, don't you?" said Easy.

"Yes, I'm afraid I do. Furthermore, I just don't believe that we've run into another intelligent species. Don't compare me with the people who refused to believe that dePerthe's rocks were man-made tools. Some things are just intrinsically improbable."

Hoffman chuckled. "Human ability to judge likelihood, you might call it statistical insight, has always been pretty shaky," he pointed out, "even if you skip purely classical examples like Lois Lane. Actually, the chances don't seem to be that low. You know as well as I do that in the very small volume of space within five parsecs of Sol, with only seventy-four known stars and about two hundred sunless planets, what we have found in the way of intelligence: twenty races at about our own stage of development, safely past their Energy Crisis; eight, including Tenebra and Mesklin, which haven't met it yet; eight which failed to pass it and are extinct; three which failed but have some hope of recovery; every one of them, remember, within a hundred thousand years of that key point in their history, one way or the other! That's in spite of the fact that the planets range in age from Panesh's nine billion years or so to Tenebra's maybe a tenth of that. There's more than coincidence there, Alan.".

"Maybe Panesh and Earth and the older planets

have had other cultures in the past; maybe it happens to any world every few tens of millions of years."

"It hasn't happened before unless the earlier intelligent races were so intelligent from the beginning that they never tapped their planet's fossil fuels. Do you think man's presence on Earth won't be geologically obvious a billion years from now, with looted coal seams and the beer bottle as an index fossil? I can't buy that one, Alan."

"Maybe not, but I'm not mystical enough to believe that some super-species is herding the races of this part of space toward one big climax."

"Whether you like that Demon Hypothesis or prefer the Esfa Theory doesn't matter. There's certainly more than chance involved, and therefore you can't use the laws of chance alone to criticize what Barlennan has suggested. You don't have to assume he's right, but I strongly urge you to take him seriously. I do."

Dondragmer would have been interested in hearing this discussion, just as he would have appreciated attending the staff meeting of some hours before. However, he would have been too busy for either, even if attendance had been physically possible. With the return of most of his crew (some, of course, had stayed behind to continue setting up the life-support equipment) there was much to oversee and quite a lot to do himself. Twenty of his men were set to helping the trio already chipping ice from the main lock. As many more went under the hull with lights and tools to find and secure any power units not too solidly frozen in. The captain kept his promise to Benj, ordering this group to check most carefully for signs of Beetchermarlf and Takoorch. However, he emphasized the importance of examining the ice walls closely, and as a result the group found nothing. Its members emerged in a few minutes with the two power boxes from the trucks which the helmsmen had used, and two more which had been freed by the action of the heater. The rest, which according to Dondragmer's recollection and the laws of arithmetic must number six, were unapproachable, even though the sailors could make a reasonably well-founded guess as to which trucks they were on.

Meanwhile, the rest of the crew had been entering the cruiser by the available locks: the small one at the bridge, the larger ones through which the fliers were launched and the pairs of one-man-at-a-time emergency traps at the sides near bow and stern. Once inside, each crewman set about an assigned job. Dondragmer had been thinking as well as talking to human beings during their absence. Some packed food to last until the life-support equipment resumed cycling normally; others readied coils of rope, lights, power units and other equipment for transportation.

Many were at work improvising carrying devices; one awkward result of the *Kwembly's* being fusion-powered was a great shortage of wheels aboard. There were tiny pulleys carrying the control cables around corners. These were too small for wheelbarrows or similar devices and Dondragmer had firmly forbidden any dismantling of the vehicle. There was nothing like a fork-lift or even a dolly aboard. Such devices, the former muscle-powered, of course, were known and used on Mesklin for medium-to-long-distance carrying; but there was nothing on the *Kwembly* which could be moved at all which a Mesklinite could not easily carry to any part of the vehicle without mechanical assistance. Now, with miles to go and the necessity of moving many items complete rather than in pieces, improvisation was in order. Litters and travois were making their appearance. The corridors leading to the main lock were rapidly being stacked with supplies and equipment awaiting the freeing of the exit.

None of the bustle and thumping, however, penetrated the mattress where Beetchermarlf and Takoorch still lay concealed. As nearly as could be judged later, they must have sought this shelter within a very few minutes of the time the resistance heater went into action. The thick, rubbery material of the mattress itself, which had been so difficult for even a Mesklinite-wielded knife to penetrate, blocked the sounds made by the crackling steam-bubbles around the hot metal and the calls of the workers who entered later. Had these last been forced to communicate with anyone at a distance, their resonant hooting might well have made its way even through that tough material; but there was little for them to say even to each other; they all knew their jobs perfectly well. The slit through which the helmsmen had found their entrance was held tightly enough closed by the elasticity of the fabric so that no light reached them. Finally, the Mesklinite personality trait most nearly described as a combination of patience and fatalism assured that neither Beetchermarlf nor his companion was likely to check outside their refuge until the breathing hydrogen in their suits became a serious problem.

As a result, even if Dondragmer had heard Benj's appeal, there would have been nothing for him to signal. The helmsmen, some three feet above some of their companions and a like distance below many others, were not found.

Not quite all the *Kwembly's* crew were engaged in preparation for the move. When the most necessary aspects of that operation had been arranged, Dondragmer called two of his sailors for a special detail.

"Go to the stream, head northwest and you can't miss it, and go upstream until you find Kabremm and the *Gwelf*," he ordered. "Tell him what we are doing. We will set up a livable site as quickly as we can, you tell him where; you've been there and I haven't. We will set up the human machines so they are looking into the lighted, active portion of that area. That will make it safe for him to bring the *Gwelf* down and land her anywhere outside that area, with no risk of being seen by the human beings. Tell him that the commander seems to be starting the native-life part of the play early, apparently to account for Kabremm's being seen in this neighborhood. He's suggested no details, and will probably stick to the original idea of letting the human beings invent their own.

"When you have seen Kabremm, go on upstream until you find Stakendee, and give him the same information. Be careful about getting into the view field of his communicator; when you think you may be getting near him, shut off your lights every little while and look for his. I'll be in touch with him through the human beings, of course, but not with *that* message. You understand."

"Yes, Sir," the two replied in unison, and were gone.

The hours passed. The main lock was freed and opened, and nearly all the material to be taken was outside when a call came from above. The communicator which had been in the laboratory was now outside, so Dondragmer could be reached directly. Benj was still the speaker.

"Captain, Stakendee reports that the stream he is following is getting noticeably broader and swifter, and that the clouds are becoming rain. I've told him to start back, on my own responsibility." The captain looked up at the still cloudless sky, then westward toward the place where Stakendee's fog might have shown if it had been daylight.

"Thanks, Benj. That's what I would have ordered. We're leaving the *Kwembly* right now before the stream gets too big to cross with the equipment. I have lashed the communicator down to the bridge and will leave the lights on as Mr. McDevitt requested. We'll hope you can tell us that it's safe to come back, before too long. Please report this to Barlennan, and tell him that we will watch as carefully as possible for the natives; if, as he seems to be suggesting, they are using Kabremm as a means of getting in touch with us, I will do my best to set up cooperative relations with them. Remember, I haven't seen Kabremm myself yet, and you haven't mentioned him since the first time, so I'm entirely in the dark about his status so far.

"Be sure to keep me informed of Barlennan's thoughts and plans, as far as you can; I'll do the same from here, but things may happen too quickly for any possible advance warning. Watch your screens. That's all for now; we're starting."

The captain uttered a resonant hoot which, fortunately for human ears, was not faithfully amplified by the set. The Mesklinites fell into rough line, and within two minutes were gone from the field of view of the bridge communicator.

The other set was being borne near the tail of the line, so the screen far above showed the string of lights bobbing in front of it. Little else could be seen. The nearest sailors, those within two or three yards of the lens, could be made out in reasonable detail as they wound among the boulders with their burdens, but that was all. The line could have been flanked on both sides twenty feet away by a legion of natives, without any human being the wiser. Aucoin was neither the first nor the last to curse Dhrawn's 1500-hour rotation period; there were still over six hundred hours to go before the feeble daylight from Lalande 21185 would return.

The stream was still small when the group splashed through it, though Stakendee's set a few miles west had confirmed the report that it was growing. Benj, noticing this, suggested that the small party also cross so that its members could meet the main body on the other side of the valley. Fortunately he made this suggestion to Dondragmer before acting on his own; the captain, remembering the two messengers he had sent upstream, hastily advised that the crossing be postponed as long as possible so that Stakendee and his men could compare more accurately the size of the stream with what it had been when they had passed the same area earlier. Benj and Easy accepted this excuse. Ib Hoffman, quite aware that the foot party was carrying no time measuring devices and could give no meaningful report on the rate of change, was startled for a few seconds. Then he smiled, privately.

For minutes, which stretched into one hour and then another, there was little to watch. The crew reached and climbed the bare rock sides of the valley at the spot where the first load of equipment had been left, and set about constructing something which might have been called either a camp or a town. Life-support equipment had first priority, of course. It would be many hours yet before any air-suits would need recharging, but the time would come. For organisms as profligate of energy as the Mesklinites, food was also a matter of immediate concern. They set about it quickly and efficiently; Dondragmer, like the rest of the cruiser captains, had given plenty of advance thought to the problem of abandoning ship.

Stakendee's group finally crossed the river and, somewhat later, reached the encampment. The crossing had been approved by Dondragmer after he had received through Benj a message which contained, quite incidentally, the name of one of the messengers the captain had sent from the *Kwembly.*

Consequently no one, either member of the *Kwembly* crew or human being, was able to watch the growth of the ammonia-water stream. It would have been an interesting sight. At first, as the witnesses had reported, it was little more than a trickle running from hollow to hollow on the bare rock in the higher reaches of the river bed, men winding among the boulders lower down. As the drops of liquid in the fog coalesced and settled out more rapidly, tiny new tributaries began to feed into the main stream from the sides, and the stream itself grew deeper and faster. On the bare rock it meandered more violently, overflowing the basins which had originally contained it. Here and there it froze temporarily, as water, supplied by the frozen puddles upstream, and ammonia from the fog, shifted about the eutectic, which was liquid at the local temperature: about 174 degrees on the human Kelvin scale, roughly 71 on that used by the Mesklinite scientists.

Among the boulders, as it neared the *Kwembly*, it accumulated more and more water-ice, and the progress grew more complicated. The ammonia dissolved water for a time, the mixture flowing away as the composition entered the liquid range. Then the stream would stop and build up, as Benj had pictured it, like hot wax on a candle, solidifying temporarily from addition of ammonia. Then it would slump away again as underlying ice reacted with the mixture.

It finally reached the hole which had been melted along the *Kwembly's* starboard side, where the human beings could watch once more. By this time the "Stream" was a complex network of alternate liquid, solid, and slush perhaps two miles across. The solid, however, was losing out. While there were still no clouds this far downstream, the air was nearly saturated with ammonia: saturated, that is, with respect to a pure liquid-ammonia surface. The ammonia vapor pressure needed for equilibrium over an ammonia-water mixture is lower; so condensation was taking place on the mostly-water and low-ammonia ice. As it reached the appropriate composition for liquefaction its surface flowed away and exposed more solid to the vapor. The liquid tended to solidify again as it absorbed still more ammonia vapor, but its motion also gave it access to more water-ice.

The situation was a little different in the space under the *Kwembly's* hull, but not greatly so. Where liquid touched ice the latter dissolved and slush appeared; but more ammonia diffusing from the free surface at the side melted it again. Slowly, slowly, minute after minute, the grip of the ice on the huge vehicle relaxed so gently that neither the human beings watching with fascination from above nor the two Mesklinites waiting in their dark refuge could detect the change, the hull floated free.

By now the entire river bed was liquid, with a few surviving patches of slush. Gently, very unlike the flood of a hundred hours or so before when three million square miles of water-snow had been touched by the first ammonia-fog of the advancing season, a current began to develop. Imperceptibly to all concerned, the *Kwembly* moved with that current: imperceptibly, because there was no relative motion to catch the eyes of the human beings, and no rocking or pitching to be felt by the hidden Mesklinites.

The seasonal river, which drains the great plateau where the *Kwembly* had been caught, slices through a range of hills, for Dhrawn, respectable mountains; the range extends some four thousand miles northwest-southeast. The *Kwembly* had gone parallel to this range for most of its length before the flood. Dondragmer, his helmsmen, his air scouts, and indeed most of the crew had been quite aware of the gentle elevation to their left, sometimes near enough to be seen from the bridge and sometimes only a pilot's report.

The flood had carried the cruiser through a pass near the southeastern end of this range to the somewhat lower and rougher regions close to the edge of Low Alpha before she had grounded. This first flood was a rough, rather hesitant beginning of the new season as

Dhrawn approached its feeble sun and the latitude of the sub-stellar belt shifted. The second was the real thing, which would only end when the whole snow plain was drained, more than an Earth year later. The *Kwembly's* first motions were smooth and gentle because she was melted free so slowly; then they were smooth and gentle because the liquid supporting her was syrupy with suspended crystals; finally, with the stream fully liquid and up to speed, it was smooth because it was broad and deep. Beetchermarlf and Takoorch may have been slightly dazed by decreasing hydrogen pressure, but even if they had been fully alert the slight motions of the *Kwembly's* hull would have been masked by their own shifting on the flexible surface that supported them.

Low Alpha is not the hottest region on Dhrawn, but the zone-melting effects which tend to concentrate any planet's radioactive elements have warmed it to around the melting point of water ice in many spots, over two hundred Kelvin degrees hotter than Lalande 21185 could manage unassisted. A human being could live with only modest artificial protection in the area, if it were not for the gravity and pressure. The really hot area, Low Beta, is forty thousand miles to the north; it is Dhrawn's major climate-control feature.

The *Kwembly's* drift was carrying it into regions of rising temperature, which kept the river fluid even though it was now losing ammonia to the air. The course of the stream was almost entirely controlled by the topography, rather than the other way around; the river was geologically too young to have altered the landscape greatly by its own action. Also, much of the exposed surface of the planet in this area was bed rock, igneous and hard, rather than a covering of loose sediment in which a stream could have its own way.

About three hundred miles from the point at which

she had been abandoned, the *Kwembly* was borne into a broad, shallow lake. She promptly but gently ran aground on the soft mud delta where the river fed into it. The great hull naturally deflected the currents around it, and set them to digging a new channel alongside. After about half an hour she tilted sideways and slid off into the new channel, righting herself as she floated free. It was the rocking associated with this last liberation which caught the attention of the helmsmen and induced them to come out for a look around.

XIV
SALVAGE CREW

It would be untrue to say that Benj recognized Beetchermarlf at first glance. As a matter of fact, the first of the caterpillarlike figures to emerge from the river and clamber up the hull was Takoorch. However, it was the younger helmsman's name which echoed from four speakers on Dhrawn.

One of these was on the *Kwembly's* bridge and went unheard. Two were in Dondragmer's encampment a few hundred yards from the edge of the broad, swift river which now filled the valley. The fourth was in Reffel's helicopter, parked close beside the bulk of the *Gwelf*.

The flying machines were about a mile west of Dondragmer's camp; Kabremm would go no closer, not wanting to take the slightest chance of repeating his earlier slip. He would probably not have moved at all from the site where Stakendee had found him if the river had not risen. For one thing, he had been fogbound and had no wish to fly at all. Reffel had been even less eager to move. However, there had been no choice, so Kabremm had allowed his craft to float upward on its own lift until it was in clear air. Reffel hovered as close to the other machine's running lights as he dared. Once above the few yards of ammonia droplets, they could navigate, and had flown toward

Dondragmer's lights until the dirigible's commander had decided they were close enough. Letting the *Gwelf* come to the attention of the men in orbit above would have been an even more serious mistake than the one he had made already; Kabremm was still trying to decide what he was going to say to Barlennan about that the next time they met.

Both he and Reffel had also spent some uncomfortable hours before concluding, from the lack of appropriate comment, that Reffel had shuttered his vision set quickly enough after coming within sight of the *Gwelf*.

In any event, Dondragmer and Kabremm had at last achieved almost direct communication, and had been able to coordinate what they would say and do if there were any further repercussions from Easy's recognition. One load was off the captain's mind. However, he was still taking steps connected with that mistake.

The cry of "Beetch!" in Benj's unmistakable voice distracted him from one of these steps. He had been checking over his crew for people who looked as much as possible like Kabremm. The job was complicated by the fact that he had not seen the other officer for several months. Dondragmer had not yet had time to visit the *Gwelf*, Kabremm would come no closer to the camp for any reason, and Dondragmer had never known him particularly well anyway. His plan was to have all crewmen who might reasonably be mistaken for the *Esket's* first officer appear unobtrusively and casually but frequently in the field of view of the vision sets. Anything likely to undermine the certainty of Easy Hoffman that she had seen Kabremm was probably worth trying.

However, the fate of the *Kwembly* and his helmsmen had never been very far from the captain's mind in the twelve hours since his cruiser's lights had vanished, and at the sound from the speaker he snapped to full attention.

"Captain!" the boy's voice continued. "Two Mesklinites have just appeared and are climbing up the hull of the *Kwembly*. They came out of the water; they must have been somewhere underneath all the time, even if you couldn't find them. It couldn't be anyone but Beetch and Tak. I can't talk to them until they get to the bridge, of course, but it looks as though we might get your ship back after all. Two men can drive it, can't they?"

Dondragmer's mind raced. He had not blamed himself for abandoning the cruiser, even though the flood had been such an anticlimax. It had been the most reasonable decision at the time and with the available knowledge. By the time the actual nature of the new flood had been clear, and it was obvious that they could have remained in the cruiser with perfect safety, it had been impossible to get back. Being a Mesklinite, the captain had wasted no time on thoughts of the "if only" variety. He had known when he left his vehicle that the chances of getting back were rather small, and when she had drifted downstream intact instead of a shattered ruin they had grown smaller. Not quite to zero, perhaps, but not large enough to take seriously any more.

Now suddenly they had expanded again. The *Kwembly* was not only usable, but his helmsmen were alive and aboard her. Something might be done, if . . .

"Benj!" Dondragmer spoke as his thoughts reached this point. "Will you please get your technical men to determine as closely as they can just how far from us the *Kwembly* is now? It is perfectly possible for Beetchermarlf to drive her alone, though there are other problems in the way of general maintenance which will keep him and Takoorch busy. However,

they should be able to manage. In any case, we must
find out whether the distance involved is fifty miles
or a thousand. I doubt the latter, since I don't think
this river could have carried them so far in twelve
hours, but we'll have to know. Get your people at it,
and please tell Barlennan what is happening."

Benj obeyed quickly and efficiently. He was no longer
overtired, worried, and resentful. With the abandon-
ment of the *Kwembly* twelve hours before he had
given up hope for his friend's life and had left the
communication room to get some long overdue sleep.
He had not expected to be able to accomplish this,
but his own body chemistry had fooled him. Nine
hours later he had returned to his regular duties in
the aerology laboratory. It had been chance alone which
had brought him back to the screens within a few
minutes of the helmsmen's emergence. He had been sent
by McDevitt to collect general data from the other
cruisers, but had lingered for a few minutes to watch
at the *Kwembly* station. The weather man had come
to depend heavily on Benj's knowledge of the Mesklinite language.

The sleep, and the sudden discovery that Beetchermarlf was alive after all, combined to dispose of Benj's
lingering resentment of Dondragmer's policy. He acknowledged the captain's request, called his mother
to take his place, and headed for the laboratory decks
as rapidly as his muscles would take him up the ladders.

Easy, who had also had some sleep, reported Benj's
departure and her own presence to Dondragmer, briefed
Barlennan as requested, and switched back to the
captain with a question of her own.

"That's two of your missing men. Do you think there
is still any chance of finding your helicopter pilots?"

Dondragmer almost slipped on his answer, carefully as he picked his words. He knew, of course, where

Reffel was, since messengers had been passing steadily between the camp and the *Gwelf;* but Kervenser, to his disappointment, had not been seen by the crew of the dirigible or anyone else. His disappearance was perfectly genuine, and the captain now regarded his chances for survival as even lower than those of the *Kwembly* an hour before. It was safe, of course, to talk about this; his slip consisted of failing to mention Reffel at all. The Stennish forms equivalent to "him" and "them" were as distinct as the human ones, and several times Dondragmer caught himself using the former when talking about his lost pilots. Easy seemed not to notice, but he wondered afterward.

"It is hard to judge. I have not seen either one. If he went down in the area now flooded it is hard to see how they could be alive now. It is very unfortunate, not only because of the men themselves but because with even one of the helicopters we might be able to transfer more men to the *Kwembly* and get her back here more easily. Of course most of the equipment could not be carried that way; on the other hand, if it turns out that the two men cannot bring the cruiser back here for any reason, having one of the fliers could make a great difference to *them*. It is a pity that your scientists cannot locate the transmitter which Reffel was carrying, as they can the one on the *Kwembly*."

"You're not the first to feel that way," agreed Easy. The matter had been brought up shortly after Reffel's disappearance. "I don't know enough about the machines to tell why the signal strength depends on the picture brightness; I always thought a carrier wave was a carrier wave; but that seems to be it. Either Reffel's set is in total darkness or it has been destroyed.

"I see your life-support equipment is set up and working."

The last sentence was not entirely an effort of Easy's

to change the subject; it was her first good look at the equipment in question, and she was genuinely curious about it. It consisted of scores, perhaps over a hundred, of square transparent tanks covering altogether a dozen square yards, each about a third full of liquid, with the nearly pure hydrogen which constituted Mesklinite air bubbling through it. A power unit operated the lights which shone on the tanks, but the pumps which kept the gas circulating were muscle-driven. The vegetation which actually oxidized the saturated hydrocarbons of Mesklinite biological waste and gave off free hydrogen was represented by a variety of unicellular species corresponding as nearly as might be expected to terrestrial algae. They had been selected for edibility, though not, as Easy had been given to understand, for taste. The sections of the support equipment which used higher plants and produced the equivalent of fruit and vegetables were too bulky to move from the cruiser.

Easy did not know how the non-gaseous items in the biological cycle were gotten into and out of the tanks, but she could see the charging of air-suit cartridges. This was a matter of muscle-driven pumping again, squeezing hydrogen into tanks which contained slugs of porous solid. This material was another strictly non-Mesklinite product, a piece of molecular architecture vaguely analogous to zeolite in structure, which adsorbed hydrogen on the inner walls of its structural channels and, within a wide temperature range, maintained an equilibrium partial pressure with the gas which was compatible with Mesklinite metabolic needs.

Dondragmer answered Easy's remark. "Yes, we have just about enough food and air. The real problem is what to do. We have saved very little of your planetological equipment; we can't carry on your work. Conceivably we might make our way back to the Settlement on foot, but we'd have to carry the life-support material by stages. That would mean setting up a camp only a few miles from here, transferring the equipment, recharging the air cartridges after cycling has resumed, and then repeating the process indefinitely. Since the distance to the settlement is about thirty thousand, excuse me, in your numbers about twelve thousand, of your miles, it would take us years to get there: that's no metaphor, nor do I mean your short years. If we're to be any further use to your project, we really must get the *Kwembly* back here."

Easy could only agree, though she could see an alternative which the captain had not mentioned. Of course, Aucoin would disapprove, or would he, under the circumstances? A trained and efficient exploring crew represented quite an investment, too. That might be a useful line to follow.

It was several more minutes before Benj returned with his information, and incidentally with a following of interested scientists.

"Captain," he called, "the *Kwembly* is still moving, though not very fast, something like twenty cables an hour. She is located, or was six minutes ago, 310.71 miles from your transmitter, in our figures. In your numbers and units that's 233,750 cables. There's a small error if there's much difference in elevation. · That's great circle distance; we don't have too good an idea of the length of the river, though they have about twenty position readings taken along it since your ship started drifting, so there's a rough river map up in the lab."

"Thank you," came the captain's answer in due course. "Are you in verbal contact with the helmsmen yet?"

"Not yet, but they've gone inside. I'm sure they'll find the communicator on the bridge pretty soon, though

I suppose there are other places they'd want to check first. The air must be pretty low in their suits."

This was perfectly correct. It took the helmsmen only a few minutes to ascertain that the cruiser was deserted, and to note that much of the life-support equipment was gone; but this left them with the need to check the air now aboard for contamination with oxygen from outside. Neither of them knew enough basic chemistry to invent a test, and neither was familiar with the routine ones used by Borndender and his colleagues. They were considering the rather drastic procedure of testing by smell when it occurred to Beetchermarlf that a communicator might have been left aboard for scientific reasons, and that the human beings might be of help. There was none in the laboratory, but the bridge was the next most likely spot, and Beetchermarlf's voice was on its way up to the station some ten minutes after the helmsmen had come aboard.

Benj postponed greetings when he heard Beetchermarlf's question, and relayed it at once to Dondragmer. The captain called his scientists and outlined the situation, and for over half an hour the relay was very busy: Borndender explained things, and Beetchermarlf repeated the explanations, then went to the lab to examine material and equipment, then came back to the bridge to make sure of some minor point . . .

Eventually both parties in the conversation felt sure that the instructions had been understood. Benj, at its pivot point, was nearly sure. He knew enough physics and chemistry himself to judge that nothing was likely to blow up if Beetch made a mistake; his only worry was that his friend might perform the tests sloppily and so miss a dangerous amount of oxygen. Was the risk simply one of poisoning, or did hydrogen-oxygen mixtures present other dangers? He wasn't quite sure; hydrogen-oxygen mixtures have other qualities.

He remained rather tense until Beetchermarlf returned to the bridge with the report that both tests were complete. The catalyst which disposed of free oxygen by accelerating its reaction with ammonia was still active, and the ammonia-vapor concentration in the ship's air was high enough to give it something to work on. The helmsmen had already removed their air-suits and neither could smell any oxygen, though, as with human beings and hydrogen sulfide, smell is not always a reliable test.

At least, the two could live on board for a time. One of their first acts had been to "hand"-pump the feed tank which kept air bubbling through the life-support medium, and to satisfy themselves that most of the plants were still alive. The next problem was navigation.

Benj told his friend as much as possible about his location, that of the rest of the crew, and the *Kwembly's* present rate and direction of travel. There was no problem about using the information. Beetchermarlf could determine direction easily enough. The stars were visible and he had a perfectly good magnetic compass. Dhrawn's magnetic field was a good deal stronger than Earth's, to the consternation of the scientists who had long since taken for granted a correlation between magnetic field and rotation rate for ordinary planets.

The discussion which produced a detailed operation plan was shorter than the one preceding the oxygen test, though it still involved the long relay. Neither Dondragmer nor the helmsmen had any serious doubts about what to do or how to do it.

Beetchermarlf was far younger than Takoorch, but there seemed no question as to who was in charge aboard. The fact that Benj always signalled Beetch by name, rather than signalling the *Kwembly* formally, may have contributed to the young one's authority. Easy and several of the other human beings suspected that Takoorch, in spite of his willingness to discuss his own past accomplishments, was in no great hurry to take on too much responsibility. He tended to agree with Beetchermarlf's suggestions either at once or after only token arguments.

"We're still adrift, and unless this river has some very funny loops farther down we'll never get any closer to the others with its help," the younger Mesklinite summarized at last. "The first job will be to get paddles on some of the powered trucks. Trying to do it with all of them will take forever; a couple of outboard-row ones aft, and maybe a central one forward should give control. With power available on other drivers we can either pull off or get safely ashore if we run aground. Tak and I will go outside and start work right now. You keep an eye on us as much as you can, Benj; we'll leave the set where it is."

Beetchermarlf did not wait for an answer. He and his companion suited up once more and broke out the paddles which were designed to be pinned onto the treads of the drivers. These had been tested on Mesklin but had never yet been used on Dhrawn; no one really knew how well they would work. Their area was small, since there was little clearance for them above the trucks, and some of that small area was taken up by a plastic shield designed to fold them flat as they were riding forward on the top side of the trucks. However, it had been proved that they would supply some thrust. What this would accomplish remained to be seen; the *Kwembly* was floating higher in the ammonia-water solution of Dhrawn, of course, than she had in the liquid hydrocarbon ocean of the world where she had been made.

Installation of the fins and shields was a long and awkward job for two workers. The pieces could be taken out only one at a time, since there was nowhere to put them down with the cruiser afloat. Safety lines persistently got in the way. Mesklinite pincers are rather less effective handling organs than are human fingers, though this is somewhat offset by the fact that their owner can use all four pairs of them simultaneously and in coordination—he has no asymmetry corresponding to human right- or left-handedness.

The need for artificial lights was still another bother. As it turned out, getting twelve paddles and one shield on each of three drivers took a total of almost fifteen hours. It could, Beetchermarlf assured Benj, have been accomplished in two with four workers on each truck.

By this time the trackers had learned that the *Kwembly* was not getting any farther from the camp, though she was still moving. Apparently she had been caught in an eddy some four miles in diameter. Beetchermarlf took advantage of this when he was finally ready to apply power; he waited until the human analysts could tell him that he was being carried south before he set the three finned trucks running. For some seconds it was not apparent that the power was doing any good; then, very slowly, helmsmen and humans alike saw that the great hull was moving gently forward. The Mesklinites could see from the bridge a feeble excuse for a bow wave; the human beings, looking aft, were able to detect small ripples spreading back from the sides. Beetchermarlf swung his helm hard over to bring the bow in line with Sol and Fomalaut. For nearly half a minute he was left wondering whether there would be any response; then the stars began to swing overhead as the long hull swerved majestically. Once started it was hard to stop; he overcontrolled many times and for a period of many minutes, sometimes by as much as a full right angle, before getting the feel of the vessel. Then for nearly an hour he managed to hold a southerly heading, though he had no idea of his actual course at first. He could guess from the earlier information that the eddy would be bearing him in the same direction at the start, but then it would presumably carry him eastward.

It was some time, however, before the directional antennae on the shadow satellites and the computers in the station could confirm this guess. About the time they did, the *Kwembly* ran gently aground.

Beetchermarlf instantly shifted drive power to the two trucks farthest forward which had power boxes, letting the paddle-equipped ones idle, and pulled his cruiser out on the shore.

"I'm out of the lake," he reported. "Minor problem. If I travel for any distance on land with the paddles in place I'll wear them out. If it turns out that I'm on an island, or have to go back to the water for any other reason, an awful lot of time will have been wasted taking them off and putting them on again. My first thought is to do some exploring on foot, leaving the ship right here, to get some idea of what the chances of staying ashore may be. It will take a long time, but not nearly as long as waiting for daylight. I'll be glad of advice from you humans or orders from the captain; we'll wait."

Dondragmer, when this was relayed to him, was prompt with his answer.

"Don't go out. Wait until the map-makers up above can decide whether you are on the same side of the river as we are, or not. As I picture the map they've described, there's a good chance that the eddy carried you to the east side, which would be the right bank; we're on the left. If they are even moderately sure of this, get back into the water and head west until they think you're past it, no, second thought. Go until they think you're opposite its mouth, then head south once more. I'd like to find out whether you can travel upstream with any speed at all. I know it will be slow; it may turn out that you can't travel at all in some places along the bank."

"I'll tell Beetch and the map people, Captain," answered Benj. "I'll try to get a copy of their map and keep it up to date down here; that may save some time in the future."

The directional data was not, as it happened, definitive. The location of the *Kwembly* could be established well enough, but the course of the river down which she had come was much less certain. The checks were many miles apart, but sufficient in number to show that the river was decidedly crooked. After some further discussion, it was decided that Beetchermarlf should get back afloat and head westward as close to shore as he could; preferably within sight of it, if the range of his lights and the slope of the lake bottom would permit it. If he could find the river mouth by sight, he was to head up it as Dondragmer had wished; if not, he was to continue along the shore until the men above were reasonably certain that he had passed the rivermouth, then turn south.

It did prove possible to keep the shore within range of the *Kwembly's* lights, but it took over two hours to reach the river. This had made a wide westward bend which had been missed in the checks of the cruiser's position during the downstream drift; then it turned again and entered the lake on an eastward slant which presumably caused the counterclockwise eddy. One of the planetographers remarked that you couldn't blame the eddy on Coriolis force because the lake was only seven degrees from the equator and on the south side, at that, of a planet which took two months to rotate.

The delta, which caused the shoreline to turn north briefly, was a warning. Beetchermarlf at the helm and Takoorch at the port wing of the bridge sent the

Kwembly groping around the rather irregular peninsula, slowing noticeably several times as the trucks dragged in soft bottom silt, and finally found their way into a clear channel and headed into its current.

This was not swift, but the *Kwembly* still wasn't afloat. The Mesklinites were in no hurry; Dondragmer gave six hours and more to the experiment of fighting the stream. They made about ten miles progress in that time. If that rate could be maintained, the cruiser would be back at the camp by a day or two after midnight, that is, in a week or so by human reckoning.

It was impatience which changed the travel plans. This could not, of course, be blamed on any Mesklinite; it was Aucoin, of all people, who decided that a mile and a half an hour was not satisfactory. Dondragmer did not feel strongly about the matter; he agreed that research might as well be worked into the trip if possible. At the planner's suggestion he sent Beetchermarlf angling westward toward what was presumably the near bank of the river. The land seemed traversable. With some misgiving he had the helmsmen remove the paddles.

Removal proved much easier than installation, since the vehicle was now on dry land. Things could be laid down and life lines were not needed. Benj, on his next visit to the communication room, found the *Kwembly* cruising smoothly south at about ten miles an hour over flat country, interrupted by an occasional outcropping of rock and studded here and there with scrubby brush, the highest life form so far encountered on Dhrawn. The surface was firm sediment; the planetologists judged the area to be a flood plain, which seemed reasonable even to Benj.

Beetchermarlf was willing to talk as usual, but it could be seen that his attention was not entirely on conversation. Both he and Takoorch were looking ahead as sharply as their eyesight and the *Kwembly's* lights would permit. There was no assurance that the going was safe; without air-scouting, the ten-mile speed was all they dared use. Anything faster would have been overrunning their lights. Whenever other duties, such as airplant maintenance, had to be performed, they stopped the cruiser and did the work together. One set of eyes, they felt, was not enough for safe travel.

Every now and then, as the hours wore on, whoever was at the helm would begin to feel the treacherous assurance that there could be no danger; that they had, after all, come scores of miles now without having to change heading except to keep the river in sight. A human being would have increased the running speed bit by bit. The Mesklinite reaction was to stop and rest. Even Takoorch knew that when he was feeling tempted to act against the dictates of elementary common sense, it was time to do something about his own condition. Discovering the vehicle halted when he came to the screens on one occasion, Aucoin assumed it was a regular air-maintenance stop; but then he saw one of the Mesklinites sprawled idly on the bridge; the set had been put back in its old location, giving a view forward over the helm. Asking why the cruiser was not travelling, Takoorch simply replied that he had found himself getting casual. The administrator left in a very thoughtful mood.

Eventually, this care paid off, or seemed to.

For some miles the outcroppings of bed rock had been more and more frequent, though generally smaller, closer together, and more angular. The planetologists had been making guesses, futile, really, with so little information, about the underlying stratigraphy. The basic surface was still hard-packed sediment, but the watchers suspected that it might be getting shallower, and that some time soon the *Kwembly* might find herself on the same sort of bare rock that formed the substrate at Dondragmer's camp.

The helmsmen occasionally found it necessary now to weave slightly left or right to avoid the rock outcroppings; he even had to slow down a little from time to time. Several times in the past few hours the planetologists had rather plaintively suggested that the cruiser stop before it was too late, and pick up samples of the sediment she was running over even if the rocks were too big to collect. Aucoin simply pointed out that it would be a year or two before the sample could get up to the station anyway, and refused; the scientists retorted that a year was much better than the time which would be needed if the specimens weren't collected.

But when the *Kwembly* stopped, it was on Beetchermarlf's initiative. It was a minor thing, or seemed to be; the soil ahead seemed a little darker, with a very sharp boundary between it and the surface under the cruiser. The line was not noticeable on the vision screen, but the Mesklinites spotted it simultaneously and, without words, agreed that close examination was in order. Beetchermarlf called the station to inform the human beings and his captain that he and Takoorch would be going outside for a time, and described the situation. Easy, translating the message, was promptly begged by two planetologists to persuade the Mesklinites to bring samples aboard. She assumed that even Aucoin would hardly object under the circumstances, and agreed to ask them when she called back with Dondragmer's clearance.

The captain, this time, approved the sortie, suggesting only that it be preceded by a careful look around from the bridge with the aid of the spotlights. This proved useful. A hundred yards ahead, not too far out of the range of the running lights, a small stream ran across their path and emptied into the river.

Sweeping the light to starboard, this tributary could be seen arcing around parallel to the cruiser's path from the north, then reversing its curve somewhat astern of the big vehicle and disappearing to the northwest. The *Kwembly* was on a peninsula some two hundred yards wide and not quite as long, bounded on the east— left—by the main river she had been following and on the other sides by the small tributary. It seemed likely to Mesklinites and human beings alike that the change in soil color which had caught the helmsmen's attention was caused by wetting from the smaller stream, but no one was sure enough of it to cancel the proposed trip outside. Aucoin was not present.

Outside, even with the aid of extra lights, the line of demarcation between the two kinds of soil was much less visible than before. Eye distance, Beetchermarlf judged, was the main cause. The crew scraped up and packaged samples of material from both sides of the line; then they went on to the stream itself. This proved to be a swift-running but shallow brook three or four body-lengths in width, its level an inch or two below the soil through which it was cutting its way. After a brief consultation, the two Mesklinites began to follow it away from the river. They had no way of telling its composition, but a bottle of its contents was secured for later testing.

By the time they reached the spot where it was curving away, even the Mesklinites could see that the stream had not been in existence very long. It was eating with visible speed into its banks, washing the sediment on toward the main river. Now that they were on the outside of its curve, the undercutting of the near bank could be seen and even felt; Beetchermarlf, standing at the edge, felt it crumble suddenly away under him and found himself in the stream.

It was only an inch or so deep, so he took advantage of the occasion to take another sample from its bottom before climbing out. They decided to continue upstream for another ten minutes or so, with Beetchermarlf wading and Takoorch on the bank. Before the time was up they had actually found the source of the watercourse. It was a spring, not half a mile from the *Kwembly*, roiling violently in the center of its basin where an underground source fed it. Beetchermarlf, investigating the middle, was knocked from his feet and carried half a body length by the upward current.

There was nothing in particular to do; they had no camera equipment, no one had seriously suggested that they bring the vision set with them, and there was nothing obvious to be gained by collecting more samples. They returned to the *Kwembly* to give a verbal description of what they had found.

Even the scientists agreed that the best step now was to get the samples back to the camp where Borndender and his fellows could do something useful with them. The helmsmen eased their cruiser into motion once more.

It approached the stream and nosed through it; the mattress took up the slight dip as the trucks crossed the bottom of the widening valley, and nothing could be felt on the bridge.

Not for another eight seconds.

The hull was rather more than half way across the little brook when the distinction between solid and liquid began to blur. A slight lurch could be felt on the bridge; it showed on the screen far above as a tiny upward jerk of the few outside features visible.

Forward motion stopped almost instantly, though the drivers kept churning. They could accomplish nothing when completely immersed in slimy mud, which the surface had so suddenly become. There was neither support nor traction. The *Kwembly* settled until the trucks were buried; settled until the mattress was nearly out of sight; settled almost, but not quite, to the level where she would have been literally floating in the semiliquid muck. She was stopped by two of the rock outcrops, one of which caught her under the stern just aft of the mattress, and the other on the starboard side some ten feet forward of the main lock. There was an ugly scraping sound as the cruiser's hull canted forward and to port, and then came to rest.

And this time, as Beetchermarlf's sense of smell warned him only too clearly, the hull had failed somewhere. Oxygen was leaking in.

XV
ESSENCE

"It boils down to this," Aucoin said from the head of the table. "We have the choice of sending down the barge, or not. If we don't, the *Kwembly* and the two Mesklinites aboard her are lost, and Dondragmer and the rest of her crew are out of action until a rescue cruiser such as the *Kalliff* can reach them from the Settlement. Unfortunately, if we do try to land the barge there's a good chance that it won't help. We don't know why the ground gave under the *Kwembly,* and have no assurance that the same thing won't happen anywhere else in the vicinity. Losing the barge would be awkward. Even if we first landed near Dondragmer's camp and transferred him and his crew to the cruiser, we might lose the barge and there is no assurance that the crew could repair the *Kwembly*. Beetchermarlf's report makes me doubt it. He says he has found and sealed the major leaks, but he's still getting oxygen inside the hull from time to time. Several of his life-support tanks have been poisoned by it. So far he has been able to clean them out each time and restock them from the others, but he can't keep going forever unless he stops the last of these leaks. Also, neither he nor anyone else has made any concrete suggestion for getting that cruiser loose from the muck or whatever it's stuck in.

"There is another good argument against landing the barge. If we use remote, live control, there is the sixty-second reaction lag, which would make handling anywhere near the ground really impossible. It would be possible to program its computer to handle a landing, but the risks of that were proved the hard way the first time anyone landed away from Earth. You might as well give the Mesklinites a quick lesson in flying the thing for themselves!"

"Don't try to make that last sound too silly, Alan," Easy pointed out gently. "The *Kwembly* is merely the first of the cruisers to get into what looks like final trouble. Dhrawn is a very big world, with very little known about it, and I suspect we're going to run out of land-cruisers for rescue or any other purpose sooner or later. Also, even I know that the barge controls are computer-coupled, with push-the-way-you-want-to-go operators. I admit that even so, the chances are ten to one or worse that anyone trying a ground-to-ground flight with that machine on Dhrawn without previous experience would kill himself, but do Beetchermarlf and Takoorch have even that much chance of survival on any other basis?"

"I think they do," replied Aucoin quietly.

"How, in the name of all that's sensible?" snapped Mersereau. "Here all along we've—" Easy held up her hand, and either the gesture or the expression on her face caused Boyd to fall silent.

"What other procedure *which you could conscientiously recommend* would stand any real chance of saving either the *Kwembly* herself, or her two helmsmen, or the rest of Dondragmer's crew?" she asked.

Aucoin had the grace to flush deeply, but he answered steadily enough.

"I mentioned it earlier, as Boyd remembers," he said. "Sending the *Kalliff* from the Settlement to pick them up."

The words were followed by some seconds of silence, while expressions of amusement flitted across the faces around the table. Eventually Ib Hoffman spoke.

"Do you suppose Barlennan will approve?" he asked innocently.

"It boils down to this," Dondragmer said to Kabremm. "We can stay here and do nothing while Barlennan sends a rescue cruiser from the Settlement. I assume he can think of some reason for sending one which won't sound too queer, after he failed to do it for the *Esket*."

"That would be easy enough," returned the *Esket's* first officer. "One of the human beings was against sending it, and the commander simply let him win the argument. This time he could be firmer."

"As though the first time wouldn't have made some of the other humans suspicious enough. But never mind that. If we wait, we don't know how long it will be, since we don't even know whether there's a possible ground route from the Settlement to here. You came from the mines by air, and we floated part of the way.

"If we decide not to wait, we can do either of two things. One is to move by stages toward the *Kwembly*, carrying the life equipment as far as the suits will let us and then setting it up again to recharge them. We'd get there some time, I suppose. The other is to move the same way toward the Settlement to meet the rescue cruiser if one comes or get there on foot if it doesn't. I suppose we'd even get *there*, eventually. Even if we reach the *Kwembly*, there is no certainty that we can repair her; if the human beings have relayed Beetchermarlf's feelings at all adequately, it seems rather doubtful. I don't like either choice because of the wasted time they both involve. There are better things to do than crawl over the surface of this world on foot.

"A better idea, to my way of thinking, is to use your dirigible either to rescue my helmsmen if it is decided to give up on the *Kwembly,* or to start ferrying my crew and equipment over to where she is."

"But that—"

"That, of course, sinks the raft as far as the *Esket* act is concerned. Even using Reffel's helicopter would do that; we couldn't explain what happened to the vision set he was carrying without their seeing through it, no matter what lie you think up. I'm simply not sure that the trick is worth the deliberate sacrifice of those lives; though I admit it's worth the *risk,* of course; I wouldn't have gone along with it otherwise."

"So I heard," returned Kabremm. "No one has been able to make you see the risk of being completely dependent on beings who can't possibly regard us as real people."

"Quite right. Remember that some of them are as different from *each other,* as they are from us. I made up my mind about the aliens the time one of them answered my question about a differential hoist clearly and in detail, and threw in my first lesson in the use of mathematics in science, gratis. I realize the humans differ among themselves as we do; certainly the one who talked Barl out of sending help to the *Esket* must be as different as possible from Mrs. Hoffman or Charles Lackland—but I don't and never will distrust them as a species the way you seem to. I don't think Barlennan really does, either; he's changed the subject more than once rather than argue the point with me, and that's not Barlennan when he's sure he's right. I still think it would be a good idea to lower the sails on this act and ask directly for human help with the *Kwembly,* or at least take a chance on their finding out by using all three dirigibles there."

"There aren't three, any more." Kabremm knew the point was irrelevant, but was rather glad of a chance to change the subject. "Karfrengin and four men have been missing in the *Elsh* for two of this world's days."

"That news hadn't reached me, of course," said Dondragmer. "How did the commander react to it? I should think that even he would be feeling the temptation to ask for human help, if we're starting to lose personnel all over the map."

"He hasn't heard about it, either. We've had ground parties out searching, using trucks we salvaged from the *Esket,* and we didn't want to make a report until it could be a complete one."

"How much more complete could it be? Karfrengin and his men must be dead by now. The dirigibles don't carry life-support gear for two days."

Kabremm gave the rippling equivalent of a shrug. "Take it up with Destigmet. I have troubles enough."

"Why wasn't your flyer used for the search?"

"It was, until this evening. There are other troubles at the mine, though. A sort of ice river is coming, very slowly, but it will soon cover the whole second settlement if it doesn't stop. It's already reached the *Esket* and started to tip it over; that's why we were able to salvage the trucks so easily. Destigmet sent me to follow back up the glacier and try to find out whether it is likely to keep coming indefinitely, or was just a brief event. I really shouldn't have come this far, but I couldn't make myself stop. It's this same river for the whole distance, sometimes solid and sometimes liquid along the way; it's the weirdest thing I've seen yet on this weird world. There isn't a chance of the ice's stopping, and the *Esket* settlement is as good as done for."

"And of course Barlennan hasn't heard about this either."

"There's been no way to tell him. We only discovered the ice was moving just before dark. It was just a cliff a few dozen cables from the mine up to then."

"In other words, we've lost not only my first officer and a helicopter but a dirigible with five men, and as an afterthought the whole *Esket* project, with my *Kwembly* probably on the same list. And you still think we shouldn't end this trickery, tell the human beings the whole story, and get their help?"

"More than ever. If they learn we're having this much trouble, they'll probably decide we're no more use to them and abandon us here."

"Nonsense. No one just abandons an investment like this project; but never mind arguing; it's a futile point anyway. I wish—"

"What you really wish is that you had an excuse for leaking the whole barrel to your oxygen-breathing friends."

"You know I wouldn't do that. I'm quite ready to use my own judgement in the field, but I know enough history to be afraid of making spot-changes in basic policy."

"Thank goodness. It's all right to like some humans, but they're not all like the Hoffman one. You admitted that yourself."

"What it boils down to," Barlennan said to Bendivence, "is that we were much too hasty in sending Deeslenver to the *Esket* with orders to shutter its vision sets. The whole *Esket* question seems to have quieted down, and that will bring it to life again. We're not ready for the main act yet, and won't be for a year or more. I wasn't sorry for the chance to start the human beings thinking along the lines of a native-menace idea, but Destigmet's crew won't be able to play the part until they have a lot more home-made mechanical and electrical equipment, things that the humans know we don't have. Certainly, unless the native menace seems real, the human beings aren't very likely to take the steps we want.

"If there were any way to go after Dee now and cancel his orders, I'd do it. I wish I'd dared let you go ahead with radio experiments, and had a set on the *Deedee* right now."

"It shouldn't be too risky, and I'd be more than glad to work on it," answered Bendivence. "The waves could be detected by the human beings, of course, but if we confined ourselves to brief and rare transmissions and used a simple off-on code they probably wouldn't realize what the source was. However, it's too late to get Deeslenver, anyway."

"True. I wish I knew why no one up there has said another word about Kabremm. The last time I talked to Mrs. Hoffman, I got the impression that she wasn't quite as sure as before that she'd really seen him. Do you suppose she really made a mistake? Or are the human beings trying to test *us*, the way I wanted to do with them? Or has Dondragmer done something to get us off that reef? If she were really wrong, we'll have to start thinking all over again . . ."

"And what about that other report we've heard no more of, something sliding across the *Esket's* floor?" countered the scientist. "Was that still another test? Or is something really happening there? Remember, we haven't had any contact with that base for over a hundred and fifty hours. If the *Esket* is really being moved by something, we're much too badly out of date to do anything sensible. You know, without saying anything against the *Esket* act, it's an awful nuisance not to be able to trust your data."

"If there's real trouble at the *Esket* we'll just have to trust Dee's judgement," said the commander, ignoring Bendivence's closing sentence. "Actually, even that isn't the chief problem. The real question is what to do about Dondragmer and the *Kwembly*. I suppose he had good reason to leave his ship and let her drift away, but the results have been very awkward. The fact that a couple of his men got left aboard makes it almost more so; if they hadn't been, we could just forget about the cruiser and send out the *Kalliff* to pick up the people."

"Why can't we do that anyway? Didn't the human Aucoin suggest it?"

"He did. I said I'd have to think it over."

"Why?"

"Because there is less than one chance in ten, and probably less than one in a hundred, that the *Kalliff* could get there in time to do those two men any good. The chances are small enough that she could get there at all. Remember that snow field the *Kwembly* crossed before her first flood? What do you suppose that area is like now? And how long do you think two men, competent men, but with no real technical or scientific training, are going to keep that leaking hull habitable?

"Of course, we could confess the whole act, tell the humans to get in touch with Destigmet through the watch he keeps at the *Esket's* communicators; then they could tell him to send a rescue dirigible."

"That would be wasting a tremendous amount of work, and ruining what still seems a promising operation," Bendivence replied thoughtfully. "You don't want to do that any more than I do; but of course we can't abandon those two helmsmen."

"We can't," Barlennan agreed slowly, "but I just wonder whether we'd be taking too much of a chance on them if we waited out one other possibility."

"What's that?"

"If the human beings were convinced that we could not possibly carry out the rescue, it's just possible,

especially with *two* Hoffmans to do the arguing, that
they'd decide to do something about it themselves."

"But what could they do? The ship they call the
'barge' will only land here at the Settlement by its automatic controls, as I understand Rescue Plan One. They
certainly can't fly it around on this world from out at
the orbiting station; if it took them a whole minute to
correct any mistake, they'd crash it right away. They
certainly can't fly it down personally. It's set up to
rescue *us,* with our air and temperature control, and
besides Dhrawn's gravity would paint a human being
over the deck."

"Don't underestimate those aliens, Ben. They may
not be exactly ingenious, but there's been time for
their ancestors to think up a lot of ready-made ideas
we don't know about yet. I wouldn't do it if I felt
there was a real chance of our getting there ourselves,
but this way we're not putting the helmsmen in any
worse danger than they are already; I think that we'll
let the human beings get the idea of making the rescue
themselves. It would be much better than giving up
the plan."

"What it boils down to," said Beetchermarlf to Takoorch, "is that we somehow have to find time between
plugging leaks and cleaning poison out of the air units
to convince people that the *Kwembly* is worth salvag-
ing.

"The best way would be to get her going ourselves,
though I doubt very much that we can do it. It's
the cruiser that's going to set the policy. Your life
and mine don't mean very much to the humans, except maybe to Benj, who isn't running things up
there. If the ship stays alive, if we can keep these
tanks going to supply us with food and air, and incidentally keep from being poisoned by oxygen our-

selves, and make real, reportable progress in repairing and freeing the cruiser, *then* maybe they'll be convinced that a rescue trip is worth while. Even if they don't, we'll have to do all those things for our own sakes anyway; but if we can have the humans tell Barlennan that we have the *Kwembly* out and running, and will get her back to Dondragmer by ourselves, it should make quite a few people happy, especially the commander."

"Do you think we can do it?" asked Takoorch.

"You and I are the first ones to convince," replied the younger helmsman. "The rest of the world will be easier after that."

"What it boils down to," said Benj to his father, "is that we won't risk the barge for two lives, even though that's what it's here for."

"Not quite right on either count," Ib Hoffman answered. "It's a piece of emergency equipment, but it was planned for use if the whole project collapsed and we had to evacuate the Settlement. This was always a possibility; there was a lot that just couldn't be properly tested in advance. For example, the trick of matching outside pressure in the cruisers and airsuits by using extra argon was perfectly reasonable, but we could not be sure there would be no side effects on the Mesklinites themselves; argon is inert by the usual standards, but so is xenon, which is an effective anaesthetic for human beings. Living systems are just too complicated for extrapolation ever to be safe, though the Mesklinites seem a lot simpler physiologically than we are. That may be one reason they can stand such a broad temperature range.

"But the point is, the barge is preset to home in on a beam transmitter near the Settlement; it won't land itself anywhere else on Dhrawn. It can be handled by remote control, of course, but not at this range.

"We could, I suppose, alter its on-board computer program to make it set itself down in other places, at least, on any reasonably flat surface; but would you want to set it down anywhere near your friend either by a built-in, unchangeable program or by long-delayed remote control? Remember the barge uses proton jets, has a mass of twenty-seven thousand pounds, and must put up quite a splash soft-landing in forty gravities, especially since its jets are splayed to reduce cratering." Benj frowned thoughtfully.

"But why can't we get closer to Dhrawn, and cut down the remote-control lag?" he asked, after some moments' thought. Ib looked at his son in surprise.

"You know why, or should. Dhrawn has a mass of 3,471 Earths, and a rotation period of just over fifteen hundred hours. A synchronous orbit to hold us above a constant longitude at the equator is therefore just over six million miles out. If you use an orbit a hundred miles above the surface you'd be travelling at better than ninety miles a second, and go around Dhrawn in something like forty minutes. You'd remain in sight of one spot on the surface for two or three minutes out of the forty. Since the planet has about eighty-seven times Earth's surface area, how many control stations do you think would be needed to manage one landing or lift-off?"

Benj made a gesture of impatience.

"I know all that, but there is already a swarm of stations down there, the shadow satellites. Even I know that they all have relay equipment, since they're all reporting constantly to the computers up here and at any given moment nearly half of them must be behind Dhrawn. Why can't a controller riding one of these, or a ship at about the same height, tie into their relays and handle landing and lift-off from there? Delay shouldn't be more than a second or so even from the opposite side of the world."

"Because," Ib started to answer, and then fell silent. He remained so for a full two minutes. Benj did not interrupt his thinking; the boy usually had a good idea when he was ahead.

"There would have to be several minutes of interruption of neutrino data while the relays were being preempted," Ib said finally.

"Out of the how many years that they've been integrating that material?" Benj was not usually sarcastic with either of his parents, but his feelings were once more growing warm. His father nodded silently, conceding the point, and continued to think.

It must have been five minutes later, though Benj would have sworn to a greater number, that the senior Hoffman got suddenly to his feet.

"Come on, Son. You're perfectly right. It will work for an initial space-to-surface landing, and for a surface-to-orbit lift-off, and that's enough. For surface-to-surface flight even one second is too much control delay, but we can do without that."

"Sure!" enthused Benj. "Lift off into orbit, get your breath, change the orbit to suit your landing spot, and go back down."

"That would work, but don't mention it. For one thing, if we made a habit of it there *would* be a significant interruption of neutrino data transmission. Besides, I've wanted an excuse for this almost ever since I joined this project. Now I have one, and I'm going to use it."

"An excuse for what?"

"For doing exactly what I think Barlennan has been trying to maneuver us into doing all along: put Mesklinite pilots on the barge. I suppose he wants his own interstellar ship, some time, so that he can start leading the same life among the stars that he used to do on

Mesklin's oceans, but he'll have to make do with one quantum jump at a time."

"Is *that* what you think he's been up to? Why should he care about having his own space pilots so much? And come to think of it, why wasn't that a good idea in the first place, if the Mesklinites can learn how?"

"It was, and there's no reason to doubt that they can."

"Then why wasn't it done that way all along?"

"I'd rather not lecture on that subject just now. I like to feel as much pride in my species as circumstances allow, and the explanation doesn't reflect much credit either on man's rationality or his emotional control."

"I can guess, then," replied Benj. "But in that case, what makes you think we can change it now?"

"Because, now, at the trifling cost of descending to the same general level of emotional reasoning, we have a handle on some of man's less generous drives. I'm going down to the planetology lab and filibuster. I'm going to ask those chemists why they don't know what trapped the *Kwembly,* and when they say it's because they don't have any samples of the mud, I'm going to ask them why they don't. I'm going to ask them why they've been making do with seismic and neutrino-shadow data when they might as well be analyzing mineral samples carted up here from every spot where a Mesklinite cruiser has stopped for ten minutes. If you prefer not to descend to that level, and would rather work with mankind's nobler emotions, you be thinking of all the heart-rending remarks you could make about the horror and cruelty of leaving your friend Beetchermarlf to suffocate slowly on an alien world parsecs from his home. We could use that if we have to take this argument to a higher authority, like the general public. I don't think we'll really need to, but right now I'm in no mood to restrict myself to clean fighting and logical argument.

"If Alan Aucoin growls about the cost of operating the barge (I think he has too much sense), I'm going to jump on him with both feet. Energy has been practically free ever since we've had fusion devices; what costs is personal skill. He'll have to use Mesklinite crews anyway, so that investment is already made; and by letting the barge drift out here unused he's wasting *its* cost. I know there's a small hole in that logic, but if you point it out in Dr. Aucoin's hearing I'll paddle you for the first time since you were seven, and I don't think the last decade has done too much to my arm. You let Aucoin do his own thinking."

"You needn't get annoyed with *me,* Dad."

"I'm not. In fact, I'm not as much annoyed as I am scared."

"Scared? Of what?"

"Of what may happen to Barlennan and his people on what your mother calls 'that horrible planet.' "

"But why? Why now, more than before?"

"Because I'm coming gradually to realize that Barlennan is an intelligent, forceful, thoughtful, ambitious, and reasonably well-educated being, just as my only son was six years ago; and I remember your diving outfit much too well. Come on. We have an astronautics school to get organized, and a student body to collect."

EPILOGUE: LESSONS

At two hundred miles, the barge was just visible as a starlike object reflecting Lalande 21185's feeble light. Benj had watched the vessel as it pulled up to that distance and moved into what its pilot considered a decent station-keeping orbit, but neither he nor the pilot had discussed technical details. It was so handy to be able to hold a conversation without waiting a full minute for the other fellow's answer that Benj and Beetchermarlf had simply chattered.

These conversations were becoming less and less frequent. Benj was really back at work now and, he suspected, making up for lost time. Beetchermarlf was often too far away on practice flights to talk at all, and even more frequently too occupied to converse with anyone but his instructor.

"Time to turn it over, Beetch," the boy ended the present exchange as he heard Tebbetts' whistling from down the shaft. "The taskmaster is on the way."

"I'm ready when he is," came the reply. "Does he want to use your language or mine this time?"

"He'll let you know; he didn't tell me. Here he is," replied Benj.

The bearded astronomer, however, spoke first to Benj after looking quickly around. The two were drifting weightless in the direct-observation section at the

268

center of the station's connecting bar, and Tebbetts had taken for granted that the barge and his student would be drifting alongside. All his quick glance caught was the dull ember of a sun in one direction and the dimly lit disc of Dhrawn, little larger than Luna seen from Earth, in the other.

"Where is he, Benj? I thought I heard you talking to him, so I assumed he was close. I hope he isn't late. He should be solving intercept orbits, even with nomographs instead of highspeed computers, better than that by now."

"He's here, sir." The boy pointed. "Just over two hundred miles away, in a 17.8 minute orbit around the station."

Tebbetts blinked. "That's ridiculous. I don't think this heap of hardware would whip anything around in that time at a distance of two hundred feet, let alone that many miles. He'd have to use power, accelerating straight toward us—"

"He is, sir. About two hundred G's acceleration. The time is the rotation period of Mesklin, and the acceleration is the gravity value at his home port. He says he hasn't been so comfortable since he signed up with Barlennan, and wishes there were some way to turn up the sunlight."

The astronomer smiled slowly.

"Yes. I see. That does make sense. I should have thought of it myself. I have some more practice exercises for him here, but that's about as good as any of them. I should do more of that sort of thing. Well, let's get at it. Can you stay to check my language? I think I have the Stennish words for everything in today's work, and space is empty enough so that his mistakes and mine should both be relatively harmless, but there's no need to take chances."

"It's too bad the *Kwembly* couldn't be salvaged after all," remarked Aucoin, "but Dondragmer's crew is doing a very good and effective study of the area while they're waiting for relief. I think it was a very good idea to send the *Kalliff* after them with a skeleton crew and let them work while they waited, instead of taking them back to the Settlement in the barge. That would have been pretty dangerous anyway, until there are practiced Mesklinite pilots. The single landing near the *Kwembly* to get the two helmsmen, and a direct return to space while they were trained, was probably the safest way to do it.

"But now we have this trouble with the *Smof*. At this rate we'll be out of cruisers before we're half way around Low Alpha. Does anyone know the *Smof*'s commander the way Easy knows Dondragmer? You don't, I suppose, Easy? Can anyone give a guess at his ability to get himself out of trouble? Or are we going to have to risk sending the barge down before those two Mesklinites are fully trained?"

"Tebbetts thinks Beetchermarlf could handle a surface landing now, as long as it wasn't complicated by mechanical emergencies," pointed out an engineer. "Personally I wouldn't hesitate to let him go."

"You may be right. The trouble is, though, that we certainly can't land the barge on an ice pack, and not even the barge can lift one of those land cruisers, even if there were a way of fastening them together without an actual landing. Beetchermarlf and Takoorch may as well continue their training for the moment. What I want as soon as possible, Planetology, is the best direction and distance for the *Smof*'s crew to trek if they do have to abandon the cruiser, that is, the closest spot where the barge *could* land to pick them up. If it's close to their present location, don't tell them, of course; I want them to do their best to save the cruiser, and there's no point in tempting them with an easy escape."

Ib Hoffman stirred slightly, but refrained from comment. Aucoin, from one point of view, was probably justified. The administrator went on, "Also, is there definite word on the phenomenon that trapped the *Kwembly*? You've had specimens of the mud, or whatever it is, that Beetchermarlf brought up, for weeks now."

"Yes," replied a chemist. "It's a fascinating example of surface action. It's sensitive to the nature and particle size of the minerals present, the proportions of water and ammonia in the lubricating fluid, the temperature, and the pressure. The *Kwembly's* weight, of course, was the main cause of trouble; the Mesklinites could walk around on it, in fact, they did, safely enough. Once triggered by a pressure peak, the strength went out of the stuff in a wave—"

"All right, the rest can serve for a paper," Aucoin nodded. "Is there any way to identify such a surface without putting a ship onto it?"

"Hmm. I'd say yes. Radiation temperature should be information enough, or at least, it would warn that further tests should be made. For that matter, I wouldn't worry about its ever getting the barge; the jets would boil the water and ammonia out of such a surface safely before touchdown."

Aucoin nodded, and passed on to other matters. Cruiser reports, publication reports, supply reports, planning prospectuses.

He was still a little embarrassed. He had known his own failing, but like most people had excused it, and felt sure it wasn't noticeable. But the Hoffman's had noticed it, maybe others had, he'd have to be careful, if he wanted to keep a responsible and respected job. After all, he repeated firmly to himself, Mesklinites *were* People, even if they looked like bugs.

Ib Hoffman's attention wandered, important though he knew the work to be. His mind kept going back to the *Kwembly,* and the *Smof,* and to a well-designed, well-built piece of diving gear which had almost killed an eleven-year-old boy. The reports, punctuated by Aucoin's sometimes acid comments, droned on; slowly Ib made up his mind.

"We're getting ahead," remarked Barlennan. "There was good excuse for taking the vision sets out of the *Kwembly,* since she was being abandoned, so we've been able to work on her with no restrictions. We could use Reffel's helicopter, since the humans think it's lost, too. Jemblakee and Deeslenver seem to feel that the cruiser can be back in running state in another day." He glanced at the feeble sun, almost exactly overhead. "The human chemists were certainly helpful about that mud she was in. It was funny how the one who talked to Dee about the stuff kept insisting that he was only guessing, while he made suggestion after suggestion. It's too bad we couldn't tell him how successful most of his ideas were."

"Self-doubt seems to be a human trait, if it's safe to make such a sweeping remark," replied Guzmeen. "When did this news get in?"

"The *Deedee* came in an hour ago, and is gone again. There's too much for that machine to do. It was bad enough when we lost the *Elsh,* and with Kabremm and his *Gwelf* overdue things are piling up. I hope we find him. Maybe the *Kalliff* will turn up something; he was supposed to be scouting a route to get her to Don's camp, so maybe one of Kenanken's scouts will spot him. He's less than a day overdue, so there's still a chance . . ."

"And with all this, you say we're ahead?" cut in Guzmeen.

"Sure. Remember, the whole aim of the *Esket* act was to persuade the human beings to let us use space ships. The self-support business was incidental, though useful. We expected to work the local-life myth up to a major menace before we could persuade Aucoin to let us fly, and spend months building up to it. We're far ahead on time, and haven't lost very much, the base at the *Esket* site, of course, and the *Elsh* and its crew, and just possibly Kabremm and his."

"But even Kabremm and Karfrengin aren't exactly expendable. There aren't very many of us. If Dondragmer and his crew don't keep alive until the *Kalliff* reaches them, we'll have taken a really serious loss; at least our dirigible crews weren't our scientists and engineers."

"Don's in no real danger. They can always be picked up by Beetchermarlf in the human space ship—I mean our space ship."

"And if anything goes wrong with *that* operation we're out not only our only space ship but our only space pilots."

"Which suggests to me," Barlennan said thoughtfully, "that we should try to regain some lost ground. As soon as the *Kwembly* is ready she should start hunting a suitable place and start replacing the *Esket* settlement. Don's scientists should have little trouble finding a good location; Dhrawn seems to be rich in metal ores. Maybe we should have him search closer to here so that communication will be quicker, though.

"We'll have to build more dirigibles; the one we have left isn't nearly enough for the work. Maybe we ought to design bigger ones."

"I've been wondering about that," a technician who had been listening silently up to this point spoke up. "Do you suppose that it would be smart to find out more, tactfully, of course, from the humans about dirigibles? We've never discussed the subject with them; they taught you about balloons years ago, and some of our own people got the idea of using the human power sources with them. We don't know if *they* ever used them at all. Maybe it isn't just bad luck that we've lost two out of our three in such a short time. Maybe there's something fundamentally wrong with the whole idea."

The commander gave a gesture of impatience.

"That's silly. I didn't try to pick up a complete scientific education from the aliens, since it was obviously going to take too long; but one thing I did gather was that the underlying rules are essentially simple. Once the humans started concentrating on basic rules, they went from sailing ships to space ships in a couple of hundred years. Balloons, powered or not, are simple devices; I understand them perfectly myself. Putting an engine aboard doesn't change that; the same rules have to be working."

The technician eyed his commander thoughtfully, and thought briefly of electron tubes and television circuits before replying.

"I suppose," he said thoughtfully, "that a piece of a tent being blown away by the gale, and a ship being tacked into the wind, are also examples of the same rules at work."

Barlennan didn't want to give an affirmative answer, but he could find nothing better.

He was still trying to shrug off the technician's remark, but only succeeding in growing more and more doubtful of his situation, some twenty hours later when a messenger called him to the communication room. As soon as he entered, Guzmeen spoke briefly into a microphone; a minute later, a human face which neither of them recognized appeared on the screen.

"I am Ib Hoffman, Easy's husband and Benj's father," the stranger began without preamble. "I'm speaking to you two, Barlennan and Dondragmer, alone. The rest of the observing crew here are concentrating on a new emergency involving one of the cruisers. I'm using your language as best I can, with my wife standing by; she knows what I want to say, and will correct me if I slip too badly. I have decided that it is time to clear up some misunderstandings, but I don't plan to tell everyone here about them; you'll see why before I finish, if you don't already. I'm bothered mostly because I hate to call anyone a liar in any language.

"First, Barlennan, my hearty congratulations. I am just about certain that when we turned the barge over to a Mesklinite pilot we fulfilled one of your chief plans, probably well before you meant or expected it to mature. That's fine. I wanted that to happen. Probably you want to make interstellar flights on your own later on, too; that's also fine with me. I'll help.

"You seem to feel that many or most human beings would try to thwart you in this, and I have to admit that some would, though I think we have the most effective one under control now. You can't be sure that I'm being sincere now, for that matter; you're tricky enough yourself to expect it of other people. Too bad. How much you believe of what I say is beyond my control; I still have to say it.

"I don't know how much of the basic situation you set up, but I can guess. I'm nearly sure the *Esket* disappearance was not genuine. I'm uncertain of the real status of the *Kwembly*. You probably know more of Dhrawn than you've reported. I won't say I don't care, because I do; we're here to learn as much as possible about Dhrawn, and what you don't tell us is a loss to the project. I can't threaten you with penalties for breach of contract, since I'm not completely certain you've broken it and am in no position to carry out threats. And in any case have less than no desire to even make threats. I do want to persuade you, though, that it will be better for both of us if we do without secrets. We're at a point where anything less than complete frankness is likely to cost us a lot and cost you everything. To make that point, I'm going to tell you a story.

"You know that human beings breathe oxygen much as you do hydrogen, though being so much larger we need a more complicated pumping system to get it through our bodies. Because of the details of that system, we suffocate if deprived of gaseous, free oxygen within a certain rather narrow range of pressures.

"About three quarters of Earth is covered by water. We cannot breathe under water without artificial equipment, but the use of such equipment is a common human sport. It consists essentially of a tank of compressed air and a valve system which releases the air to our breathing system as needed; simple and obvious.

"Six of our years ago, when Benj was eleven years old, he made such a device, designing it himself with my assistance. He made the pressure tank and regulator, using ordinary fabricating equipment such as may be found in most home workshops, just as he had made more complex things such as small gas turbines. He tested the parts with my help; they worked perfectly. He calculated how long the air in the tank would last him, and then tested the whole assembly under water. I went along as a matter of common-sense safety, using a commercial diving device.

"I am sure you know the principles of hydrostatics and the gas laws, at least, Easy has given me words for them in your language. You can see that at a certain depth, a lungful of air would have only half its volume at the surface. Benj knew this too, but reasoned that it would still be a lungful as far as oxygen content was concerned, so that a one-hour tank would be a one-hour tank regardless of depth, as long as tank pressure was above that of the water.

"To make a long story short, it didn't. He ran out of air in less than a third of the calculated time, and I had to make an emergency rescue. Because of the quick pressure change and some human peculiarities which you don't seem to share, he was very nearly killed. The trouble turned out to be that the human breathing rate is controlled, not by the oxygen in our blood, but by the carbon dioxide, one of the waste products. To maintain a normal equilibrium of that, we have to run normal *volumes* of air through our lungs, regardless of oxygen content or total pressure; hence, an hour's air supply at normal pressure is only half an hour thirty-three feet under water, a third of an hour at sixty-six, and so on.

"I don't want to insult anyone's intelligence by asking if he understands my point, but I'd like some comment from both of you on that story."

The answers were interesting, both in nature and arrival time. Barlennan's popped from the speaker with very little more than light-travel delay; Dondragmer's came much, much later, and did not overlap with his commander's.

"It is obvious that incomplete knowledge can lead to mistakes," said Barlennan, "but I don't see why that is especially applicable to the present case. We know that our knowledge can't be complete, and that our work here is dangerous for that reason. We have always known it. Why emphasize the point now? I'd much rather hear your report on the cruiser you say is in trouble. You make me suspect that you are leading up gently to the information that I have lost another cruiser because of something its designing engineers didn't know. Don't worry, I won't blame you for that. None of us could foresee everything."

Ib smiled sourly at the revelation of yet another human characteristic.

"That's not just what I had in mind, Commander, though there are valid aspects to what you have just said. I'd like to wait for Dondragmer's answer before I say any more, though."

It was another full minute, a slightly strained one, before the voice of the *Kwembly's* captain arrived.

"Your account is plain enough and you would probably have been briefer had you not meant to imply more. I suspect that your key point is not so much that your son got into trouble through ignorance, but that he did so even under your experienced adult supervision. I would take the implication to be that even though you aliens do not claim omniscience or omnipotence, we are in a certain amount of danger here no matter how closely you supervise and assist us, and we are adding unnecessarily to our danger any time we act on our own, like the student chemist who experiments on his own." Dondragmer had spent much more time at the College than had his commander.

"Right. Just what I meant," said Ib. "I can't . . ."

"Just a moment," interrupted Easy. "Hadn't you better relay Don's remark to Barlennan first?"

"Right." Her husband gave a one-sentence summary of the captain's speech, and went on, "I can't force any policy on you, and would prefer not to even if I could. I don't expect you to make a complete revelation of everything that's gone on on Dhrawn since you first built the Settlement. In fact, I'd advise strongly against it; I have enough complications up here with the administration as it is. However, if Easy just happened to get an occasional talk with her old friends Destigmet and Kabremm, just as an example, I would have a better idea of what has gone on and be in a better position to keep things running smoothly at this end. I don't expect a spot decision on any matter of major policy change, Commander, but please think it over."

Barlennan, being a sea captain by training and trade, was accustomed to the need for quick decisions.

Furthermore, circumstances had already compelled thoughts on similar lines to circulate in his tiny head. Finally, his only really basic policy was to ensure his own survival and that of his crew. He answered Ib promptly.

"Easy may get her talk with Destigmet, but not right away; the *Esket* is a long distance from here. I will also have to wait to tell you all that I'd like to, because I must first hear from you the details of the trouble you mentioned when you first called. You said that another of my cruisers was in trouble.

"Please tell me just what has happened, so I can plan what help to request from you."

Ib and Easy Hoffman looked at each other and grinned in mingled relief and triumph.

But it was Benj who made the key remark. This was later on, in the aerology lab, when they were recounting to him and McDevitt all that had been said. The boy looked up at the huge globes of Dhrawn, and the tiny area where the lights indicated partial knowledge.

"I suppose you think he's a lot safer now, down there."

It was a sobering thought.

About the Author

Hal Clement (Harry Clement Stubbs) was born in Massachusetts in 1922. He has been a science lover from early childhood, at least partly as a result of a 1930 *Buck Rogers* panel in which villains were "headed for Mars, forty-seven million miles away." His father, an accountant, couldn't answer the resulting questions, and led little Hal to the local library. The result was irreversible brain influence.

He majored in astronomy at Harvard, and has since acquired master's degrees in education and in chemistry. He earns his basic living as a teacher of chemistry and astronomy at Milton Academy, in Massachusetts, and regards science-fiction writing and painting as hobbies. His first two stories, "Proof" and "Impediment," were sold when he was a junior in college; their impression on Harvard's $400 per year tuition secured family tolerance for that crazy Buck Rogers stuff.

He has since produced half a dozen novels, of which the best known are *Needle* and *Mission of Gravity*. His reputation among science-fiction enthusiasts is that of a "hard" writer—one who tries to stick faithfully to the physical sciences as they are currently understood; like Arthur C. Clarke and the late Willy Ley, Clement would never dream of having a space ship fall into the sun merely because its engines broke down. He can do his own orbit computing, and does.

He leads a double life, appearing frequently at science fiction conventions as Hal Clement and spending the rest of his time in Milton as the rather square science teacher with a wife of twenty-five years and three grown children, Harry Stubbs. He does occasional merit badge counselling for the Boy Scouts, has served on his town's finance committee, and is an eleven-gallon Red Cross blood donor.

The MS READ-a-thon needs young readers!

Boys and girls between 6 and 14 can join the MS READ-a-thon and help find a cure for Multiple Sclerosis by reading books. And they get two rewards — the enjoyment of reading, and the great feeling that comes from helping others.

For complete information call your local MS chapter, or call toll-free (800) 243-6000. Or mail the coupon below.

Kids can help, too!